The Presentati

H. De Vere Stacpoole

Alpha Editions

This edition published in 2024

ISBN 9789362098016

Design and Setting By

Alpha Editions

www.alphaedis.com

Email - info@alphaedis.com

As per information held with us this book is in Public Domain.
This book is a reproduction of an important historical work.
Alpha Editions uses the best technology to reproduce historical work
in the same manner it was first published to preserve its original nature.
Any marks or number seen are left intentionally to preserve.

Contents

BOOK I .... - 1 -

CHAPTER I THE DUC DE CHOISEUL'S BALL .... - 2 -

CHAPTER II THE HOUSE OF THE DUBARRYS .... - 10 -

CHAPTER III A COUNCIL OF WAR .... - 21 -

CHAPTER IV THE METHODS OF MONSIEUR DE SARTINES .- 33 -

CHAPTER V FERMINARD .... - 37 -

CHAPTER VI THE COMTESSE DE BÉARN .... - 47 -

CHAPTER VII THE ARTIST .... - 51 -

CHAPTER VIII THE PRESENTATION .... - 52 -

CHAPTER IX THE REWARD .... - 61 -

CHAPTER X THE ORDER OF ARREST .... - 63 -

CHAPTER XI FLIGHT .... - 67 -

CHAPTER XII A DUEL OF WITS .... - 70 -

BOOK II .... - 72 -

CHAPTER I A LODGING FOR THE NIGHT .... - 73 -

CHAPTER II THE GRATITUDE OF THE DUBARRYS .... - 83 -

CHAPTER III THE PAIR OF SPECTACLES .... - 89 -

CHAPTER IV THE ARREST OF ROCHEFORT .... - 93 -

CHAPTER V CAPTAIN ROUX .... - 100 -

BOOK III .... - 111 -

CHAPTER I THE POISONING OF ATALANTA .... - 112 -

CHAPTER II MONSIEUR BROMMARD .... - 117 -

CHAPTER III CHOISEUL'S LETTER.. - 126 -

CHAPTER IV THE DECLARATION OF CAMUS .... - 129 -

CHAPTER V THE HOUSE OF COUNT CAMUS.............................. - 133 -

CHAPTER VI THE LABORATORY .... - 139 -

CHAPTER VII THE FAWN AND THE SERPENT.......................... - 144 -

CHAPTER VIII THE CATACOMBS OF PARIS .... - 147 -

BOOK IV .... - 149 -

CHAPTER I NEWS FROM VINCENNES.. - 150 -

CHAPTER II THE TWO PRISONERS .... - 154 -

CHAPTER III THE TWO PRISONERS (continued)........................... - 160 -

CHAPTER IV THE TWO PRISONERS (continued)........................... - 165 -

CHAPTER V M. DE ROCHEFORT REVIEWS HIMSELF............. - 169 -

CHAPTER VI THE ESCAPE .... - 172 -

CHAPTER VII ROCHEFORT'S PLAN.. - 176 -

CHAPTER VIII THE HONOUR OF LAVENNE................................ - 183 -

CHAPTER IX THE GATHERING STORM... - 192 -

CHAPTER X THE DUC DE CHOISEUL'S RECEPTION .... - 195 -

CHAPTER XI ROCHEFORT AND CHOISEUL................................. - 203 -

CHAPTER XII ENVOI .... - 211 -

ns
BOOK I

CHAPTER I

THE DUC DE CHOISEUL'S BALL

IT was the night of the Duc de Choiseul's ball, that is to say, the night before the expected presentation of the Comtesse Dubarry at Court, and Versailles was in a ferment, the seething of which reached to the meanest streets of Paris.

France had long been accustomed to the rule, not of kings, but of favourites and ministers, and at the present moment in the year of our Lord, 1770, she was under the rule of the most kind-hearted of women since the harmless La Vallière and the most upright minister since Colbert.

The mistress was Dubarry and the minister de Choiseul.

It was a strange government. To-day Dubarry, who hated Choiseul much more than she hated the devil, would be in the ascendant over Louis the Voluptuous. To-morrow Choiseul would have the long ear of the King, who was, in fact, only the table on which these two gamblers played with loaded dice for the realm of France.

Behind the two gamblers stood their backers. Behind Choiseul, when he was winning, nearly the whole Court of Versailles. Behind Dubarry, when she was losing, only her family, the Vicomte Jean, and a few inconsiderable people who had learned to love her for her own sake.

This adherence of the courtiers to Choiseul was caused less by the prescience of self-interest than by hatred of the Comtesse, and this hatred, always smouldering and ready to burst into flame, was one of the strangest features in the Court mind of France.

Why did they hate her, these people? Or, rather, why did they hate her with such intensity—they who had raised few enough murmurs against the rule of the frigid and callous Pompadour?

They hated her, perhaps, because she was an epitome of the virtues and the vices of the people whom they had trampled under foot for centuries. She had that goodness of heart and simplicity of thought rarer even than rectitude in Court circles, and her very vices had a robustness reminiscent of the soil.

Dubarry was, in fact, a charming woman who might have been a good woman but for Fate, the Maison Labille, and Louis of France.

The question of her presentation at Court, an act which would place her on the same social footing as her enemies, had been the main topic of conversation for a month past. The women had closed their ranks and united against the common enemy. Not one of them would act as sponsor. The King, who cared little enough about the business, had, still, interested himself in the matter. The Comtesse, her sister Chon, and the Vicomte Jean Dubarry had ransacked the lists of the most venial of the nobility. Bribes, threats, promises, all had been used in vain; not a woman would stir or raise a finger to further the ambition of the "shop girl," so that the unfortunate Comtesse was on the point of yielding to despair when a brilliant idea occurred to the Vicomte Jean.

Away down in the provinces, mouldering in a castle on the banks of the Meuse, lived a lady named the Comtesse de Béarn. A lady of the old *régime*, a litigant with a suit pending before the courts in Paris, poor as Job, proud as Lucifer, and seemingly created by Providence for the purpose of the presentation.

This lady had been brought to Paris by a trick, installed in the town house of Madame Dubarry, and wheedled into consenting to act as sponsor by pure and rank bribery. One can fancy the consternation of the Choiseul party when this news leaked out.

The presentation was assured; nothing, one might fancy, could possibly happen to prevent it, and yet to-night, standing with the Duchess to receive their guests, the face of Choiseul showed nothing of his threatened defeat.

The Rue de Faubourg St. Honoré was alight with the torches of the running footmen and filled with a crowd watching the carriages turning into the courtyard of the Hôtel de Choiseul from the direction of the Rue St. Honoré, the Rue de la Bonne Morue, the Rue d'Anjou, and the Rue de la Madeleine.

It was a great assemblage, for the Court for the moment was in Paris, the King having changed his residence for three days, returning to Versailles on the morrow, and the people, with that passion for display which helped them at times to forget their misery and hunger, watched the passing liveries of the Duc de Richelieu, M. de Duras, M. de Sartines, the Duc de Grammont, and the host of other notabilities, content if by the torchlight they caught a glimpse of some fair face, the glimmer of a jewel, or the ribbon of an order.

The Maréchal de Richelieu's carriage had drawn away from the steps, having set down its illustrious occupant, when another carriage drew up, from which stepped two young men. The first to alight was short, dark, with a face slightly pitted with smallpox, and so repellent, that at first sight the mind recoiled from him. Yet such was the extraordinary vigour and personality behind that repulsive face that men, and more especially women, forgot the ugliness in the hypnotism of the power. This was the celebrated Comte Camus, a descendant of Nicholas Camus, who had arrived in France penniless in the reign of Louis XIII., married his daughter to Emery, superintendent of finance, and died leaving to his heirs fifteen million francs.

The gentleman with him, tall, fair complexioned, and with a laughing, devil-may-care face, marred somewhat by a sword-cut on the right side reaching from cheek-bone to chin, was the Comte de Rochefort.

Rochefort was only twenty-five, an extraordinary person, absolutely fearless, always fighting, one of those characters that, like opals, seem compounded of cloud and fire. Generous, desperate in his love and hate, a rake-hell and a roué, open-handed when his fist was not clenched, and always laughing, he was fittingly summed up in the words of his cousin, the Abbé du Maurier, "It grieves me to think that such a man should be damned."

Rochefort, followed by Camus, passed up the steps and through the glass swing-doors to the hall. It was like entering a palace in fairy-land. Flowers everywhere, clinging to the marble pillars, gloated on by the soft yet brilliant lights of a thousand lamps, and banking with colour the balustrades of the great staircase up which was passing a crowd of guests, or, one might better say, a profusion of diamonds, orders, blue ribbons, billowing satin, and the snow of lace and pearls. Over the light laughter and soft voices of women the music of Philidor drifted, faintly heard, from the band of violins in the ball-room, and, clear-cut and hard through the murmur and sigh of violins, voices and volumes of drapery, could be heard the business-like voice of the major-domo announcing the guests.

"Monsieur le Maréchal Duc de Richelieu!"

"Madame la Princesse de Guemenée!"

"Madame de Courcelles!" etc.

Camus and Rochefort, having made their bow to Madame de Choiseul and saluted the minister, lost each other completely. Each had a host of acquaintances, and Rochefort had not made two steps in the direction of the ball-room when a hand was laid on his arm and, turning, he found himself face to face with Monsieur de Sartines, the Lieutenant-General of Police.

"Is this an arrest, monsieur?" said Rochefort, laughing.

"Only of your attention," replied de Sartines, laughing in his turn. "My dear Rochefort, how well you are looking. And what has brought you here to-night?"

"Just what brought you, my dear Sartines."

"And that?"

"The invitation of Choiseul."

"But I thought you were of the other party?"

"Which other party?"

"The Dubarry faction."

"I—I belong to no faction—only my own, and that includes all the pretty women and pleasant fellows in Paris. *Mordieu*, Sartines, since when have you imagined me a man of factions and politics? I keep clear of all that simply because I wish to live. Look at Richelieu, he has aged more in the last six months with hungering after Choiseul's portfolio than he aged in the whole eighty years of his life. Look at Choiseul grinning at Richelieu, whom he expects to devour him; he has no more wrinkles simply because he has no more room for them. Look at yourself. You are as yellow as a louis d'or, and your liver can't grow any bigger on account of the size of your spleen—politics, all politics."

"I!" said Sartines. "I have nothing to do with politicians—my business is with criminals."

"They are the same thing, my dear man," replied Rochefort. "The criminals stab each other in the front and the politicians in the back; that is all the difference. Ah, here we are in the ball-room. More flowers! Why, Choiseul must have stripped France of roses for this ball of his."

"Yes, but there is a Rose that he has failed to pluck with all these roses."

"Dubarry?"

"Precisely."

Though Rochefort pretended to know nothing of politics, his acute mind told him at once a secret hidden from others. Sartines belonged to the Dubarry faction. He read it at once in the remark and the tone in which it was made.

Sartines moved through the circles of the Court, mysterious, secretive, professing no politics, yet with his thumb in every pie, and sometimes his whole hand.

He was Fouché with the aristocratic particle attached—a policeman and a noble rolled into one. With the genius of Mascarille for intrigue, of Tartuffe for hypocrisy, acting now with the feigned stupidity of a Sganarelle, and always ready to pounce with the pitilessness of a tiger, this extraordinary man exercised a power in the Court of Louis XV., equalled only by the power of the grey cardinal in the time of Richelieu—with this difference—he was feared less, on account of his assumed bonhomie, an attribute that made him even more dangerous than *son éminence gris*.

He stood now with his hands behind his back, leaning slightly forward, his lips pursed, and his eyes upon the minuet that had just formed like a coloured flower crystallized from the surrounding atmosphere by the strains of Lully.

"Ah," said the Minister of Police, catching sight of a familiar figure, "so the Comte Camus is among the dancers. He came with you to-night?"

"Yes; we arrived in the same carriage."

"Then take care," said Sartines, "that you do not end your life in the same carriage."

"Pardon!"

"The carriage that takes men to the Place de la Grève."

"Monsieur!" cried Rochefort.

"It is my joke; yet, all the same, a joke may have a warning in it. Rochefort, beware of that man."

"Of Comte Camus?"

"Yes."

"And why?"

"*Mordieu*, why! He is a poisoner—that's all."

"A poisoner!"

"Precisely. He poisoned his uncle with a plate of soup, he poisoned his wife with a pot of rouge, and he would poison me with all his heart if he could get into my kitchen. You ask me how I know all this? I know it. Yet I cannot touch him because my evidence is not as complete as my knowledge. But the rope is ready for him, and he will fall as surely as my name is Sartines, for he is an expert in the art, and my eye is always upon him."

Rochefort, who had recovered from his shock, laughed. He did not entirely believe Sartines; besides, his attention was distracted from the thought of Camus by a face.

"Who is that lady seated in the alcove beside Madame de Courcelles?" asked he.

De Sartines turned.

"That?" said he. "Why, it is La Fleur de Martinique. How is it possible that you do not know her?"

"I have been away from Paris for two months. She must have bloomed in my absence, this flower of Martinique. Her name, my dear Sartines? I am burning to know her name."

"Mademoiselle Fontrailles. But beware of her, Rochefort; she is even more dangerous than Camus."

"Why, does she poison people?"

"No, she only makes eyes at them. It's the same thing. Now, what can she be doing here to-night—for she is a friend of the Dubarrys?"

"What can she be doing here? Why, where are your eyes? She is making Choiseul's ball-room more beautiful, of course. *Mon Dieu*, what a face; it makes every other face look like a platter. Sartines, introduce me."

"That I will not."

"Then I will introduce myself."

"That is as may be."

Rochefort turned on his heel and walked straight towards Mademoiselle Fontrailles, whilst Sartines looked on in horror. He knew that Rochefort would stick at nothing, but he did not dream that he would dare the act on which he was now evidently bent.

Rochefort walked straight up to Madame de Courcelles, with whom he had a slight acquaintance, and bowed.

"How delightful to find you here, and you, too, Mademoiselle Fontrailles. I was just complaining of the profusion of the flowers—I thought Choiseul must have gathered together a hundred million roses in this room—till, turning to your alcove, I found there were only two."

He bowed, and Madame de Courcelles laughed as she rose to greet Sartines, with whom she wished a few minutes' conversation.

"Since you two know each other, I will leave you to talk nonsense together," said she. "Ah, Sartines, I thought you were eluding me. You looked twice in my direction, and not one sign of recognition."

"I am growing short-sighted, madame," replied de Sartines, as she took his arm, "and had it not been for the keen sight of Monsieur de Rochefort, I might altogether have missed you."

They passed away in the crowd that now thronged the room, leaving Rochefort and Mademoiselle Fontrailles together.

She was very beautiful. Graceful as the *fleur d'amour* of her native land, dark, yet without a trace of the creole, and with eyes that had been compared to black pansies. Those same eyes when seen by daylight discovered themselves not as pansies, but as two wells of the deepest blue.

The Flower of Martinique looked at Rochefort, and Rochefort looked at the Flower of Martinique.

"Monsieur," said the Flower, "I have met many surprising things in Paris; but nothing has surprised me more than your impertinence."

"Not my impertinence, dear Mademoiselle Fontrailles," replied Rochefort, "but my philosophy. Have you not noticed that when two people get to know each other they generally bore each other? Now in Paris society two people cannot possibly know each other without being introduced; and, since we have never been introduced, it follows logically that we can never bore each other."

"I am not so sure of that," replied the lady, looking at her companion critically. "Many people to whom I have never been introduced bore me by the expression of their faces and the tone of their voices. I was noticing that fact even whilst I was watching you talking to Monsieur de Sartines a moment ago."

"Ah," said Rochefort, "you noticed that about him! It is true he is a bit heavy."

She laughed. In her Paris experience she had met no one like Rochefort. Impudence she had met, and daring, laughter, raillery, good looks and ugliness. Yet she had never met them all combined, as in the case of Rochefort. For it seemed to her that he was now almost ugly, now almost good-looking, and she set herself for a moment to try and read this man whose face had so many expressions, and whose mind had, seemingly, so many facets.

She was a keen reader of character, yet Rochefort baffled her. The salient points were easy enough to discern. Courage, daring and sharp intelligence were there; but the retreating angles, what did they contain? She could not tell, but she determined, whatever his character might be, it would be improved by a check.

"I have not weighed Monsieur de Sartines," she said, rising to rejoin Madame de Courcelles, who was approaching on the arm of the minister, "but I have weighed Monsieur Rochefort, and I find him——" she hesitated with a charming smile upon her lips.

"And you have found him——?"

"Wanting."

Next moment she was passing away with Madame de Courcelles, and Rochefort found himself face to face with the Minister of Police.

At the word "wanting," she had swept him from head to foot with her eyes, and the charming smile had turned into an expression of contemptuous indifference worse than a blow in the face. It was the secret of her loveliness that it could burn one up, or freeze one, or entrance one at will. Rochefort had been playing with a terrible thing, and for the first time in his life he felt like a fool. He had often been a fool, but he had never felt like a fool before.

"Well," said de Sartines, with a cynical smile, "and what have we been talking about to Mademoiselle Fontrailles?"

"Why," said the young man, recovering himself, "the last subject we were discussing was your weight, Sartines."

"My weight?"

"She said that you impressed her as being rather heavy."

He turned away and walked off, mixing with the crowd, trying to stifle his mortification, his fingers clutching his lace ruffles and his eyes glancing hither and thither for someone to pick a quarrel with or say a bitter thing to. He found no one of this sort, but he found Mademoiselle Fontrailles. Twice in the crowd he passed her, and each time her eyes swept over him without betraying the least spark of recognition.

CHAPTER II

THE HOUSE OF THE DUBARRYS

CAMUS, meanwhile, having finished dancing, went into the card-room. He seemed to be in search of someone, and passed from table to table like an uneasy spirit, till, reaching the farthest table, he found the man he wanted.

It was the Comte de Coigny.

Coigny was standing watching a game of picquet; when he raised his eyes and saw Camus, he gave a sign of recognition, left the game, and coming towards him, took his arm.

"Let us go into the ball-room," said Coigny; "we can talk there without being overheard in the crush. Did you get my note asking you to be sure to come to-night?"

"Yes, I got your note. Why were you so anxious for me to come?"

"For a very good reason. There are great things in the air."

"Ah! Something about the Dubarry, I wager."

"You are right. The case is desperate, and you know the only cure for a desperate case is a desperate remedy."

"Go on."

"She is due at Versailles at nine o'clock to-morrow evening. Well, we are going to steal her carriage, her dress and her hairdresser."

"Dubarry's?"

"Yes, Dubarry's."

"And you want me——"

"To help."

"And when is this theft to be made?"

"To-morrow, at six o'clock in the evening. We cannot entrust this business to servants. I have a friend who will look after the milliner, I myself will attend to the hairdresser, and you, my dear Camus, must look after the carriage."

"Let us clearly understand each other," said Camus. "You propose to suppress a hairdresser, a carriage and a gown. Is this to be done by brute force, or how?"

"By bribery."

"Have you approached the milliner, the hairdresser, and the coachman on the subject?"

"Heavens no! The thing is to be done at the last moment; give them time to think and they would talk."

"And who is to pay the bribes?"

"Choiseul; who else? It will cost three hundred thousand francs; but were it to cost a million, the million is there."

"And suppose they resist?"

"That has also been taken into consideration. If they resist, then force must be used. You must have five companions ready to your call, should you need them."

"I can easily find five men," said Camus. "I have only to whisper the name of Dubarry, and they would spring from the pavement."

"They must all be gentlemen," said Coigny, "for in an affair of this sort, nothing must be trusted to servants."

"Just so. Who are the coach people?"

"Landry, in the Rue de la Harpe. The carriage is finished, and the varnish is drying on it. But Landry has nothing to do with it. Your business concerns the coachman, Mathieu. You must get hold of this man, and, having put him out of the way, assume the Dubarry livery, call for the coach at Landry's, and drive it to the devil—or anywhere you like but the Rue de Valois."

"And the footmen?"

"Your genius must dispose of those. Send them into a cabaret for a drink, and drive off while they are drinking. That is all detail."

"But Landry will recognize that I am not Mathieu."

"You can easily meet that. You can say he is ill, or better, drunk. He has a reputation for getting drunk, and there is nothing like a bad reputation to help a good plan, sometimes."

"*Ma foi!*" said Camus, "if that is the case, you ought to use Dubarry's reputation. Well, I agree. But Choiseul ought to make me a duke at least, for it would be worth a dukedom to see Dubarry's face when she finds out the trick, and I will be out of all that."

"Rest assured," said Coigny, "that Choiseul will not forget the men who have helped him; but your reward will come less from him than another quarter."

"And where is that?"

"Why, all the women of the Court. And a man with the women on his side can do anything. Ah, there is Madame de Courcelles with the charming Fontrailles. Now, what can Mademoiselle Fontrailles be doing here to-night, for, if I am not greatly mistaken, she is a friend of Dubarry's?"

Camus caught sight of Mademoiselle Fontrailles.

"*Mon Dieu!*" said he, "what a lovely face! Where has she come from?"

"What?" said Coigny, "do you not know her? She is from Martinique. They call her the 'Flower of Martinique'—but surely you have seen her before?"

"I have been away from Paris for some weeks, hunting with Rochefort," said Camus, his eyes still on the girl.

"Ah! that accounts for it," said Coigny. "She is a new arrival."

"Introduce me."

"Certainly."

In a moment the introduction was made. Camus's success with women was due less, perhaps, to his force and personality, than to his knowledge of them. Like Wilkes, he only wanted ten minutes' start of the handsomest man in town to beat him. With Mademoiselle Fontrailles he was charming, courtly, deferential and graceful.

He knew nothing of Rochefort's experience with the girl, but he needed no warning, and when the Duc de Soissons came up to claim her as partner, he fancied that he had made a very good impression, as, indeed, he had.

He watched her dancing. If he had made a good impression on her, she had made a deep impression upon him. He watched her with burning eyes, as one might fancy a tiger watching a gazelle, then, turning away, he passed through the crowd to the supper-room.

Here, drinking at a buffet, he met a friend, Monsieur de Duras, a stout gentleman—one of those persons who know everything about everyone and their affairs. Camus questioned him about Mademoiselle Fontrailles, and learned her origin and history. Her father was the chief banker in Martinique. She had come to Paris for her health. Attended by whom?

"*Mon Dieu!*" said de Duras, "now you ask me a question. She has come attended by no one but an old quadroon woman, and she lives, now in apartments in the Rue St. Dominic, and now at Luciennes. She is a friend of the Dubarry, to whom old Fontrailles owes many a concession that has helped to make his fortune. But you may save yourself trouble, my dear Camus—she is entirely unapproachable, one of those torches that turn out to be icicles when you take a hold of them."

"Indeed!" said Camus. He stayed for a little while in the supper-room, talking to several people; then he returned to the ball-room.

Mademoiselle Fontrailles had disappeared. It took him some time to ascertain this fact, searching hither and thither among the hundreds of guests. The corridors, the landings, the hall, he tried them in succession without result. The lady had vanished.

The mind of Camus was of that type which can turn from one subject to another, leaving the most burning questions to await their answer whilst it is engaged in some alien consideration. Having failed to find the woman who had charmed him, he turned his attention to the Dubarry business.

He had to find five friends whom he could trust, men absolutely devoted to Choiseul, that is to say, sworn enemies of Dubarry. By midnight he had picked out four gentlemen fit for the purpose, that is to say, four titled rake-hells and blackguards, who would stick at nothing, and who held the honour of women and the life of men equally cheap. He made an appointment with these people to meet him at breakfast on the morrow at his house in the Rue de la Trône, and was casting about for a fifth when his eye fell on Rochefort, who, flushed with wine and winnings at cards, had almost recovered his temper.

Rochefort was just the man he wanted to complete his party. He thought that he knew Rochefort thoroughly, and, taking him by the arm, he turned to the entrance hall.

"It is after midnight," said Camus, "and I am off. Will you walk part of the way with me, for I have something particular to say to you?"

"You are going home?"

"Yes."

"Well, I don't mind coming with you. I have won two hundred louis, and if I stay I will be sure to lose them again. What is this you wish to say?"

"Wait till we are in the street," replied Camus.

They got their cloaks and hats and left the hôtel, crossing the courtyard thronged with carriages, and turning to the right down the Rue du Faubourg St. Honoré in the direction of the Rue St. Honoré.

"Look here," said Camus, taking the other's arm, "we have made a famous plan about the washerwoman."

"Dubarry?"

"Who else? Her presentation is as good as cancelled."

"Oh, I thought it was assured."

"It was."

"And what has happened to cancel it?"

"Nothing. But things are going to happen."

"Explain yourself, my dear fellow; you are as mysterious as the Sibyl. Are you going to strangle the Comtesse de Béarn?"

"No, but we are going to steal Dubarry's coach."

"Steal her coach?"

"And not only her coach, but her gown and her hairdresser."

"Are you serious?" said Rochefort.

"Perfectly. Is it not a splendid plan? It is all to take place at the last moment—that is to say, at six o'clock to-morrow, or rather, to-day, for it is now after midnight. Look you, this is the way of it."

Camus, bursting with laughter, made a sketch of what he proposed to do. "I shall want five men at my back," said he, "I have four; will you be the fifth?"

Rochefort made no reply for a moment. Then he said:

"You know I am no friend of the Dubarrys, and that I would give a good deal to see this shop-girl in her proper place. Yet what you propose to me does not seem a work I would care to put my hand to. I would carry off the Comtesse with pleasure, but to steal her carriage—well—to that I can only reply, I am not a thief."

Camus withdrew his arm from that of Rochefort. He knew Rochefort as a man who cared absolutely nothing for consequences—as a gambler, a drinker, and a fighter who could have given points to most men and beaten them at those amusements. He had failed to take into his calculations the fact that Rochefort was a man of honour. This desperado of a Rochefort had mired his clothes with all sorts of filth, but his skin was clean. He always fought fair, and he never cheated at play. Even in love, though his record was bad enough, he played the game without any of those tricks with which men cheat women of their honour.

Camus, absolutely without scruple and with the soul of a footman, despite the power of his mind and personality, had utterly failed to read Rochefort aright, simply because, being blind to honour himself, he could not see it in others. One may say of a man like Camus that he may be clever as Lucifer, but he can never be a genius in affairs, simply because of that partial blindness which is one of the adjuncts of evil.

"Oh, oh," said he, "we have suddenly become very strait-laced!"

"I?" said Rochefort. "Not at all! But your plan seems to me equivalent to robbing a person of his purse so as to prevent him from taking the stage to Versailles. It is a trick, but it is not a clever one, and if you will excuse me for saying so, it is not the trick of a gentleman. Coigny originated it, you say? I believe you. He has the mind of a lackey and the manners of one—he only wants the livery."

"Ah!" said Camus, with a sneer, "it is easy to see you are for the Dubarry party. Why do you not wear their colours then, openly, instead of carrying them in your pocket with your conscience?"

Rochefort laughed.

"I do not wear my colours," said he, "my servants wear them. They are grey and crimson, not rose. I have nothing to do with the Dubarrys, nor do I wish to have anything to do with them. The Comtesse can go to Versailles or go to the devil for all I care—but what is that?"

They had turned to the left up the broad way bordered by trees which cut the Rue du Faubourg St. Honoré, and led from the Pont Tournant of the Tuileries to the Hôtel de Chevilly. Rochefort's attention had been attracted by a woman's screams coming from the narrow Rue de Chevilly that ran by the hôtel. The moon had risen, and by its light he could see a group of three people struggling; two men were attacking a woman.

Always ready for a fight, he whipped his sword from its scabbard, and calling on Camus to follow, ran at full speed towards the ruffians, who, dropping their hold on the woman, took to their heels, doubling down the road that led past the Bénédictines de la Ville l'Évêque. Rochefort, forgetting Camus, the woman and everything else, pursued hot-foot to the road corner, where the two men parted, one running down the Rue de la Madeleine towards the river, the other up the street leading to the Hôtel de Soyecourt.

Rochefort pursued the latter, and for a very good reason. The man was running into a cul-de-sac. The pursued one did not perceive this till suddenly he found himself faced by the barrier, closed at night, which extended from the wall of the Bénédictines to the wall of the cloister of the Madeleine. Then he turned like a rat and Rochefort in the moonlight had a full view of him.

He was quite young, perhaps not more than eighteen, with a white, degenerate, evil face—one of those faces that the Cour des Miracles invented and constructed, that the Revolution patented and passed on to the *banlieue* of Paris, and that the *banlieue* handed to us under the title of "Apache."

"Ah," said Rochefort, "I have got you!"

The words were within an ace of being his last. The ruffian's hand shot up and a knife whistled past Rochefort's neck, almost grazing it. Instantly, and like a streak of light, the sword of Rochefort passed through the chest of the knife-thrower, pinning him to the door of the barrier, where he dandled for a moment, flinging his arms about like a marionette. Then, unpinned, he fell all of a heap on the cobble-stones. The sword had gone clean through his heart. He was as dead as Calixtus.

Rochefort had done the only thing possible to do with him—put him out of existence; and feeling that the world was well rid of a ruffian, he looked about for something to wipe his sword upon. A piece of paper was blowing about in the wind and the moonlight; it was a scrap of an old ballad then being hawked about Paris. He used it to wipe his sword, returned the blade to its sheath, and, well content with the clean and very sharp-cut business he had completed, returned on his tracks.

Nearing again the Rue de Chevilly, he again heard the cries of a woman, and next moment, turning the corner at a run, he saw two forms struggling together, the form of a woman and the form of a man. Camus, with his arm round the waist of the woman they had rescued, was trying to kiss her. In a moment Rochefort was up to them. His quick blood was boiling. To rescue a woman and then to assault her would, in cold blood, have appeared to him the last act—in hot blood it raised the devil in him against Camus. He ran up to them, crooked his arm in that of the count, and, swinging him apart from his prey, struck him an open-handed blow in the face that sent him rolling in the gutter. Then he drew his sword.

Now Camus was reckoned a brave man, and undoubtedly he was, but courage has many qualities. Caught acting like a ruffian and smitten open-handed in the face and cast in the gutter, he sat for a moment as if stunned. Then, rising with his clothes and gloves soiled, he stood for a moment gazing at Rochefort, but he did not draw his sword. His spirit for the moment was broken.

He had been caught acting like a blackguard, and that knowledge, and the blow, and Rochefort's anger, and the horrible indignity of the whole business, paralysed the man in him, quelled his fury, and disabled his arm.

"We will see about this later on," he said, and stooping for his three-cornered hat, which was lying on the ground, he walked away in the direction of the Rue de la Madeleine. Twenty yards off he turned, gazed back at Rochefort, and then went on till the corner of the street hid him from sight.

Rochefort sheathed his sword, and turned to the woman, who was leaning, trembling and gasping, against the wall of the Hôtel de Chevilly.

"Oh, *mon Dieu*," said she, "what a night! Ah! monsieur, how can I ever thank you for saving me!"

She was young and pretty. The hood of her cloak had fallen back, showing her dark hair and her face, on which the tears were still wet. She was evidently a servant returning from some message, or perhaps some rendezvous. Rochefort laughed as he stooped to pick up her handkerchief, which had fallen on the ground.

"There is nothing to thank me for," said he. "Come, little one, pick up your courage. And here is the handkerchief which you dropped. Have they robbed you, those scamps?"

"No, monsieur," replied the girl; "the letter which I was carrying is safe."

"Ah, they were after a letter! But how did they know you had a letter in your possession? Have they been following you?"

"They followed me, monsieur, from my mistress's home to the house where I went to receive the letter, and from that house they followed me, always at a distance, till I reached the street where they attacked me. They asked me for the letter——"

"Ah, they asked you for the letter!"

"Yes, monsieur, promising to let me go free if I gave it to them."

"And you?"

"I refused, monsieur."

"Well, mademoiselle, your courage does you credit; and now take my arm, and I will see you safe back to your home. *Mordieu*, many a man would have given up letter and purse as well to escape from ruffians like those. What is thy name, little one?"

"Javotte," replied the girl, taking his arm.

"Well, Mademoiselle Javotte, your troubles are now at an end, and your letter will arrive safely at its destination. Which way shall we turn?"

"I am going to the Rue de Valois, monsieur."

"Ah, well then, our quickest way is straight ahead and through the Rue des Capucines. *En avant!*"

As they went on their way they talked. Javotte was not a Parisienne by birth—she hailed from Poictiers—but she had a fresh and lively mind of her own, and to the Comte de Rochefort it came as a revelation that this girl of humble extraction could be both interesting and amusing.

The extraordinary circumstances attending their meeting and the fact that he was playing the rôle of her protector served to destroy, in part, those social differences which would otherwise have divided them. The whole thing was new and strange, and to a mind like Rochefort's, these elements were sufficiently captivating.

In the Rue de Valois, Javotte paused at a postern door and drew a key from her pocket.

"This is the house, then," said Rochefort. "What an ugly door to be the end of our pleasant journey!"

Javotte with a little sigh put the key in the lock of the ugly door and opened it gently.

"Monsieur," said she in a low voice, "I can never thank you enough. I am only a poor girl, and have few words; but you will understand."

Something in the tone of her voice made Rochefort draw close to her, and as he took the step she retreated, so that now they were in the passage on which the door opened.

"You will say good-night?" he whispered.

"Yes," she replied in a murmur, "Good-night, monsieur."

"Ah! not in that way—this."

She understood. Their lips met in the semi-darkness and his hand was upon her waist when the door behind them, as if resenting the business, closed with a snap. Almost on the sound, a door in front of them opened, a flood of light filled the passage, and Rochefort, drawing away from the girl, found himself face to face with a man, stout, well but carelessly dressed, and holding a lamp in his hand.

It was the Vicomte Jean Dubarry!

Rochefort was so astounded by the recognition that for a moment he said no word. The Vicomte, who did not recognize Rochefort at once, was so astonished at the sight of a man in the passage with Javotte that he was equally dumb. The unfortunate Javotte, betrayed by the bad luck that had dogged her all the evening, covered her face with her hands.

After the first second of surprise, Rochefort remembered that the Dubarry town house was situated in the Rue de Valois, and the fact that he must be standing in the Comtesse's house, and that he had saved her maid and her letter, brought a laugh to his lips with his words.

"*Mordieu!*" cried he. "Here's a coincidence."

"Ah!" cried Dubarry, now recognizing his man. "Why, it is Monsieur le Comte de Rochefort!"

"At your service," said Rochefort, with another laugh.

Dubarry bowed ironically. He knew Rochefort's reputation, and he fancied that the presence of this Don Juan was due to some intrigue with Javotte. He had Rochefort at a disadvantage, but he did not wish to press it. Rochefort was not the man to press. As for Javotte, Jean Dubarry would not have cared had she a dozen intrigues on hand. He wanted the letter for which she had been sent.

"Monsieur," said he, "the hour is rather late. To what do I owe the honour of this visit?"

"Why," said Rochefort, "I believe you owe it to the letter which Mademoiselle Javotte has in her pocket and of which two men tried to rob her in the Rue de Chevilly half an hour ago."

"Monsieur le Vicomte," said Javotte, recovering herself, "I was followed to the address you gave me by two men. Then, when I was returning with this letter, they attacked me and would have taken it from me but for this brave gentleman, who beat them off. He escorted me home. I was saying good-night to him here when the door shut to and you entered." She took the letter from her pocket and handed it to him.

Jean Dubarry's manner instantly changed as he took the letter. He knew that Rochefort belonged to no party, and to attach this powerful firebrand to the Dubarry faction would be a stroke of very good policy. Also, he wished to know more about the affair.

"Monsieur Rochefort," said he, smiling, "you have done us a service. We are deeply beset by enemies, and if you wanted proof of that, the fact that our servant has been attacked to-night, on account of this letter, would supply you with it. In the name of the Comtesse, I thank you. And now, will you not come in? This cold passage is but the entrance to a house that is still warm enough, thank God, for the entertainment of our friends. And though the hour is late, it is of importance that I should have a word with you on the matter."

"Thank you," said Rochefort, "I shall be glad also to have a moment's talk with you."

He felt slightly disturbed in mind. If everything was as it appeared to be, then the man he had killed was not a common robber, but a creature of Choiseul's; and, however vile this creature might have been, Choiseul would visit the man who had killed him with his vengeance, should he discover the fact.

Truly, this was a nice imbroglio, and he was even deepening it now by accepting an invitation to enter the house of Choiseul's most bitter enemy. But Rochefort was a man who, when in a difficulty, always went forward, depending on the strength of his own arm to cut his way through. If he was bound to be involved in politics, and Court intrigue, fate had ordained that he would have to fight against Choiseul, and if that event came about, it would be better to have the Dubarrys at his back than no one.

En avant! was his motto, and, following the broad back of the Vicomte, and being followed, in turn, by little Javotte, he left the passage and entered the house of the Dubarrys.

CHAPTER III

A COUNCIL OF WAR

THE Vicomte led the way along a corridor with painted walls and a ceiling wherefrom impossibly fat cupids pelted one in gesture with painted roses.

He opened a door, and with a courtly bow, ushered Rochefort into a small room exquisitely furnished, and lit by a swinging crystal lamp of seven points burning perfumed oil. This house of the Dubarrys had once belonged to Jean de Ségur, a forbear of General Philippe de Ségur, that ardent Royalist who, at the sight of Murat's dragoons galloping through the gate of the Pont Tournant, forgot his grief at the destruction of the old *régime*, and became a soldier of Napoleon's.

It was furnished regardless of expense. Boucher had supervised the paintings that adorned the ceilings, the Maison Grandier had produced the chairs and couches, Versailles had contributed porcelain idols, bonbonnières, and a hundred other knicknacks. Ispahan and Bussorah had contributed the carpets, at a price, through the great Oriental house of Habib, Gobelins the tapestry, Sèvres the china, and the glass manufactory of the Marquis de Louviers the glass. It was for this house, perhaps, rather than for Luciennes, that the Comtesse had refused Fragonard's exquisite panels, "The Romance of Love and Youth," a crime against taste which, strangely enough, found no place in the *procès-verbal*.

Dubarry, excusing himself for a moment, closed the door, and Rochefort glanced round the room wherein he found himself.

Everything was in white or rose; the floor was of parquet, covered here and there with white fur rugs; on the rose-coloured silk of one of the settees lay a fan, as if cast there but a moment ago; and a volume of the poems of Marot, bound in white vellum and stamped with the Dubarry arms and their motto, "*Boutez en avant*" lay upon a chair, as if just put down in haste.

A white-enamelled door, half-hidden by rose-coloured silk curtains, faced the door by which he had entered, and from the room beyond, Rochefort, as he paced the floor and examined the objects of art around him, could hear a faint murmur of voices. Five minutes passed, and Rochefort, having glanced at the fan, peeped into the volume of poems, set the huge Chinese mandarin that adorned one of the alcoves wagging his head, and wound up and broken a costly musical-box, turned suddenly upon his heel.

The door leading into the next room had opened, and a woman stood before him, young, plump, fair-haired and very pretty, exquisitely dressed.

It was the Comtesse Dubarry.

Behind her, Jean Dubarry's gross figure showed, and behind Jean the dark hair of a girl, who was holding a fan to her face as though to conceal her mirth or her features—or both.

"Monsieur le Comte de Rochefort, Madame la Comtesse Dubarry," came Jean's voice across the Countess's shoulder, and then the golden voice of the woman, as she made a little curtsey:

"Monsieur le Comte de Rochefort. Why, I know him!"

Rochefort bowed low. He had met Madame Dubarry at Versailles—that is to say, he had made his bow to her with the thousands of others who thronged the great halls, but he had never hung about the ante-chambers of her special apartment with the other courtiers. He fancied her recognition held more politeness than truth, but in this he was mistaken. Madame Dubarry knew everybody and everything about them. She had a marvellously retentive and clear memory, and an equally quick mind. An ordinary woman in her position would have been lost in a week.

"And though I have had no proof of his friendship before, I know him now to be my friend. Monsieur Rochefort, I thank you."

She held out her hand, which he touched with his lips.

Raising his head from the act, he saw the girl with the fan looking at him; she had lowered the fan from her face. It was Mademoiselle Fontrailles!

"Madame," said he, replying to the Comtesse, "it was nothing. If I have served you, it has been through an accident, yet I esteem it a very fortunate accident that has enabled me to use my sword in your service."

Though he ignored Mademoiselle Fontrailles, his heart had leaped in him at the recognition. It seemed to him that Fate had willed that he should find his interests entangled in those of the beautiful woman who had smitten him in more ways than one. But, as yet, he did not know whether it was to be an entanglement of war or peace, an alliance or a feud.

"Camille," said the Comtesse, "this is Monsieur de Rochefort." She smiled as she said the words, and Rochefort, as he bowed, knew instantly that the Flower of Martinique had told of the incident at the ball, nor did he care, for the warm glance in her dark eyes and the smile on her lips said, as plainly as words: "Let us forget and forgive." From that moment he was Dubarry's man.

"I had the pleasure of seeing Mademoiselle Fontrailles at Monsieur de Choiseul's to-night," said he, "in the company of my friend, Madame de Courcelles." Then, turning sharply to the Comtesse: "Madame, there are so many coincidences at work to-night, that it seems to me Fate herself must have some hand in the matter. Now, mark! I go to Monsieur de Choiseul's, and I meet Mademoiselle Fontrailles, who is your friend; as if the alchemy of that friendship had touched me, on my walk home through the streets, I had the honour to be of service to you by protecting your messenger; I offer her my protection and escort and I find myself at your house; I meet the Vicomte Dubarry, and he invites me in to talk over the matter, and here, again, I meet Mademoiselle Fontrailles."

He bowed to the girl, who bowed in return with a charming little laugh, whilst Jean Dubarry closed the door, and pushed forward chairs for the ladies to be seated.

"But that is not all," continued Rochefort, addressing his remarks again to the Comtesse; "for if it has been my good luck to have served you in the matter of the letter, it will perhaps be my good fortune to assist you on a matter more serious still. You know, or perhaps you do not know, that I am a man of no party and no politics, yet it would be idle for me to shut my eyes to the finger that points my way, and my ears to the voice that whispers to me that my direction is the direction of the Rue de Valois."

He bowed slightly, and his bow included Mademoiselle Fontrailles. The Comtesse had been looking at him attentively all this while, and her quick mind divined something of importance behind his words.

"Monsieur Rochefort," said she, indicating a chair, whilst she herself took her seat on a settee by the side of Mademoiselle Fontrailles, "you have something to tell me. I have the gift of second sight, and I guess that this something is of importance; in my experience, I find that the important things are always the unpleasant things of life, so put me out of my anxiety, I pray you."

"I will, madame; you have divined rightly. My news is unpleasant, simply because it relates to a conspiracy against you."

"Ah! ah!" said Jean Dubarry, who had not taken a seat, but was standing by the mantelpiece, snuff-box in hand. "A conspiracy."

"Yes, Monsieur le Vicomte, a conspiracy."

"Against my life?" asked the Comtesse, with a laugh. "It would be a bright idea for some of them to attack that instead of my poor reputation. Unfortunately, however, these gentlemen are incapable of a bright idea."

"No, madame, they do not propose to take your life; they propose to steal your coachman, your hairdresser and the robe that you are to wear to-morrow evening."

Jean Dubarry almost dropped his snuff-box; he swore a frightful oath; and the Countess, fully alive to the gravity of the news, stared open-eyed at Rochefort. Mademoiselle Fontrailles alone found words, other than blasphemies, to express her feelings.

"Ah, the wretches!" said she. "I thought they would leave no stone unturned by their vile hands."

"Monsieur," said the Comtesse, finding voice, "are you certain of what you say?"

"Why, madame, they invited me to take a part in the business."

"And you refused?"

"I refused, madame, not because I was of your party—in fact, to be perfectly plain, at that moment I was rather against you—I refused because I considered the whole proceeding a trick dishonouring to a gentleman; and I told Monsieur Camus my opinion of the business in a very few words."

"Comte Camus? Was he the agent who brought you this proposition?"

"He was, madame. I can say so now openly, since we are no longer friends. We quarrelled on a certain matter to-night, and if you are desirous of knowing the details of our little quarrel, Javotte will be able to supply them."

But the Comtesse had no ears for anything but the immediate danger that threatened her, and Rochefort had to tell the whole story from the beginning to the end.

"Death of all the devils!" cried Jean Dubarry, when the story was finished. "What an escape!"

"The question is," said Madame Dubarry, "have we escaped and shall we be able to prevent these infamous ones from carrying out their plan?"

"Prevent them!" cried Jean. "I will pistol the first man that lays hands on the carriage. I will lock the hairdresser up in the cellar till the moment comes when he is wanted. As for the modiste, we will arrange that she will be all right. Prevent them! *Mordieu!* Yes, we will prevent them."

"Excuse me," said Rochefort, "but if I may be allowed to give my advice, I would say to you, do not prevent them; let them carry out their plan."

"And let them take my carriage?"

"And the dress!" cried Mademoiselle Fontrailles.

"And the hairdresser!" put in Jean.

"Precisely," said Rochefort. "With that power which is at your disposal, madame, can you not have a new dress created, a new carriage obtained, and a new hairdresser found in the course of the few hours before us? My reason is this. Should they fancy that their plan is successful they will try nothing else. Should we thwart them openly, I would not say at what they would stop."

"Certainly," cried Jean, "there's truth in that. Can we not find a carriage, a dress and a coiffeur! Let us think—let us think!" He walked up and down the room, twisting his ruffles.

"No one can dress my hair like Lubin," said the Countess.

"Excuse me," said Rochefort, "but I believe there is a man whom I know who is a genius in the art. He is unknown; but the day after tomorrow, should you employ him, I believe he will be known to all Europe."

"As to the dress," said Mademoiselle Fontrailles, "you know, dear madame, that I was to be presented also. And our figures, are they not nearly the same?"

"*Dame!*" cried Jean, hitting himself a smack on the forehead. "I have the carriage! It is at Vaudrin's, in the Rue de la Madeleine. I saw it yesterday. It has been made to the order of the Comtesse Walewski, who, it seems, has not arrived yet; and all it requires is that the Dubarry arms should be painted over those of the Comtesse. We only want a loan of it, and five thousand francs will pay the bill."

The Comtesse turned to Rochefort.

"Monsieur Rochefort, I can trust your taste as I trust your friendship. All I ask you as a woman is this: Are you sure of your hairdresser?"

"Absolutely, madame; he is an artist to the tips of his fingers. I will stake my reputation on him."

The Comtesse inclined her head. She turned to Mademoiselle Fontrailles.

"Camille, have you thought that this act of generosity will ruin your presentation, for if I am to wear your dress, which is divinely beautiful and has cost you a hundred thousand francs, how, then, are you to appear before his Majesty?"

"Madame," said the girl, "I will have a cold; my presentation will be put off, that is all. And I esteem it a very small sacrifice to make for one who has benefited my family so deeply. Besides, madame, even if my presentation never occurred, it would not give me a sleepless night. The world has very few attractions for me."

Her dark eyes met those of Rochefort for a moment. There are seconds of time that carry in them the essence of years, and it seemed to Rochefort, in these few seconds, that some magic in the dark gaze of the eyes that held him had seized upon his mind, indelibly altering it.

The Comtesse's only reply was to lay her hand in a caressing way upon the beautiful arm of her friend. She turned to Jean:

"Jean, are you sure of the carriage?"

"*Mordieu*, yes. Vaudrin is ours entirely."

"Will it be possible to have the arms altered in this short time?"

"He will do it. I will call upon him to-morrow morning at six o'clock."

"Well," said the Comtesse, "I accept. I accept everything—your advice, Monsieur de Rochefort, and your sacrifice, Camille. But it is a debt I can never repay."

This sweet sentence was suddenly broken upon by a shriek of laughter from Jean. Dubarry rarely laughed, but when he did so it took him like convulsions—a very bad sign in a man. He flung himself on a couch and slapped his thigh.

"Their faces," cried he, "when you appear, when the usher cries, 'Madame la Comtesse de Béarn, Madame la Comtesse Dubarry.' Choiseul's face!"

"And Polastron's!" cried the Comtesse, catching up the laugh. "And de Guemenée's!"

Mademoiselle Fontrailles clasped her hands and laughed too. One might have fancied that they were quite assured of their victory over the profound and duplex Choiseul. They were laughing like this when a man-servant appeared. He had knocked at the door, but as he had received no answer and his business was urgent, he entered.

"Madame," said the servant, "Monsieur de Sartines has arrived, and would speak a word with you on a matter of importance."

"Monsieur de Sartines," said the Comtesse, rising, "at this hour! Show him in."

Everyone rose, and as they stood waiting, the little clock on the mantel chimed the hour. It was two o'clock in the morning. A minute passed, and then the servant returned, opening wide the door.

"Monsieur de Sartines."

Sartines bowed to the Comtesse, and then, individually, to each present. He showed scarcely any surprise at the presence of Rochefort.

Sartines was the burning centre of this conspiracy to present the Comtesse Dubarry at Court in the teeth of all the opposition of the nobles, and he wished his part in it to be as secret as possible; yet he did not question Rochefort's presence. He knew quite well that, Rochefort being there, he must have joined hands with the Comtesse. He was a man who never wasted time.

"Madame," said he, "I have grave news to tell you."

"Aha!" said the Comtesse, "more bad news. But stay, perhaps we know it. Is it the plot to rob me of my carriage and my hairdresser?"

"No, madame, I know nothing of any plot to rob you of your carriage. It is about the Comtesse de Béarn I have come to speak. Did she not receive a present to-day?"

"Yes, a basket of flowers from an old lady who belongs to her province. A Madame Turgis."

"Yes," said de Sartines, "and a Secret Service agent has just brought me news that amidst the flowers in that basket was a note."

"A note!"

"A letter, I should say, giving the Comtesse de Béarn a full and true account of the little plan by which she was induced to come to Paris."

"Oh, *mon Dieu!*" cried Madame Dubarry. "If the old fool only gets to know that, we are ruined! I know her as well as if I had constructed her. Once her pride and self-esteem are touched, she is hopeless to deal with."

"At what hour did this basket of flowers arrive?" asked de Sartines.

"At four o'clock."

"It has been in her private apartments ever since?"

"Yes."

De Sartines looked at the clock on the mantel.

"Ten hours and seven minutes. Well, madame, if in that time the Comtesse de Béarn has not discovered the note, you are saved. Go at once, madame, to her apartments, and if you can capture the accursed basket and its contents, for Heaven's sake do so. We must give her no chance to find it in the morning."

Madame Dubarry left the room without a word. She passed through the next room and down a corridor, where, taking a small lamp from a table, she turned with it in her hand to a narrow staircase leading to the next floor. Here she paused at a doorway, listened, and then, gently opening the door, entered the Comtesse de Béarn's sitting-room.

On a table near the window stood the fateful basket of flowers. The folding-doors leading to the bedroom were slightly open, and the intruder was approaching to seize the basket, when a sound from the bedroom made her pause, a low, deep groan, as if from someone in mortal pain.

"Help!" cried a muffled voice. "Who is that with the light? Ah! how I suffer!"

Without a word the Comtesse passed to the folding-doors, opened them, and next moment was in the bedroom. On the bed, half-covered with the clothes, lay the Comtesse de Béarn, on the floor near the stove lay a chocolate-pot upset, and the contents staining the parquet.

"*Mon Dieu!*" cried Madame Dubarry. "What has happened?"

"Ah, madame!" cried the old woman, "I am nearly dead. Here have I lain for hours in my misery. The pot of chocolate which I was heating on the stove upset—and look at my leg!"

She protruded a leg, and Madame Dubarry drew back with a cry. Foot and ankle and the leg half-way up to the shin bone were scalded in a manner that would be unpleasant to describe; but it was not the scalded leg that evoked Madame Dubarry's cry of anguish. It was the knowledge that her presentation was now hopeless. For the Comtesse de Béarn to undertake the journey to Versailles with a leg like that was clearly impossible.

The Choiseuls had taken all precautions, their bow had many strings. This was the fatal one. The old woman on the bed, though suffering severely, could not suppress the gleam of triumph that showed in her eyes, now fixed on those of the Comtesse.

"Ah, madame!" said Dubarry, "this was ill done. Had you known what personal issues to yourself were involved, you would have been more careful!" Then, lest she should lose all restraint over herself, and fling the lamp in her hand at the head of the scalded one, she rushed from the room, seized the basket of flowers, and with basket in one hand and lamp in the other reached the ground floor, taking this time the grand staircase. She broke into the room, where de Sartines and the others were seated, flung the basket on a chair, so that it upset and the contents tumbled pell-mell over the floor, and broke into tears.

Everyone knew.

"Has she found out?" cried Jean.

"Madame," said de Sartines, waving the Vicomte aside, "calm yourself; all may not yet be lost."

"Ah, monsieur, you do not know," sobbed the unfortunate woman. "Not only has she found out, but she has scalded her leg, so that the affair is now absolutely hopeless." She told her tale, and as she told it her sobs ceased, her eyes grew bright, and she finished standing before them with clenched hands and sparkling eyes, more beautiful than ever.

Mademoiselle Fontrailles had been collecting the flowers; there was no sign of a letter among them. Jean Dubarry, white and beyond speech and unable to vent his spleen on anything else, had cuffed the China mandarin on to the floor, where it lay shattered. Rochefort, carried away by the tragedy, was cursing. De Sartines only was calm.

"It is impossible, then, for her to appear at Versailles?" said he.

"Utterly, monsieur."

"Well, madame," said de Sartines, "courage; all is not yet lost."

"Ah, Monsieur de Sartines," said the Comtesse, "what do you mean? Do you not know as well as I do that, failing the Comtesse de Béarn, the thing is impossible? Even were I to find someone qualified to take the place of this old woman, there would still be all the formalities of the application. Monsieur de la Vrillière would have to inquire into the antecedents of the lady, and Monsieur de Coigny would have to receive the request, only to lose it for Monsieur to find and cancel on account of the delay."

"Madame," cut in de Sartines, "the plan which has just occurred to me has nothing to do with the finding of a substitute. Madame la Comtesse de Béarn shall present you; or, let us put it in this way: to-morrow evening at ten o'clock you will be presented to his Majesty at the Court of Versailles. I am only mortal, and therefore fallible; but if you will leave the matter in my hands the thing shall be done, always saving the direct interposition of God."

"You are, then, a magician?" cried the Comtesse.

"No, madame; or only a white magician who works through human agency."

"Ah, Monsieur de Sartines," cried the Comtesse, hope appearing again in her eyes, "if you can only help me in this, I shall pray for you till my dying day!"

"Oh, madame," replied de Sartines, with a laugh, "I would never dream of imposing such a task upon the most beautiful lips in the world. I only ask you now to work with me, for this immediate end."

"And what can I do?"

"Carry on all your preparations for to-morrow night. Monsieur Rochefort has explained to me the plot for the stealing of the carriage, the dress and the coiffeur. Let the Vicomte attend to the carriage, let Mademoiselle Fontrailles supply you with her dress, and let your most trusted servant fetch the coiffeur that Monsieur Rochefort knows of."

"I will fetch him myself," said Rochefort.

"No, Rochefort," said de Sartines, "I have need of you for something else. May I put my reliance on your obedience in this crisis?"

"Implicitly, Sartines," replied the Comte. "Call upon me for what you will. *Mordieu!* I have fought many a duel, but never has a fight stirred my blood like this. I will act any part or dress for any part except the part of spectator."

"I will find enough for you to do, and now I must be going. It is after three o'clock, and if you will take a seat in my carriage, I will give you a lift on your way home, and explain what I want."

"And I will see you again, monsieur?" said the Comtesse, addressing the Minister of Police.

"Not till after the presentation, Madame, when I hope to have the honour of kissing your hand. You understand, I have nothing to do with this affair. You must even abuse me to your friends, who are absolutely sure to be in communication with your enemies. And now, if I were you, I would send for your physician to attend to Madame de Béarn's leg."

He bade his adieux.

Rochefort, having scribbled the name of the coiffeur on a piece of paper supplied by Jean, gazed into the eyes of Mademoiselle Fontrailles, as he lifted his lips from her hand. He fancied that her glance told him all that he wished, and more than he had hoped.

In the hall Sartines enveloped himself in a black cloak, put on a broad-brimmed hat, and, followed by Rochefort, entered the carriage that was waiting in the courtyard. It was a carriage, perfectly plain, without adornment, such as the Minister used when wishing to mask his movements.

"You did not come in your own carriage, then?" said Rochefort, as they drove away.

"Oh, dear, no," said Sartines. "My carriage is still waiting at Choiseul's. I slipped away, having already sent an agent for this plain carriage to meet me at the third lamp-post on the right, as you go up the Rue St. Honoré from the Rue du Faubourg."

"You had an agent in attendance, then?"

"My dear Rochefort, three of Choiseul's servants are my agents, and it was from one of them that I learned of this precious plot about the basket of flowers. You live in the Rue de Longueville!"

"Ah, you know my new address!" said Rochefort, laughing.

"I know everything about you, my dear Rochefort. Now, will you put your head out of the window, and tell the coachman to drive to the Rue de Longueville? I cannot go back to the Hôtel de Sartines at once. I must crave the shelter of your apartments; we are being followed."

"Followed?"

"*Mordieu*, yes! The Dubarrys' house has been watched all day. When I drove up in this carriage, I saw one of Choiseul's agents, who, without doubt, tried to question my coachman whilst I was in the house; a perfectly useless proceeding, as my coachman is Sergeant Bonvallot. I know quite well, now, that there is a man running after us, so do as I say."

Rochefort put his head out and gave the direction.

"My faith!" said he, as he resumed his place, "but they are keen, the Choiseuls."

"They are more than that. You cannot guess at all the way this matter has stirred the whole court. Of course, when the thing is over and done with, and the presentation an accomplished matter, the Comtesse will not be able to number her friends. But she is lost if Choiseul succeeds, and if she succeeds Choiseul is lost. Once give her an accredited place at court, and the breaking of Choiseul will be only the matter of a few months."

"Sartines," said the young man with that daring which gave him permission to say things other men would not have dreamed of saying, "you are not doing this for love of the Dubarry?"

"I?" said de Sartines. "I am doing it to break Choiseul."

The carriage which had entered the Rue de Longueville stopped at a house on the left, and the two men got out.

CHAPTER IV

THE METHODS OF MONSIEUR DE SARTINES

DE SARTINES said a word to his coachman and, without even glancing down the street to see if he were followed or not, entered the house, the door of which Rochefort had opened with a key. They passed upstairs to the apartments of the Count. In the sitting-room de Sartines cast off his cloak, flung it on a chair with his hat, and took his seat.

"Now let us talk for a moment," said he. "And first, a word about yourself. It is unfortunate that you killed that man, considering that he was one of Choiseul's agents."

"I killed him in self-defence," said Rochefort; "or at least, I can say that he attempted my life before I took his."

"Oh, the killing is nothing," said de Sartines. "The vermin is well out of the way. What really matters is, that you balked Choiseul in his attempt to spy upon Dubarry's secrets. Of course, he may never know the truth of the matter; but, if he does—well, you will need a lot of protection, and we will endeavour to find it for you. Now to the Comtesse's business. It is quite clear that the old Béarn woman is literally out of court. Every other woman in Paris or Versailles is equally impossible, or, at least, seemingly so. I, as Minister of Police, have great power; but I am powerless to help, for to help I would have to declare my hand openly, which, as you well may guess, is impossible to one in my position. Besides, my power has limits. I cannot say to one of these Court women: 'You *shall* present Madame Dubarry to-night.' No; yet all the same, I am powerful enough to ensure that presentation, I believe."

Rochefort listened with interest. It was rarely that de Sartines unbosomed himself, and when he did it was generally only to show a cuirass of steel painted to imitate flesh; but to-night was different. He knew Rochefort to be absolutely reliable to those who trusted him.

"You talk in enigmas, my dear Sartines," said the young man. "You say you are powerless, and then you say you are powerful enough to assure the presentation. Please explain yourself."

"No man can explain himself, with the exception, perhaps, of Monsieur Rousseau, whose 'Confessions' you have perhaps read. But a man may explain his methods. Well, my methods are these. Being by nature a rather stupid and lazy man, I seek out the cleverest and most active men I can find to act for me. People fancy that my life is spent in searching for criminals, political offenders, and so forth; on the contrary, it is spent in looking for clever men. I have one gift, without which no man can hold a position like mine. I know men.

"More than that, I hunt for men and buy them just as M. Boehmer hunts for and buys diamonds. The consequence is that I have more genius at my command in the Hôtel de Sartines than his Majesty has at Versailles or Choiseul at the Ministry. I have Escritain, the greatest linguist in France, who knows not only all European languages, but all dialects. I have Fremin, the first cryptographer. I have Jumeau, the first accountant, who could reduce the value of the universe to francs and sous and, more important, discover an error in his work of one centime. I have Beauregard, the bravest man in France; Verpellieux, the best swordsman; Valjean, whose tongue would talk him into the nether regions and whose hand, if it caught hold of some new Eurydice, would bring her out, even though it fetched everything else with her. I have Formineux, a blind man whose sense of smell is phenomenal; and I have Lavenne, the greatest Secret Service agent in the world. Bring me a book you can't translate, the name of a man you can't find, a crime you can't fathom, a suspicion you want verified, you will find the answer at the Hôtel de Sartines. One of these brave men, who are mine, will read the riddle.

"But outside the Hôtel de Sartines I have other men at my service. Yes, you will find a lot of people attached to us. You yourself, my dear Rochefort, have just become one of us. The Hôtel de Sartines has touched you."

Rochefort laughed. "If it does not touch me any more unpleasantly than now, I shall not mind," said he. "But you have not yet explained."

"What?"

"Your plans as to the Dubarry."

"Oh, that. I was coming to that; let me come to it in my own way. I have shown you the power at my disposal. I have all sorts of brains ready to work for me, all sorts of hands ready to do my bidding; but all those brains and hands would be useless to me had I not an intimate knowledge of their capacities, and had I not the power of selection. More than that, my dear Rochefort; I have, I believe, the dramatist's gift of valuing and using shades of character. Dealing, as I do, with the most complex and highly civilized society in the world, I would be lost without this gift, which might have made me a good dramatist if Fate had not condemned me to be a policeman. In fact, my work at Versailles and in Paris has mainly to do with the reading backwards through plots, far more complicated than the plots of Molière, to find the authors' names.

"Now I come to the Dubarry business. This woman must be presented to-morrow night. Choiseul has as good as stolen her carriage and her dressmaker—that will be put right. Choiseul has succeeded in making Madame de Béarn half boil herself to death. But Choiseul, who fancies that he has the whole business in the palm of his hand, has reckoned without the Hôtel de Sartines and the geniuses whom I have collected for years past, just as Monsieur d'Anjou collects seals or Monsieur de Duras Roman coins.

"I am about to employ one of these geniuses to work a miracle for Madame Dubarry. His name is Ferminard. He lives at the Maison Gambrinus—which is a tavern in the Porcheron quarter—and, as you have promised to serve us, you will go there to-morrow at noon, or a little before, with my agent Lavenne, and conduct this Ferminard to the Rue de Valois. Lavenne will not go to the Rue de Valois, for I will have other work for him to do, and besides, it is just as well for him not to go near the Dubarrys' house, for, clever as he is in the art of disguise, Choiseul will have men watching all day who have the scent of hounds. We must run no risks."

"Let us understand," said Rochefort. "I am to meet your agent, Lavenne—where?"

"He will call for you here."

"Good! Then I am to go with him to the Maison Gambrinus, find Ferminard, and conduct him to Madame Dubarry's house in the Rue de Valois—all that seems very simple."

"Perhaps. But you must be on your guard, for this Ferminard is a *bon viveur*. Taverns simply suck him in, and were he to get lost in one, you would find him next drunk and useless."

"A drunkard?"

"No, a man who drinks. Never look down on these people, Rochefort. Drink may be simply the rags a beggar walks in, or the robes and regalia that a royal mind adorns itself with to enter the kingdom of dreams."

"And what am I to tell this Ferminard to do?"

"You are to tell him nothing, simply because you are a stranger to him, and he would look on orders from a stranger as an impertinence. Lavenne, however, knows him to the bone, and is a friend of his. Lavenne will give him private instructions, and then hand him over to you."

"Very well. I will obey your orders, though they completely mystify me."

"I assure you," said de Sartines, "that I have no intention of mystifying you; but I cannot explain my idea to you simply because I have to explain it to Lavenne. It is after four in the morning, and I must get back to the Hôtel de Sartines. There is a man still watching at the corner of the street; he must not follow me. Now, do as I tell you. Take my black cloak and broad-brimmed hat, and put them on. We are both about the same size. Go out, walk down the street, go down the Rue de la Tour, and then through the Rue Picpus, returning here by the Rue de la Vallière. The fool will follow you all the time."

"And you?"

"And I," said de Sartines, putting on Rochefort's cloak and hat, "will slip away to the Hôtel de Sartines, whilst you are leading that *sot* his dance."

"But he will follow me back here."

"Of course he will, and he will see you go in and shut the door. Lavenne will bring you back your cloak and hat in a parcel. The point is, that they will never know that the man in the black cloak and hat, who left the Hôtel Dubarry with Monsieur Rochefort, returned to the Hôtel de Sartines."

"But your carriage?"

"I told the coachman to take the carriage back to the place it came from. They will not follow an empty carriage; were they to do so, they would get nothing for their pains, as it came from a livery stable managed by the wife of Jumeau, that accountant of whom I spoke just now."

Rochefort looked in astonishment at this man, whose methods were as intricate and minute as the reasoning power that directed them; whose life was a maze to which he alone possessed the clue, and whose path was never in a straight line.

He followed implicitly the instructions he had received, conscious all the time that he was being tracked, and once glimpsing a stealthy form that slipped from house-shadow to house-shadow. When he returned, de Sartines had vanished, and, casting himself on his bed dressed as he was, wearied with the night's work, he fell asleep.

CHAPTER V

FERMINARD

WHEN he awoke, with the full daylight staring into the room, the first remembrance that came to him was that of Mademoiselle Fontrailles. The whole of the past night seemed like some page torn from a romance; only this girl from the South seemed real. He was in love, for the first time in his life, and he did not recognize the fact that his passion had bound him openly to the Dubarrys, cast him head over heels into politics, to sink or swim with that exceedingly dubious family.

Rochefort had a big stake to lose; he had estates in Auvergne, his youth and his position in society. He had no political ambitions, but he had an ambition, ever living and always being gratified, to shine in his own peculiar way. He set the fashion in coats and morals, his sayings were repeated, even though many of them were scarcely worth repetition; his eccentricities, which were genuine and not assumed, were a feature of Paris life. Paris was his true home, and though he was seen frequently at Versailles, he was seen more often at the Café de Régence. He was the first of the dandies, the predecessor of the *boulevardier* of the Boulevard de Gand and the Café de Paris, the prefiguration in flesh of Tortoni's and the Second Empire.

Our present utilitarian age could no more produce a Rochefort than one of our engineers could produce a butterfly; only the full summer of social life which fell on Athens four hundred years before Christ, which fell on France in the time of Louis XIV. and Louis XV., and which brushed England with its wing in the time of the Regency, can produce these rare and useless human flowers. Useless, that is to say, as fine pictures, Ming figures, and live dragon-flies are useless.

He had, then, a big stake to lose by venturing into the stormy arena of politics, for the hand of de Choiseul was a heavy hand, and with the famous diamond-rimmed snuff-box held many things, including confiscation, exile, and even imprisonment. But Rochefort never thought of this, and, if he had thought of it, he would have pursued his present course absolutely unchecked. This dandy and trifler with life had no thought at all for danger, and the prudence that arises from self-interest was not one of his possessions. Leaving all that aside, he was in love, and the object of his love was in the path of his present progress.

He rang for Lermina, his valet, and bathed and dressed himself with most scrupulous care. It was now half-past eleven. He ordered *déjeuner* to be served a quarter of an hour earlier than its usual time, and was seated at the meal when Lavenne was announced. He told the servant to show the visitor up, and when Lavenne entered rose from the table to greet him.

Lavenne formed a striking contrast to the elegant Rochefort. Lavenne was a man who, at first sight, seemed a young man, and at second sight, a man of middle age, soberly dressed, of middle height, and remarkable only for eyes wonderfully bright and luminous. Rochefort, who did not possess de Sartines' power of reading men, had still the gift of deciding at once whether a person pleased him or not. He liked this man's manner and appearance and face, and received him in a manner that at once made the newcomer at home.

Rochefort had not two manners, one for the rich and one for the poor. Whilst always rigidly keeping his own place, he would talk familiarly with anyone, from the king to the beggar at the corner of the street. But it would go hard with the man who presumed on this fact. Lavenne knew Rochefort quite well by name and appearance, had ranked him among the titled larvæ of the Court who were always passing under his eyes, and was surprised to find, after a few minutes' talk, what a pleasant person he was.

"I have left the hat and cloak, monsieur, with your servant," said Lavenne. "My master, the Comte de Sartines, gave me instructions to bring them with me.

"Ah, the hat and cloak!" said Rochefort. "I had forgotten them. Thanks. Will you not be seated? I have just finished *déjeuner*, and shall be quite at your disposal when the carriage arrives. I ordered it for twelve, as I suppose we had better drive to this place, which is in the Porcheron district. Will you not have a glass of wine?" He poured out a glass of Beaune, and whilst Lavenne drank it, finished his breakfast, chatting all the time, but saying nothing at all on the object of their journey till they were in the carriage and driving to their destination.

"You expect to find him in, this Monsieur Ferminard?" asked Rochefort.

"Yes, monsieur. He is very poor just now, and when in that state he avoids the streets and cafés."

"Ah, ah!" said Rochefort, wondering how this very poor man, who avoided even the streets, could be of help to the powerful Comtesse Dubarry at one of the most critical moments of her life. But he said nothing more; he did not like to appear as though he were trying to draw Lavenne out.

The Porcheron quarter lay between the Faubourg Montmartre and La Ville l'Évêque. It was sparsely populated, and here, at a tavern whose sign represented a hound running down a hare amidst long grass, the carriage drew up.

This was the Maison Gambrinus, a house of considerable repute for the excellence of its wine. Founded in the year 1614 by William Gambrinus, a Dutchman from Dordrecht, it was famous for three things—the excellence of its cookery, the goodness of its wine, and the modesty of its charges. Turgis, who now owned the place, possessed a wife who had been kitchenmaid at the Hôtel Noailles under the famous Coquellard; being a pretty girl, she had obtained from him, as a mark of his favour and as a wedding gift, a recipe for stewing veal, that he reckoned as one of his chief possessions. This same recipe brought people to the Maison Gambrinus from all over Paris, so that Turgis did a fair enough business.

As the carriage drew up, a big man appeared at the door of the inn; he was so broad that he nearly filled the doorway, which was by no means narrow. One might have fancied that the mould for his face had been cast on that great and jovial day when Nature, tired of making ordinary folk, took thought and said to herself: "Now let us make an innkeeper."

It was an ideal face of its kind—fat, material, smiling—and promising everything in the way of good cheer and comfort. Yet to-day, to Lavenne's surprise, this face, ordinarily so jovial, wore an expression that sat ill upon it, or rather, one might say, it had lost somewhat the natural expression that sat so well upon it.

"Turgis," said Lavenne, as they followed him into the big room with a sanded floor, which formed the *salle-à-manger* and bar combined, "we have come to see Monsieur Ferminard. Is he in?"

"Oh, *mon Dieu!*" cried Turgis, "is he in? Why, Monsieur Lavenne, he has not been out for a fortnight; he has driven half my customers away, and his bill is still owing. Three hams, six dozen eggs, thirty-seven bottles of wine of Anjou, bread, salt, olives; a bill for sixty-five francs, to say nothing of the money I have lost through him. Before I take another poet as a guest, I will set light with my own hand to the Máison Gambrinus. Listen to him!"

From an adjoining room came the sound of a loud and high-pitched voice, laughing, talking, bursting out now and then into snatches of song, and now low-pitched and seemingly engaged in argument. Then, all at once, came a furious stamping, a cry, and the sound of a table being overset.

"*Pardieu!*" cried Rochefort, "he seems busy. What on earth is he doing?"

"Doing, monsieur!" replied the host. "Nothing. He is writing a play."

"Does he write with his feet, then, this Monsieur Ferminard?"

"Aye, does he," replied Turgis, bending to lift a bottle from the floor and placing it on one of the tables, "and with his tongue and fists and head. Gascon that he is, he acts all his tragedies as he writes them. He has been writing a duel since noon, and has smashed, God knows how much of my furniture. Sixty-five francs he owes me, which will not be paid till his tragedy is finished; by which time, Heaven help me! I fear he will have devoured and drunk the contents of my cellar and destroyed my inn. And, were it not that he is the best fellow going and once did me a service, I would bundle him out of my place neck and crop, poems, plays and all."

The noise from the adjoining room suddenly ceased, as if the poet had become aware of the voices of the innkeeper and the new-comers. The door burst open, and a man in his shirt-sleeves—a short, rather stout, clean-shaved individual, with a mobile face and bright, piercing eyes—appeared. He held a pen in his hand.

"*Morbleu!*" cried this apparition, in a testy voice, speaking to the landlord without even a glance at the others. "Have you no thought for the comfort of your guests? With your chatter, chatter, chatter, you have spoilt one of the finest of my passages."

"And what about my tables?" burst out Turgis, suddenly flying into a rage, "and my glasses? Four broken this day, and my wainscoting pierced with the point of your rapier, and my room half wrecked—and you talk to me of your passages! What about my custom driven away? For one may not sneeze, it appears to me, without your poems being upset and your passages spoilt. What about my sixty-five francs?"

"They shall be paid," said the poet, taking a minor key. "Ah, Monsieur Lavenne!" His eye had just fallen on Lavenne.

"Pardon me," said Lavenne to Rochefort. He went towards the tragedian, took him by the arm and drew him into the adjoining room. Then he shut the door.

Turgis wiped his forehead. "His passages! I wish he would find a passage to take him to the devil. What may I get for monsieur?"

"Get me a bottle of that wine for which you are so famous," said Rochefort, taking a seat at a table, "and two glasses—that is right. He seems a strange customer, this Monsieur Ferminard."

"Oh, monsieur," replied Turgis, opening the wine and filling the glasses, "he would be right enough were he only to stick to his trade."

"And what is his trade?"

"An actor, monsieur; he is a great actor. He belonged to the Théâtre Molière; but he quarrelled with the director, and the quarrel came to blows, and Ferminard wounded the director. Yes, monsieur, he would now be in prison only for Monsieur de Sartines, who took an interest in him, having seen him act. Ah, monsieur, he was a great actor. But he was not content to be an actor. Oh, no! What does he do but write a comedy himself, to beat Molière? And what does he do but get the ear of the Duc de la Vrillière and his permission to produce this precious comedy at Versailles, with Court ladies and gentlemen to act in it. If he had acted himself in it, the thing would have been saved, but belonging to the Théâtre Molière, he was bound by agreement not to act elsewhere.

"Well, monsieur, the thing went so badly that he abused the actors and actresses when they came off the stage, and, as a result, he was caned by Monsieur de Coigny."

"Ah!" said Rochefort, "I heard something of that; but I was away from Paris, and I did not hear the details. He abused them. *Mordieu!* that's good."

"Yes, monsieur. I had the story from his own mouth. He told Madame de Duras, who was acting as one of his precious shepherdesses, that her head was as wooden as her legs. As for me, I would have been a mouse among all that company; but he—he does not care for the King himself; and so outraged does he feel even still, that could he burn Versailles down and all it contains he would be happy. He is not the man to forgive the strokes of Monsieur de Coigny's cane. Your health, monsieur! Still the pity is that the fault was not with the actors, but with the play. It is common sense, besides. I, for instance, am a very good man at selling that wine you are drinking. But if I were to go to Anjou and try to make that wine, I would not be good at the business. Just so! A man may be a very good actor, and yet may not be able to write a play that another man could act well in."

A sudden burst of laughter from the adjoining room cut Turgis short.

"What is up now, I wonder?" said he.

"He seems laughing at something that Monsieur Lavenne is telling him," said Rochefort, whose interest in the whole affair had suddenly taken on an extra keenness, and who was deeply puzzled by a business of which he could find no possible explanation. "Come, refill your glass! You deserve to drink such good wine since you choose to sell it."

The landlord did as he was told without the slightest trace of unwillingness, and they sat talking on indifferent matters till the door of the next room suddenly opened and Lavenne appeared.

He took Rochefort outside the inn to the roadway, where the carriage was still in waiting.

"Monsieur," said Lavenne, "I have arranged everything with Ferminard. But it is absolutely necessary that he should go to the Rue de Valois in such a fashion that no one can recognize him. Will you, therefore, take your seat in the carriage, and he will join you in a few minutes."

"Certainly," said Rochefort, who had drunk enough wine and on whom the conversation of the innkeeper had begun to pall. "And here is a louis to pay the score. He can keep the change."

"Thank you, monsieur," said Lavenne. "You will see me no more, for my part in this business is now over."

"Well, then, good-day to you," said the Comte, "and thank you for your pleasant company."

Lavenne bowed and returned to the inn, and Rochefort, telling his coachman to wait, got into the carriage. Five minutes passed, and then ten. He was becoming impatient, when from the inn door emerged an old man of miserable appearance who blinked at the sun, blinked at the carriage, and then came towards it and placed his hand on the door-handle.

Rochefort, who did not care for the appearance of this person, was on the point of asking him what the devil he wanted, when he caught a glimpse of Lavenne at the inn door, nodding to him to indicate that all was right. Then he grasped the fact that this incredible mass of decrepitude was Ferminard. He helped the old fellow in, and the driver, who already had his instructions, turned his horses, whipped them up, and started off in the direction of the Faubourg St. Honoré.

"Well, Monsieur Ferminard," said Rochefort, laughing, "if I had not had the honour of seeing you when comparatively young, I would not have known you in your old age."

"Oh, that is nothing, monsieur," said Ferminard; "to turn oneself into an old man is an easy matter. The great difficulty is for an actor to turn himself into a youth. Has Monsieur ever seen me act?"

"Often," said Rochefort, who, in fact, had little care for the theatre, and had never seen him act, "and I was charmed."

"Monsieur is very good to say so. As for me, I have never been charmed by my own acting, though 'twas passable enough; but the fact is, monsieur, I was not born an actor. I was born a dramatist."

"Oh, ho!"

"Yes, monsieur, that is how fate treats one. My head is full of my creations; they seize me, and make me write. Ah! whilst I am writing, then I can act; if I were impersonating one of my own characters on the stage, then I could act. But when I have to play the part of some other man's creation in character, then I feel a stick."

"You have written many plays?"

"Numerous, monsieur," said the greatest actor and worst dramatist in France.

"I hear you had one staged in Versailles."

"Oh, *mon Dieu!*" said Ferminard. "All France knows that tale. Ah, *dame*, when I think of it, I could kick this coach to pieces—I could eat the world. Well, they shall be rewarded. Ferminard will have his revenge."

He laughed and slapped his thigh.

They had entered the Rue de Pontoise, which led into the Rue de Valois.

"And now, monsieur," said Ferminard, "I will forget, if you please, that I am an actor, and remember that I am an old man."

He did, with strange effect. As the carriage turned into the courtyard of the Hôtel Dubarry, had any spy been watching the antique face of Ferminard at the window of the coach, he would have sent a report absolutely confusing to the Choiseul faction. He alighted, leaning on Rochefort's arm. In the hall, when they were admitted, Jean Dubarry, who was waiting and who evidently had been advised by de Sartines of what to expect, seized upon Ferminard as though he had been a long-lost treasure, and spirited him away down a corridor, apologizing to Rochefort, and calling back to him over his shoulder to wait for a moment until he returned.

Rochefort, left alone, was turning to look at a stand of arms, supposed to contain the pikes and swords and spears of vanished Dubarrys slain in warfare, when a step drew his attention, and turning, he found himself face to face with Javotte. He had completely forgotten Javotte. But she had not forgotten him. She had a tray of glasses in her hand, and as their eyes met she blushed, looked down, and then glanced up again with a charming smile.

He had kissed her the night before; but she was only one of the thousand girls that the light-hearted Rochefort had kissed in passing, so to speak, and without ulterior intent. The pleasantest thing in the world is to kiss a pretty girl, just as one of the pleasantest things in the world is to draw a rose towards one, inhale its perfume, and release it unharmed; but very few men have the art of doing the thing successfully. Rochefort had. Just as some old gentlemen, by sheer power of personality, can say the most *risqué* and terrible things without giving offence, so could Rochefort with women do things and say things that another man would not have dared. It was the touch of irresponsibility in his nature that gave him, perhaps, this power.

It was not the kiss lightly given the night before that made Javotte blush; it was the presence of Rochefort. Since his rescue of her, he completely filled her mind.

"Ah! little one," said he, "good-morning!"

"Good-morning, monsieur."

"And where are you going?"

"To the room of Madame la Comtesse, though I am no longer in her service."

"No longer in her service?"

"No, monsieur."

"And in whose service are you now, *petite?*"

"I belong to Mademoiselle Fontrailles, monsieur. I was only temporarily with Madame la Comtesse; and as her maid, Jacqueline, has returned to her this morning, and as I seemed to please Mademoiselle Fontrailles, who is staying here till after the presentation, I entered her service."

"Ah, ha!" said Rochefort. "And where does mademoiselle live?"

"She has apartments in the Rue St. Dominic, monsieur, where she lives with her nurse."

"Her nurse!"

"Yes, monsieur, an old Indian woman, who is as black as my shoe."

The lively Javotte was proceeding to a vivacious description of her black sister from Martinique when a step on the stairs checked her; she vanished with the glasses, and Rochefort, turning, found himself face to face with Mademoiselle Fontrailles, who had just entered the hall.

They bowed to one another ceremoniously. It seemed to Rochefort that, beautiful as she had appeared on the night before, she was even more beautiful by daylight, here in the deserted hall of the Hôtel Dubarry.

"Well, mademoiselle," said he, "and how are things progressing?"

"Marvellously, monsieur; but do not let us talk here of state secrets." She led the way into the little room where they had parted but a few hours before.

"The carriage has been arranged for, your coiffeur will, I am sure, prove a success; he has arrived, and the Vicomte Jean has put him under lock and key, with a pocketful of louis to play with, and the promise of an equal amount when his work is done; my poor dress is now being altered and promises a perfect fit. We are saved, in fact, and thanks to you."

"No, mademoiselle, thanks to luck; for if I had not gone to Choiseul's ball I would not have met you."

"You mean, you would not have discovered the plot to steal the carriage and the dress."

"But for you the plot would have lain in my mind unrevealed. I have a horror of Court intrigue. As it is, I have set myself against Choiseul, and killed one of his agents, and thwarted his best hopes; but I count all that nothing in your service."

Mademoiselle Fontrailles gazed at him steadily as he stood there with this patent declaration of homage on his lips, and all the laughter and lightness gone from his happy-go-lucky and defiant face.

She guessed now from his face and manner what was in his mind, and that the slightest weakening on her part would bring him down on his knee before her.

"I thank you, monsieur," said she. "And now to the question of the Comtesse de Béarn."

"Ah!" said Rochefort, inwardly cursing the Comtesse de Béarn, "I had forgotten the Comtesse. And how is she this morning?"

"She is still very bad."

"And to-night?"

"She will be quite unable to attend at Versailles."

Rochefort was about to make a remark when the door leading to the adjoining room opened, and Madame Dubarry herself appeared, young, fresh, triumphant and laughing.

"Did I hear you speaking of the Comtesse de Béarn?" asked she, as she extended her hand to Rochefort.

"Yes, madame, and I am grieved to hear that she is still indisposed."

"Then, monsieur, you have heard false news. Madame la Comtesse has nearly recovered, and will be quite well enough to act for me to-night."

Mademoiselle Fontrailles smiled, and Rochefort, not knowing what to make of these contradictory statements, stood glancing from one to the other of his informers.

"Not only that," continued Madame Dubarry, "but you may tell everyone the news. That Madame la Comtesse has had a slight accident and has now perfectly recovered. And now I must dismiss you, dear Monsieur Rochefort, for I have a world of business before me; but only till to-night, when we will meet at Versailles. You will be there, will you not?"

"Yes," said Rochefort, "I shall be there to see your triumph—and Mademoiselle Fontrailles?"

"I shall not be there," said the girl, "or only in spirit; but my dress will be there."

"Ah!" said Rochefort, "even that is something."

Then off he went. Light-hearted now and laughing, for it seemed to him that, though his affair had seemingly not made an inch of progress, all was well between him and Camille Fontrailles.

CHAPTER VI

THE COMTESSE DE BÉARN

TO present the mentality of the Comtesse de Béarn one would have to reconstruct the lady, and rebuild from all sorts of medieval constituents her mind, person and dress. Feudal times have left us cities such as Nuremberg and Vittoria standing just as they stood in the twilight of the Middle Ages, but the people have vanished, only vaguely to be recalled.

The Comtesse de Béarn was medieval, and carried the twelfth century clinging to her coif and mantelet right into the heart of the Paris of 1770. Arrogant, narrow, superstitious and proud as Lucifer, this old lady, impoverished by years of litigation with the family of Saluce, inveigled up to Paris by a false statement that her lawsuit was about to be settled to her advantage, entertained by the Dubarrys and filled by them with promises and hopes, had agreed to act as introducer to the Comtesse. She disliked the business, but was prepared to swallow it for the sake of the lawsuit.

Choiseul's note conveyed in the basket of flowers had acted with withering effect. It was written by a master mind that understood finely the mind it was addressing, and its one object was to convey the sentence: "You have been tricked."

She saw the truth at once; she had been fetched up to Paris to act as a servant in the Dubarrys' interests; she had been outwitted, played with. In an instant, twenty obscure and dubious happenings fell into their proper place, and she saw in a flash not only the deception but the fact that when she was done with she would be cast aside like a sucked orange; returned to her castle on the banks of the Meuse.

The unholy anger that filled the old lady's mind might have led her at once to open revolt had she not possessed a lively sense of the power of the Dubarrys, and an instinctive fear of the Vicomte Jean. To revolt and say: "I will take no part in the presentation," would have led to a pitched battle, in which she felt she would be worsted. She was too old and friendless to fight all these young, vigorous people who were on their own ground. But she would not present the woman who had tricked her at the Court of Versailles.

She boiled a pot of chocolate, and poured the contents over her foot and leg. The physical agony was nothing to the satisfaction of her mind. Madame Dubarry's face when she saw the wound was more soothing than all the cold cream that Noirmont, the Dubarrys' doctor, applied to the scald; and this morning, stretched on her back, with her leg swathed in cotton and the pain eased, she revelled in the thought of her enemy's discomfiture. She felt no fear; they could not kill her; they could not turn her out of the house; she was an honoured guest, and she lay waiting for the distraction and the wailing and tears of the Dubarry woman, and the storming of the Vicomte Jean.

Instead of these came, at twelve o'clock or thereabouts, Noirmont, the physician, accompanied by Chon Dubarry, who had just arrived from Luciennes. The charming Chon seemed in the best spirits, and was full of solicitation and pity for her "dear Comtesse."

Noirmont examined the leg, declared that his treatment had produced a decidedly beneficial effect, and, without a word as to when the patient might expect to be able to walk again, bowed himself out, leaving Chon and the Comtesse together.

"You see, my dear lady," said the old woman, "how fallible we all are to accident. But for that unlucky pot of chocolate, I would now be dressed, and ready to pay my *devoirs* to Madame la Comtesse; as it is, if I am able to leave my bed in a week's time I will be fortunate, and even then I will, without doubt, have to be carried from this house to my carriage."

"Madame," said Chon devoutly, "we are all in the hands of Providence, whose decrees are inscrutable. Let us, then, bear our troubles with a spirit, and hope for the best."

"Oh, *mon Dieu!*" cried the old woman, irritated at the extraordinary cheerfulness of the other, and feeling instinctively that some new move of the accursed Dubarrys was in progress, "it is easy for the whole in body and limb to dictate cheerfulness to the afflicted. Here am I laid up, and my affairs needing my attention in the country; but I think less of them than of the Court to-night, which I am unable to attend, and of the presentation which I am debarred from taking my part in. Not on my own account, for I have long given up the vanities of the world, but on account of Madame la Comtesse Dubarry."

"Truly, there seems a fate in it," said Chon, with great composure and cheerfulness. "Everything seemed going on so happily for your interests and ours. Well, it cannot be helped; there is no use in grumbling. The great thing now, dear Madame de Béarn, is your health, which is, after all, more important to you than money or success in lawsuits. Can I order you anything that you may require?"

The only thing Madame de Béarn could have wished for at the moment was Madame Dubarry's head on a charger, but she did not put her desire in words. She lay watching with her bright old eyes whilst Chon, with a curtsey, turned and left the room. Then she lay thinking.

She was beaten. The Dubarrys had in some way found a method of evading defeat. Unfortunate Comtesse! When she had put herself to all this pain and discomfort she little knew that she was setting herself, not against the Dubarrys alone, but against de Sartines, and all the wit, ingenuity and genius of the Hôtel de Sartines. Moss-grown in her old château by the Meuse, she knew nothing of Paris, its trickery and its artifice. She had all this yet to learn.

All that she knew now was the fact that the plans of her enemies were prospering, and the mad desire to thwart them would have given her energy and fortitude enough to leave her bed, and hobble from the house, had she not known quite well that such a thing was impossible. The Dubarrys would not let her go.

Then a plan occurred to her. She rang the bell which had been placed on the table beside her, and when the maid entered, ordered her to fetch at once Madame Turgis, the old lady from her province who had sent her the basket of flowers.

"She lives in the Rue Petit Picpus, No. 10," said she. "And ask her to come at once, for I feel worse."

The maid left the room, promising to comply with the order. Five minutes passed, and then came a knock at the door, which opened, disclosing the Vicomte Jean. He was all smiles and apologies and affability. Did the Comtesse feel worse? Should they send again for Noirmont? The maid had gone to fetch Madame Turgis, who would be here no doubt immediately. Would not Madame la Comtesse take some extra nourishment? Some soup?

Then he retired as gracefully as he had entered, and the Comtesse de Béarn waited. At one o'clock the maid came back. Madame Turgis was from home, but the message had been left, asking her to call at once on her return.

"Ah, *mon Dieu, mon Dieu!*" cried the old woman recognizing at once that she had been tricked again, and that the maid had doubtless never left the house, seeing also her great mistake in not having used bribery. "And here am I lying in pain, and perhaps before she comes I may be gone, and my dying bequests will never be known. But wait."

She took something from under her pillow. It was a handkerchief tightly rolled up. She unrolled the handkerchief carefully. There were half a dozen gold coins in it—*louis d'or*, stamped with the stately profile of the fourteenth

Louis. It was part of the hoard which she kept at the Château de Béarn, on which she had drawn for travelling contingencies. Taking a louis, and folding up the rest, she held it out between finger and thumb.

"For you," said she.

The maid advanced to take the coin.

"When Madame Turgis arrives," finished the old woman, with a snap, withdrawing the coin and hiding her hand under the bed-clothes. "So go now, like a good girl, or find some messenger to go for you. Tell Madame Turgis that the Comtesse de Béarn has need for her at once. Then the louis will be yours to do what you like with, eh? 'Tis not often a louis is earned so cheap. You'll have a young man of your own, and nothing holds 'em like a bit of fine dress; and I'll look among my things and see if I can't find you a bit of lace, or a trinket to put on top of the louis. And—put your pretty ear down to me—*don't let anyone know I've sent to Madame Turgis. It's a secret between us about some property in the country.* You understand me?"

Jehanneton, the maid, assented, and left the room, nodding her head, to acquaint immediately the powers below of this attempt at bribery and corruption.

At five o'clock a new maid arrived with a tray containing soup and minced chicken.

"What has become of Jehanneton?" asked the old woman.

"Jehanneton went out, and has not yet come back," replied the other. "I do not know where she has gone to. Does Madame feel better?"

The invalid drank her soup and ate her chicken. She had been duped again, and she knew it. Her only consolation was the fact that she had not parted with the louis.

At six she rang for a light. The maid who answered the summons not only brought a lamp, but put a lighted taper to all the candles about the dressing-table.

"*Ma foi!*" cried the Comtesse. "I did not tell you to light those."

"It is by my mistress's orders," replied the maid, lighting, as she spoke, several more candles that stood on the bureau, till the room had almost the appearance of a *chapelle ardente*—an appearance that was helped out by the corpse-like figure on the bed. Then the maid went out.

CHAPTER VII

THE ARTIST

FIVE minutes later a knock came to the door, and a man entered. It was Ferminard. He was carrying the stiff brocade dress of Madame de Béarn over his left arm. In his right hand he carried a wig-block, on which was a wig such as then was worn by the elderly women of the Court.

The thing carried by Ferminard was less a wig than a structure of hair, a prefiguration of those towers and bastions with which the ladies of the sixteenth Louis' reign adorned their heads. Hideous bastilles, which one would fancy did not require arming with guns to frighten Love from making any attack on the wearers.

Under his right arm Ferminard also carried a rolled-up parcel. He made a bow to the occupant of the bed as he entered, and then advanced straight to the dressing-table, where he deposited the wig-block and the parcel, whilst the door closed, drawn to by someone in the corridor outside.

"My hair! My dress! And, *mon Dieu!* A man in the room with me!" cried the Comtesse, seizing the bell on the table beside her and ringing it. "And the door shut! Monsieur, open that door, or I will cry for help."

"Madame," said Ferminard, placing the dress on a chair, "we are both of an age. Calm yourself, and regard me as though I were not here. Besides, I am not a man; I am an artist, and, so far from molesting you, I have come to pay you the greatest compliment in my power by producing your portrait."

He drew a chair to the dressing-table, and proceeded to unroll the bundle, which contained bottles of pigment, some brushes and a host of other materials. The old woman on the bed lay watching him like a mesmerized fowl. Her portrait, at her time of life, and in her condition! What trick was this of the Dubarrys? She was soon to learn.

CHAPTER VIII

THE PRESENTATION

THE Versailles of to-day stands alone in desolation among all the other buildings left to us by the past. That vast courtyard through whose gates the dusty and travel-stained *berlines* of the ambassadors used to pass; those thousand windows, vacant and cleaned by the municipality; those fountains and terraces, and statues and vistas—across all these lies written the word which is at once their motto and explanation: *Fuimus*—we have been.

It is the palace of echoes.

But it is more than this. It is France herself. Not the France of to-day—banker and bourgeois-ridden; nor the France of the Second Empire—vulgar and painted; nor the Napoleonic France—half a brothel, half a barrack. Across all these and the fumes of the Revolution, Versailles calls to us: "I am France. Before I was built I was born in the dreams of the Gallic people. I am the concretion in stone of all the opulence and splendour and licence of mind which found a focus in the reign of Le Roi Soleil; the Hôtel St. Pol and the Logis d'Angoulême foreshadowed me, and Chambord and all those châteaux that mirror themselves in the Loire. I am the wealth of Jacques Cœur, the bravery of Richelieu and Turenne, the laughter of Rabelais, the songs of Villon, the beauty of Marion de l'Orme, the licentiousness of Montpensier, the arrogance of Fouquet. Of all that splendour I remain, an echo and a dream."

But to-night, in the year of our Lord 1770, Versailles, living and splendid, a galaxy of lights that might have been seen from leagues away, the huge park filled with the sound of the wind in the trees and the waters of the fountains, the great courtyard ablaze with lamps and torches, and coloured with the uniforms of the Guards and the Swiss—to-night Versailles was drawing towards herself the whole world in the form of the ambassadors of Europe, the whole Court of France, and a majority of the population of Paris.

The Place d'Armes was thronged, and the Paris road, a league from the gates; bourgeois and beggar, the hungry and well-fed, the maimed, the halt and the blind, apprentice and shop-girl—all were there, a seething mass attracted to the festivity as moths are attracted by a lamp, and all filled with one idea: the Dubarry.

The news of the friction at Court had gone amongst the people. It was said that the Dubarry had been forbidden at the last moment to attend; that the presentation had been cancelled, that she was ill, that the Vicomte Jean had insulted M. le Duc de Choiseul, that the arrival of the Dauphiness had been hurried, and that she was already at Versailles, and that she had refused to see the favourite. All of which statements, and a hundred others more wild and improbable, were bandied about during the glorious excitement to be got by watching the blazing windows of the palace, the uniformed figures of the Guards, and the steady stream of carriages coming from the direction of Paris.

Rochefort arrived at nine o'clock—that is to say, an hour before the time of the ceremony; his carriage immediately followed that of the Duc de Richelieu. The entrance-hall was crowded, and the Escalier des Ambassadeurs thronged. This great staircase, now removed, led by a broad, unbalustraded flight of eleven marble steps to a landing where, beneath the bust of Louis XV., a fountain played, gushing its waters into a broad basin supported by tritons, dolphins and sea-nymphs; from here a balustraded staircase swept up to right and left, and here, just by the fountain, Rochefort found himself cheek by jowl with de Sartines, who had arrived just before M. de Richelieu.

"Ah!" said de Sartines, recognizing the other, "and when did you arrive?"

"Why, it seems to me an hour ago," replied the other, "judging by the time I have been getting thus far; to be more precise, I came immediately after M. de Richelieu. And how are your dear thieves and people getting on? I should imagine they are mostly at Versailles to-night, to judge by the crowds on the Paris road."

"Oh," replied de Sartines, "I daresay there are enough of them left in Paris to keep my agents busy. And how did you like Lavenne?"

"He was charming. If all your thief-catchers were such perfect gentlemen, I would pray God to turn a few of our gentlemen into thief-catchers. But he was not so charming as your dramatist, Monsieur Ferminard, the gentleman who writes plays with his feet, it seems to me."

Sartines nudged him to keep silence. They had reached the corridor leading to the Hall of Mirrors, and here the Minister of Police drew his companion into an alcove.

"Do not mention the name Ferminard here; the walls have ears and the statues have tongues. Forget it, my dear Rochefort. Remember M. d'Ombreval's maxim: 'Forget so that you may not be forgotten.'"

"In other words, that you may not be put in the Bastille?"

"Precisely."

"Then I will forget the name Ferminard. But, before Heaven, I will never be able to forget the person. He amused me vastly. And now, my dear Sartines, without mentioning names, how are things going?"

"What things?"

"Why, the presentation."

"Admirably."

"Then the lady with the scalded leg——"

"Hush!"

"There is no one near, and, besides, I was only inquiring after her health."

"Well, her health is still bad."

"Will she be here to-night?"

"You will see. Ask me no more about her. Besides, I have something else to talk of. Your man, whom you put out of action the night before last, has been found."

"The man I killed?"

"Yes."

"Well," said Rochefort, laughing, "I don't envy the finder—that is to say, if he has any sense of beauty."

"Rochefort," said de Sartines, "it would not trouble me a *dernier* were forty like him found every morning in the streets of Paris; but, in this case, you have to be on your guard, for he was found, not by one of my agents, but by one of Choiseul's. The news came to me through Choiseul."

"Ah!" said Rochefort, becoming serious. "Is that so?"

"With a request that I should investigate the matter. If that were all it would be nothing; the danger to you is that Choiseul, no doubt, has started investigating the matter for himself."

Sartines, having delivered himself of this warning, turned to the Comte d'Egmont, who was passing, and walked off with him, leaving Rochefort to digest his words.

Rochefort for a moment was depressed; he did not like the idea of this dead man turning up, arm-in-arm, so to speak, with Choiseul. He had no remorse at all about the ruffian, but he had a lively feeling that, should Choiseul discover the truth, he would avenge the death of this villain, deserved even though it was. Then he put the matter from his mind, and passed with the throng through the Hall of Mirrors towards the *salon*, where the presentations took place.

On the way he passed Camus, who, with his wife, was speaking to the Comte d'Harcourt. Madame Camus was rather plain, older than her husband, and afflicted with a slight limp—an impediment in her walk, to quote M. de Richelieu. Camus' marriage with this woman was a mystery. She was the third daughter of the Comte de Grigny, who owned a château in Touraine, and little else, if we except numerous debts. She was plain, without dowry, and had a limp. It may have been the comment of Froissart on women so affected, or that her plainness appealed to him in some curious way; the fact remained that Camus had married her, and—so people said—was heartily sick of his bargain.

The Hall of Mirrors gave one eyes at the back of one's head; and Camus, though his back was half-turned to Rochefort, saw his mirrored reflection approach and pass; but he did not take the slightest notice of his enemy, continuing his conversation, whilst Rochefort passed on towards the wide-open door of the Salon of Presentations.

Rochefort was one of those implacable men who never apologize, even if they are in the wrong. Camus had been his friend, or, at least, a very close acquaintance, and he had struck Camus in the face. If Camus did not choose to wipe out the insult it was no affair of Rochefort's. He was ready to fight. He was not angry now with Camus; his attitude of mind was entirely one of contempt, and he passed on haughtily to the Hall of Presentations, where he soon found enough to distract his attention from personal matters.

The Hall of Presentations—vast, lit by a thousand lights—gave to the eye a picture of magnificence and splendour sufficient to quell even the most daring imagination. The Escalier des Ambassadeurs had been thronged, the corridors and the Hall of Mirrors crowded; but here, so wide was the floor, so lofty the painted ceiling, that the idea "crowd" vanished, or at least became subordinated to the idea of magnificence. One would not dream of associating the word "solemnity" with the word "butterfly"; yet, could one see the congregation of a million butterflies, variegated and gorgeous, drawn from all quarters of the earth towards one great festival, the word "solemnity" on the lips of the gazer might not be out of place.

So, to-night, at Versailles, all these butterflies of the social world of France—coloured, jewelled, beautiful—filling the vast Salon of Presentations with a moving picture, brilliant as a painting by Diaz, all these men and women, individually insignificant, produced by their setting and congregation that effect of solemnity which Versailles alone could produce from the frivolous.

That was, in fact, the calculated effect of Versailles; to give the *fainéant* the value of the strenuous, the trivial the virtue of the vital; to give great echoes to the sound of a name, to raise the usher on the shoulders of the Suisse, the grand master of the ceremonies on the shoulders of the usher, the noble on the shoulders of the grand master of the ceremonies, and the King on the shoulders of the noble. A towering structure, as absurd, when viewed philosophically, as a pyramid of satin-breeched monkeys, but beautiful, gorgeous, solemn under the alchemy of Versailles.

The great clock of the Hall of Presentations pointed to ten minutes to ten. The King had not appeared yet, nor would he do so till the stroke of the hour.

The presentation was fixed for ten. Rochefort knew everybody, and the man who knows everybody knows nobody. That was Rochefort's position at the Court of Versailles; he belonged to no faction, and so had no especial enemies—or friends. He did not fear enemies, nor did he want friends. Outside the Court, in Paris, he had several trusty ones who would have let themselves be cut in pieces for him; they were sufficient for him, for it was a maxim of his life that out of all the people a man knows, he will be lucky if he numbers two who are disinterested. He did not invent this maxim. Experience had taught it to him.

He passed now from group to group, nodding to this person and talking to that; and everywhere he found an air of inattention, an atmosphere of restlessness, such as may be noticed among people who are awaiting some momentous decision.

They were, in fact, awaiting the decision of Fate as to the presentation of the Dubarry. Among the majority of the courtiers nothing was definitely known, but a great deal was suspected. Rumours had gone about that it was now absolutely certain that the presentation would not take place, and all these rumours had come, funnily enough, not from the Choiseuls, but from the Vicomte Jean. The Choiseul faction, or rather the head centre of it, said nothing; for them the thing was assured. They had robbed the Comtesse, not only of her dress, her coiffeur and her carriage, but of her sponsor.

Camus, who had stolen the carriage, had followed Rochefort into the Hall of Presentations, and was now speaking to Coigny, Choiseul's right-hand man. Coigny, who when he saw Camus had experienced a shock of surprise at seeing him so early, interrupted him.

"The carriage?"

"It is quite safe," replied Camus. "The deed is accomplished."

"But how are you here so soon?"

"Oh, *ma foi!*" said Camus, "am I a tortoise? Having placed the thing in the coach-house of a well-trusted friend, I went home, dressed, and came on here."

"Ah, but suppose this well-trusted friend of yours were to betray you at the last moment, harness his horses to the precious carriage, and drive it to the Rue de Valois?"

Camus laughed. "Can you drive a carriage without wheels? It took seventeen minutes only to remove the wheels and make firewood of them with a sharp axe, to knock the windows to pieces, strip out the linings, and rip to pieces the cushions. If the Dubarry drives to Versailles in that carriage—well, my friend, all I can say is, the vehicle will match her reputation."

"Thanks!" said Coigny. "You have worked well, and you have Choiseul's thanks." He moved away, drawn by the sight of another of his confederates who had just appeared.

It was the Marquis Monpavon, twenty years of age, cool, insolent, a bully and scamp of the first water, with a smooth, puerile, egg-shaped face that made respectable fingers itch to smack it.

"The dressmaker?" said Coigny.

"She was charming," replied Monpavon. "I have quite lost my heart to her. I have made an arrangement to meet her to-morrow evening at the corner of the Rue Picpus."

"But the dress?"

"What dress?"

"The Dubarry's! Good God! You did not forget about the dress?"

"No," replied Monpavon. "I did not forget about the dress. The next time you see that dress will be on a mermaid in the Morgue. It is now in the Seine. What's more, it is in a sack, which also encloses a few stones."

"Thanks, Monpavon. I will tell Choiseul." He hurried away, attracted by another new-comer. This time it was Monsieur d'Estouteville, an exquisite, who seemed to have no bones, so indolently did he carry himself.

"The coiffeur?" asked Coigny, in a low voice, as he ranged alongside of this person. "What have you done with him?"

"He is safe," replied d'Estouteville.

"Where?"

"I don't know."

"But, heavens! Did you not undertake to have him guarded? Yet you do not know where he is?"

"I only know that he is in Paris somewhere. My dear Coigny, I could have given him no better guardian than the guardian he has chosen for himself—drink."

"Oh, you made him drunk!"

"Oh, no. It was a happy accident. It was this way. I had him brought to my house on an urgent summons. He was shown into a room where some wine was set out, quite by accident, and when I came to interview him with a purse full of gold for his seduction, I found he had been at the wine. He was talkative and flushed. Now, said I to myself, why should I pay five thousand francs for what I can obtain for a bottle of wine or two? So I ordered up some Rousillon, and made him drunk."

"Ah!"

"He quite forgot that he was a hairdresser at the end of the first bottle; before he had finished the second, he grew quarrelsome, and would have drawn his sword.[A] Then he fell asleep, and my servants took him and laid him out by the wall that borders the Cemetery of the Innocents. It was then half-past six o'clock. No man, not even his Majesty's physician, could turn him into a hairdresser again before to-morrow morning. So, you see, by a stroke of luck I saved five thousand francs, and avoided the implication in this affair that a bribe given to a barber might have occasioned all of us."

"Good!" said Coigny. He knew quite well that the apparently boneless d'Estouteville was one of the elect of chicanery, was as good a swordsman almost as Beauregard, and could outslang a fish-fag on the Petit Pont were he called to the test; but he had not expected such a brilliant piece of work as this. "Good. I will tell Choiseul that story. By the way, you are expected in his private apartments after this affair is over. You will not find him ungenerous, I think. Tell Monpavon and the others that they are expected also."

He walked away to where the Duc de Choiseul was standing, talking to some gentleman. It was now after ten, and the King had not yet appeared, though the hour for the presentation had arrived. He drew the Minister aside, and informed him of the reports he had just received from d'Estouteville, Monpavon and Camus; and Choiseul was in the act of congratulating him when the whole brilliant assemblage turned as if touched by a magician's wand; conversation died away, and silence fell upon the Chamber of Presentations.

The King had entered by the door leading from his apartments. He wore the Order of the Golden Fleece. Glancing from right to left, he advanced, followed by his suite, till, seeing Choiseul, he paused whilst the Minister advanced, bowing before him.

Choiseul saw that his Majesty was in a temper. He knew quite well that the King had made his appearance thus late, not because of laziness or indifference, but simply because he had been waiting the arrival of Madame Dubarry. The King, in fact, had been kept informed of all the guests who had arrived. Ten o'clock was the hour for the presentation, and now at a quarter past ten, his Majesty, never patient of delay, had left his apartments to seek the truth for himself.

"The Comtesse is late, Choiseul," said the King.

"The journey from Paris is a long one, Sire," replied the Minister, "and some delay might have occurred on the way."

"Or some accident," said the King. "Well, Choiseul, should some accident have happened to the poor Comtesse upon the road, we shall inquire into the cause of it, and I shall place the matter in your hands to find out and to punish, if necessary. But should the accident have happened in Paris, our Minister of Police will take the matter in his hands. Ah, there is de Sartines. Sartines, it seems that the Comtesse is late."

"Yes, Sire," replied the Minister of Police. "The carriage may have been delayed by the crowds that throng the Paris roads. But she will arrive in safety, if I am not much mistaken, before the half-hour has struck."

Choiseul smiled inwardly, and those members of the Choiseul faction who were within earshot of this conversation glanced at one another. The half-hour struck, and Choiseul, freed from his Majesty, who had passed on, turned to de Sartines.

"Well, monsieur," said Choiseul, "it seems that the clock has declared you a false prophet."

"Monsieur," replied de Sartines, looking at his watch, "the clock of the Chamber of Presentations, as you ought very well to know, is always kept five minutes in advance of the hour, by an order given by his late Majesty to Noirmont, the keeper of the clocks of the Palace of Versailles. It is now twenty-four and a half minutes past ten. Ah! what is this?"

A hush had fallen on the assembly; around the door leading to the corridor of entrance the people had drawn back as the waves of the Red Sea drew back before the rod of Moses.

The usher had appeared. He stood rigid as a statue, his profile to the room, then turning and fronting the great assembly and the lake of parquet floor where his Majesty stood in sudden and splendid isolation, he grounded the butt of his wand, and announced to the grand master of the ceremonies:

"The Comtesse Dubarry. The Comtesse de Béarn."

Never had Madame Dubarry looked more beautiful than now, as she advanced, led by this lady of the old *régime*—stiff, as though awakened from some tomb of the past; proud, as though she carried with her the memory of the Austrian; remote from the present day as the wars of the Fronde and the beauty of Madame de Chevreuse. It was the youth and age of France; and de Sartines, gazing at Madame de Béarn as one gazes at a great actor, murmured to Himself:

"What a masterpiece!"

CHAPTER IX

THE REWARD

THE presentation was over. The Choiseuls were defeated. Madame Dubarry was passing hither and thither, speaking to this one and that, and poisoning her enemies with her sweetest smiles. The King was delighted; and Choiseul, devouring his own heart, was kissing the favourite's hand. Smiles, smiles everywhere, and poisonous hatred so wonderfully masked that the washerwoman to the Duc d'Aiguillon might have thought herself the best-loved woman in France.

And Madame de Béarn? Madame de Béarn had vanished. Sartines had enveloped her in a cloud, and escorted her to her carriage; she had injured her leg that day, and required rest; she had braved pain and discomfort to obey the wish of his Majesty.

The Dubarry had triumphed, and they were paying their court to her. Rochefort, who had been following the whole proceedings of the evening with an interest which he had rarely experienced before in his life, approached de Sartines, who had just returned from escorting Madame de Béarn to her carriage; with that lightness of heart with which men sometimes approach their fate, he drew the Minister of Police a bit to one side.

"And Ferminard?" said he.

"Pardon me," said de Sartines, "I do not understand your meaning. What about Ferminard?"

"Oh," said Rochefort, laughing, "I was only intending to compliment you on having discovered so consummate an actor."

The other said nothing for a moment. Then he said, speaking slowly and in a voice so low that it was only just audible to his companion:

"Rochefort, by accident you have been drawn into a little conspiracy of the Court; by luck you are able to escape from it if you choose to hold your tongue for ever on what you have seen and heard. You imagine that Ferminard came here to-night and laid his genius at the feet of Madame la Comtesse by acting for her the part of Madame de Béarn. All I can say is, imagine what you please, but say nothing; for, mark you, should anything of this be spoken of by you, friend though I am to you, my hand would fall automatically on you, and the future of M. de Rochefort would be four blank walls."

"You threaten?" said Rochefort haughtily.

"Monsieur, I never threaten; I only advise. You have acted well in this affair; act still better by forgetting it all. And now that it is over, I am deputed to hand you your reward."

"My reward!"

Sartines took a little note from his pocket and handed it to Rochefort, who opened it and read:

"You will not receive this until and unless all is successful. In that case I wish to thank you both in my own name and that of the dear Comtesse. The presentation will be over by eleven, at which time this note will be handed to you. Should you care to receive my thanks, you can reach Paris by midnight. I live at No. 9, Rue St. Dominic, and my door will be opened to you should you knock to receive my thanks.

"CAMILLE FONTRAILLES."

Rochefort stood for a moment with this note in his hand. She had been thinking of him; she had guessed his feelings towards her; and she in her turn loved him!

He glanced at the clock. It pointed to half-past eleven. A swift horse would take him in less than an hour to Paris. He turned to the door.

"Where are you going?" asked Sartines.

"To Paris, monsieur," replied Rochefort, with a bow.

CHAPTER X

THE ORDER OF ARREST

AT a quarter past eleven, that is to say, a quarter of an hour before Rochefort received the note from Mademoiselle Fontrailles, Choiseul, who had kissed the hand of the Dubarry, congratulated her on her dress, compared her to a rose in an epigram that had the appearance of being absolutely new, and watched her vanishing with his Majesty triumphantly towards the apartments lately occupied by the Princess Adélaïde, and now occupied by the favourite—at a quarter past eleven, Choiseul, furious under his mask of calm, turned towards his own apartments.

The fixed smile on his face never altered as he bowed to right and left, and as he passed along through the crowd several members of the assemblage detached themselves from the mass and fell into his train.

Choiseul's apartments in the Palace of Versailles were even more sumptuous than those relegated to the use of the Dubarry. He passed from the corridor to the *salon*, which he used for the private reception of ambassadors, and all that host of people, illustrious and obscure, which it was the duty of the Minister to receive, in the name of France.

This *salon* was upholstered in amber satin and white and gold, with a ceiling of yellow roses and joyful cupids. Ablaze with lights, as now, the place seemed like a great cell, the most gorgeous and the most brilliantly lit in that great honeycomb, Versailles.

Choiseul sat down at a table and dashed off a letter which he addressed, sealed, and sent by a servant to M. de Beautrellis, captain of the Gardes, for delivery. Then he turned to Coigny who had followed him.

"You told the others to come here to-night?"

"Yes, monsieur; they are even now waiting outside the door."

"Well, we will have them in. Coigny, how has this happened?"

"I don't know, monsieur, unless it was the devil. Everything was secure, everything was assured. Madame de Béarn was out of action, and you know what other measures we took. Yet at the last moment we are overthrown."

"Well," said Choiseul, "it only remains for us to find out the secret of our reverse, and the name of the person who has upset our plans. Call in the others."

Coigny went to the side door giving entrance to the apartments, opened it, and ushered in a number of gentlemen who had been standing outside. First came Camus, the chief of the executive of the broken-down conspiracy; after him Monpavon, cool, smug and impudent as ever, and after him, d'Estouteville, a trifle flushed; after these, the others who had helped in one way or the other in the great fiasco, as Monpavon had already named the business. Seven gentlemen in all entered to receive Choiseul's felicitations on their failure to outwit a woman, and Choiseul's tongue in a matter of this sort was sure.

"Ah, Monsieur Camus!" said he. "Good evening. Good evening, Monsieur Monpavon; Monsieur d'Estouteville, good evening. Ah! I see Monsieur d'Est, Monsieur Beaupré, Monsieur Duras—well, gentlemen, we have not succeeded in lending as much colour to his Majesty's presentation to-night as I might have wished. We have not been very brilliant, gentlemen. Monsieur Monpavon, I believe you have a very small opinion of women. Their value, of course, viewed philosophically, is an academic question; but viewed practically—well, viewed practically, the brains of those women you despise, Monsieur Monpavon, have a certain value, though you may not imagine it. Yes, Monsieur d'Estouteville, the brain of a woman has proved itself a better article to-night than all the brains in Versailles. Monsieur Camus, what explanation have you to offer?"

He expected to see Camus discomfited, but the dark, pitted face of the Count showed nothing of his feelings.

"Monsieur," said Camus, "we have been betrayed."

"That is very evident," said Choiseul. "*Mon Dieu*, Monsieur Camus, what next will you come here to tell me? That the sun does not shine at night?"

"Monsieur," said Camus, "I have not yet finished. I know the name of the man who has betrayed us."

"Ah, you know his name!"

"Yes, monsieur."

"And this man?"

"It is the Comte de Rochefort."

"Rochefort!"

"Monsieur, it is Rochefort, and no other. He alone knew of our plan."

"Who told him?"

"I did, monsieur."

"You told him?"

"He was my friend. I reckoned him a man of honour. I swore him to secrecy." As he told this lie his hand went to his pocket and produced a piece of paper. "And entrusted him with the full details of the business in hand. He refused to assist, we quarrelled. It was just after we left your ball last night, and we parted in the Rue de Chevilly.

"I turned and walked slowly away, intending to return to the Hôtel de Choiseul and inform you of the matter. Then I altered my mind, as the idea occurred to me of calling on my friend, the Marquis de Soyecourt, and I did not want to trouble you at that late hour, engaged as you were with the duties of hospitality. I came down the street leading past the Bénédictines de la Ville l'Évêque, and sought the side way to the Hôtel de Soyecourt that runs between the wall of the Bénédictines and the wall of the cloister of the Madeleine, forgetting that this side way is closed by a barrier at night. Before I had reached it a man came out hurriedly. It was M. Rochefort.

"He was carrying his sword naked in his hand and wiping it upon a piece of paper; he cast the paper away, and, sheathing his sword, walked off hurriedly in the direction of the river. He did not see me, as I had taken shelter in an alcove. I picked the piece of paper up; then I glanced down the passage to the Hôtel de Soyecourt, and there, lying by the barricade, was a man. He was dead, still warm, and he had died from a sword-thrust through the heart. I thought in him I recognized one of our agents. I walked away, and in the Rue de la Madeleine I took counsel with myself, went home, and sent a servant to apprise your major-domo of the occurrence. To-day I have been so busy ever since six in the morning that I had no time to trouble in the matter. But those are the facts, and here is the piece of paper which I picked up. And see, here are the blood marks."

Choiseul took the page of the *ballade* between finger and thumb; the marks were plain and bore out Camus' statement.

It did not matter to him two buttons whether Camus' statement were true or false, as long as his statement about the betrayal was true, and he knew now that it must be true, for his agents had brought him the report that the man in the cloak and hat who had left the Dubarrys' house the night before had been accompanied by a man like Rochefort, that they had driven to a house in which Rochefort had apartments, a report of the whole story which we know.

And you will observe that, though Rochefort had stamped himself on the spy's report in letters of fire, Sartines, the core of the whole conspiracy, was not even suspected. Sartines had managed to shovel the whole onus of the business on to the shoulders of Rochefort; he had not set out wilfully so to do, perhaps—or perhaps he had; at all events, his success was due entirely to his faultless methods. No one suspected him, and he had not made an enemy of Choiseul, despite the fact that he alone had wrecked Choiseul's most cherished plan.

Choiseul, certain that Rochefort had been the means of his defeat, turned suddenly and faced the group of gentlemen standing before him.

"M. Camus, M. de Monpavon, M. d'Estouteville," cried he, "I commission you. M. de Rochefort has not yet left the palace. Seize him and bring him here. If he has left the palace, pursue him and bring him here. I place the Gardes, and the Suisses and the police of M. Sartines at your disposal."

He turned rapidly to a writing-table, sat down, and dashed off three warrants in the following terms:

"URGENCY.

"The bearer is empowered to seize and arrest the person of Charles Eugène Montargis, Comte de Rochefort, and to call on all French citizens to assist in such arrest.

"Signed, DE CHOISEUL,
"Minister."

He sanded each paper when written and passed it over his shoulder to the hands waiting to receive it. "If possible," said he, "make the arrest yourselves, without the help of Sartines' men. You are my accredited agents."

When the three gentlemen had each received his commission and warrant they turned, led by Camus, and left the room swiftly and without a word. They entered the Chamber of Presentations, divided, passed through the room from door to door, through the thinning crowd, and drew it blank. Rochefort had left. The great clock of the chamber pointed to seven minutes past the half-hour.

CHAPTER XI

FLIGHT

WHEN Rochefort took his leave of Sartines and left the Chamber of Presentations, he made full speed for the corridor leading to the Escalier des Ambassadeurs, passed down the great staircase rapidly, pushed his way through the crowd thronging the hall, found Jaquin, the usher, on duty, and seizing him:

"Where is Monsieur Bertrand?" asked Rochefort.

"He is, no doubt, in the Cabinet of the Equipages, monsieur," replied the usher.

"Good," said Rochefort.

His carriage was waiting in the courtyard, but a carriage was too slow for his present purpose. He wanted a horse, and a swift horse, for the journey to Paris—wings, if possible, failing them, the swiftest horse in his Majesty's stables.

Bertrand was the keeper of his Majesty's horses, and Rochefort's friend. The Cabinet of the Equipages was a moderately sized apartment. Here the King arranged each day what horses, what carriages and attendants he would require, and here Rochefort found his friend, deep in accounts and reports.

"My dear Bertrand," said the Comte, "you see a man in a most desperate hurry. I must get to Paris at once. My carriage is too slow, and I have come to beg or steal a horse."

Bertrand threw up his hands.

"Impossible! I have already been called to account for lending horses to my friends in a hurry. Ask me anything else, my dear Rochefort—my purse, my life, my heart—but a horse, no, a thousand times, no."

"Ah, well," said Rochefort, "I must tell a lie, and you will know the desperate urgency of my business from the fact that it makes me lie to you. Well, then, I come from de Sartines with an order of urgency. I am commanded to ask for your swiftest horse on a matter of State business."

"So be it," said Bertrand. "I cannot resist that order, and you must settle with Sartines." He scribbled some words on a piece of paper, and, calling an attendant, gave it to him.

"The horse will be in the courtyard in a few minutes," said Bertrand. "Well, I am sure to be interrogated over this, and M. de Sartines will give you the lie. You have weighed all that?"

"Sartines will support me," said Rochefort. "We are very good friends; you need fear nothing. And now, adieu! And thank you for your good offices in this matter."

He bade good-bye to Bertrand and returned through the still crowded hall to the door that gave exit from the palace.

Carriage after carriage was leaving, and the courtyard, as Rochefort came out, was ablaze with light. Burning with impatience, Rochefort watched the endless stream of carriages, the servants, and the guards, till, catching sight of a groom in the royal livery, leading a horse by the bridle, he was about to descend the steps when a hand fell upon his shoulder. He turned and found himself face to face with Camus. Behind Camus appeared the egg-shaped face of Monpavon—a man he hated—and beside Monpavon the boneless form of d'Estouteville.

"Monsieur," said Rochefort, "you have taken a strange liberty with me."

"Monsieur," replied Camus, "I have come to take your freedom."

He handed Rochefort the warrant of Choiseul. Rochefort read it by the light of the doorway, comprehended instantly the desperate seriousness of his position and the danger of resistance—besides the bad policy.

But M. de Rochefort was going to Paris, and policy, and danger, and even Choiseul himself, would not interfere with his purpose. He handed the paper back to Camus with a smile.

"Present it to-morrow at my apartments in Paris, Monsieur Camus. I shall be there at noon. If I am late, my servants will entertain you till my return. *Au revoir.*"

He descended a step, and Camus, putting out a hand to seize him, received a blow on the belt that felled him as effectually as a blow on the head would have done. Next moment, Rochefort, dipping under the horses' heads of the carriage that had just stopped to take up, reached the groom in royal livery and the horse which he was leading, seized the bridle, mounted, and plunged his spurless heels into its flanks.

Valmajour, for so was the big roan horse named, was not of a temper to stand treatment like this without marking his resentment of it. He bucked, as much as a French horse can, filled the yard with the sound of his hoofs on the great cobble-stones; then he came to hand and struck for the gate.

But Rochefort had reckoned without Monpavon and d'Estouteville. They had raised the hue and cry, the lackeys and soldiers had taken it up. Twenty voices were crying, "Bar the gate!" and as Rochefort approached the great gateway, he saw the Suisses crossing their pikes before the gateway, pike-head across pike-head at a level four feet from the ground. Valmajour checked slightly at the pull of the bridle, rose to the touch of Rochefort's heel, and passed over the crossed pikes like a bird. A shout rose from the on-lookers as horse and rider disappeared from the zone of torchlight at the gate into the blacknesses beyond, and on the shout and like the materialized fury of it, a horse and rider shot out across the courtyard in pursuit.

It was d'Estouteville. That limp and enigmatic personage had, alone, perceived, standing amongst the equipages, the horse of M. de Beautrellis, captain of the Gardes; a groom was holding it for the gallant captain, who had entered the palace on some urgent business. D'Estouteville had seized the horse, mounted, and was now in pursuit. He knew Rochefort perfectly, and that Rochefort, in his present mood, would not be taken without a battle to the death. This, however, did not check him in the least; rather, perhaps, it was the mainspring of his suddenly found energy.

The Suisses, recognizing a pursuer, and in a pursuer authority, did not attempt to check him, and next moment he too had passed the zone of torchlight and was swallowed up by the darkness beyond.

CHAPTER XII

A DUEL OF WITS

CLOUDS were drifting across the moon's face, casting alternately light and shadow on the country; the people, attracted by the fête at the palace, had long vanished. The road was clear, and Rochefort gave free rein to Valmajour.

For two miles or so he kept at full speed; then he reined in, leaped from the saddle, eased the girths a bit, and stood for a moment gazing backwards along the road, and listening and watching to see if he were pursued.

As he listened, he heard on the breeze a faint and rhythmical sound; it was the great clock of Versailles striking midnight. It passed, and then in the silence of the night his quick ear caught another sound, also rhythmical, but continuous. It was the sound of a horse at full gallop. He was pursued.

Even as he listened and looked, the shadow of a cloud drew off, leaving to view the distant figure of a horseman and his horse, as though it had dropped them on the road. He tightened the girths and remounted, only to discover the tragic fact that Valmajour, the brave Valmajour, was lame.

Now Rochefort was a man to whom the riding of a lame horse brought more suffering than to the horse itself. It was clearly impossible to urge Valmajour into any pace, but there was a good horse behind him to be had for the taking. He turned Valmajour's head and advanced to battle.

Instantly his quick eye recognized d'Estouteville, who, advancing at a gallop, was fully exposed to view by the moonlight now strong on the road, and instantly his quick mind changed its plan. He was only too eager for a fight, but what he wanted even more was a horse. D'Estouteville was a good swordsman, and might place him, by chance, *hors de combat*, and this chance did not suit him. For M. de Rochefort was going to Paris, and he had sworn to himself that nothing should stop him.

When d'Estouteville was only a hundred yards away, Rochefort drew rein, leaped from his horse and ran away. He struck across a fence and across some park-land lying on the right of the road, and d'Estouteville, scarcely believing his eyes at the sight of his cowardice, flung himself from the saddle, left the two horses to fraternize, and gave chase.

Rochefort was striking across the grass towards some trees. One of the swiftest runners in France, he now seemed broken down and winded.

D'Estouteville overhauled him rapidly as he ran, making for a small clump of trees standing in the middle of the park-land. He doubled round this clump, d'Estouteville's hand nearly on his shoulder, and then, having turned and having the road again for his goal, a miracle happened.

The tired and broken-down runner became endowed with the swiftness of a hare; d'Estouteville, furious and hopelessly outpaced, followed, cursing no less deeply because he had no breath to curse with. On the road Rochefort, with a good thirty yards between him and his pursuer, seized the bridle of d'Estouteville's horse, which was quietly cropping the grass at the road edge, mounted, and, waving his hand to the emissary of de Choiseul, struck off for Paris.

D'Estouteville, still perfectly sure of his prey, mounted Valmajour and turned in pursuit. Then he found out the truth. Rochefort had exchanged a broken-down horse for a sound one; his flight had not been dictated by cowardice but by astuteness, and the fooled one in his fury would have driven his sword through the heart of Valmajour had not Valmajour been the King's horse and under royal protection.

BOOK II

CHAPTER I

A LODGING FOR THE NIGHT

THE horse Rochefort had captured was a powerful roan, fully caparisoned after the fashion of the officers' horses of the cavalry, with pistols in the holsters and a saddle-bag for despatches.

Having ridden half a league at full gallop, Rochefort drew rein and glanced back. He was no longer pursued. He hugged himself at the thought of d'Estouteville's position. D'Estouteville would have to return to Versailles, on a lame horse, and with what explanation? Were he to tell people that Rochefort had run away from him, he would be laughed at, for Rochefort's reputation for courage was too well founded to be shaken by a tale like that.

Then as Rochefort proceeded swiftly on his way, the saddle-bag attracted him; he was at open war with the Choiseul faction; Choiseul was in power, the Gardes were the servants of Choiseul, and the horse belonged to an officer in the Gardes. It and its trappings were loot, and to examine his loot he opened the saddle-bag as he rode, plunged in his hand, and found nothing but a letter. A large, official letter, sealed with a red seal and addressed in a big firm hand to

"Mademoiselle La Bruyère,
"In the Suite of Her Royal Highness
"At Compiègne.

"To be left with Madame de La Motte."

This was the letter which we saw Choiseul writing.

"Oh, ho!" cried Rochefort, "M. de Choiseul writing to a young lady, and that young lady in the suite of the Dauphiness. Well, I have no quarrel with Choiseul's private affairs and the letter shall go to its destination or be returned to him—but first, let me get to Paris."

He returned the letter to its place, closed the saddle-bag and urged the horse into a canter.

He did not know that Choiseul had specially commissioned M. de Beautrellis to take this letter, written immediately after the presentation, to its destination, nor the special urgency and secrecy necessary to the business, and with which Choiseul had impressed the servant. Nor would he have had time to think of these things had he known, for he was now catching up with the crowd of Parisians who had returned on foot from Versailles, and his eyes and ears and tongue were fully occupied in avoiding stragglers and warning them out of his way.

At the Octroi of Paris he was stopped by the soldiers for a moment, but he had no difficulty in passing them, despite the fact that he was in full court dress, without spurs, and riding a guard's horse. He was M. de Rochefort, known to all of them, and this was doubtless one of his many freaks. Then, with the streets of Paris before him, he struck straight for his home in the Rue de Longueville.

Burning as he was to keep his appointment, he knew the vital necessity of money and a change of clothes. Though he had outwitted d'Estouteville, he was still pursued. Choiseul would ransack Paris for him, and failing to find him there—France. He guessed Camus's part in the business, he guessed that his action in killing Choiseul's villainous agent had been traced to him, and worse than that, he guessed that the part he had played in disclosing the plan which Camus had put before him to Madame Dubarry was now perfectly well known to Choiseul.

Choiseul would never forgive him for that.

It was absolutely necessary for him to leave France for a time till things blew over, or Choiseul was out of power. Of course in a just age, he might have stood up to the business of the killing, called Javotte as a witness to the facts of the case, and received the thanks of society, not its condemnation; but in the age of the *Lettre de Cachet* and of Power without mercy, flight was the only safe course, and this child of his age knew his age, and none better.

It was two o'clock when he reached the Rue de la Harpe, adjoining the Rue de Longueville. Here he left the horse tied to a post for anyone to find who might, and taking the letter from his saddle-bag, repaired to his apartments. He let himself in with his private key, and without disturbing his valet changed his clothes, took all the money he could find, some three thousand francs in gold, tore up and burned a few letters and left the house, closing the door gently behind him.

A nice position, truly, for the man who had sworn never to touch politics, alone in the streets of Paris at half-past two in the morning, with only a few thousand francs in his possession and the whole of France at his heels.

But Rochefort, now that he was in the midst of the storm he had always avoided, did not stop to think of the fury of the wind. So far from cursing his folly and his position, he found some satisfaction in it. It seemed to him that he had never lived so vividly before.

It was only a few minutes' walk from the Rue de Longueville to the Rue St. Dominic, where Mademoiselle Fontrailles lived; one had to go through the Rue de la Harpe, and as he entered that street he saw the horse, which he had left tied to a post, being led away by a man.

"Well, my friend," said the Count, as he overtook the man, "and where are you going with that fine horse?"

"Monsieur," replied the other, "I found him tied to a post, and thinking it a pity to leave him there to be misused maybe, or stolen by the first thief, I am taking him home."

"Just so," replied the Count, taking a louis from his pocket, "and, as I may be in want of a horse in a few hours, here is a louis for you if you will take him home, give him a feed, change his saddle and be with him on the road that leads from the Porte St. Antoine at eleven o'clock, that is, nine hours from now. Be a quarter of a mile beyond the gate, and if you will do this, I will pay you ten louis for your trouble."

"Monsieur, I will do it."

"Can you obtain a plain saddle in exchange for this one?"

"I will try, monsieur."

"Do not try, simply rip all this stuff off and take the saddle-bag away, then it will be plain enough, take off the chain bridle and leave the leather, and remember ten louis for your trouble."

He handed the louis to the man, and went on his way.

It was a good idea, though risky; Rochefort, however, took risks; he was of the temper of Jean Bart, who, it will be remembered, once reefed his sails with seaweed, trusting to the wind to blow them loose at the proper moment.

In the Rue St. Dominic he paused at the house indicated in the letter. It was a medium-sized house of good appearance, and all the windows were in darkness, with the exception of the second window on the first floor. He stopped and looked up at this window. To knock at the door would mean rousing the porter. He was quite prepared to do that, but the lit window fascinated him, something told him that the person he sought was there.

He looked about to see if he could find a pebble, but the moon had gone and the roadway was almost invisible in the darkness; he rubbed the sole of his boot about on the ground, but could find nothing, so taking a louis from his pocket and taking careful aim, he flung it up at the window.

The casement was open a few inches, and, as luck would have it, the coin instead of hitting the glass, entered, struck the curtain and fell on the floor.

He waited for a moment, and was just on the point of taking another louis from his pocket, when a shadow appeared on the curtain, the curtain was drawn aside, and the window pushed open. He could see the vague outline of a form above the sill, and then came a woman's whisper:

"Who is it?"

"Rochefort," came the answer. He dared not say more, fearing that it might be some servant: then, as the form disappeared with the word, "Wait," he knew that all was right.

He searched for the door, found it, and stood waiting, his heart beating as it never had beaten before. Choiseul, Camus, his own position, everything, was forgotten.

He heard a step in the passage and then the bolts carefully withdrawn; he could scarcely believe in his luck: Camille Fontrailles, with her own hand, was opening the door for him, at dead of night, secretively, and in a way that cast everything to the winds.

Next moment he was in the hall, holding a warm hand in the darkness, whilst the other little hand of the woman who had admitted him was replacing the bolts.

"Come," whispered a voice.

He followed, still holding her hand and led as a blind man is led, up the stairs, to a landing, to a door.

The woman pushed the door open, and they entered a room lit by a lamp and with the remnants of a fire in the grate.

The light of the lamp struck on the woman's face. It was Javotte.

Rochefort dropped her hand, stared round him, and then at the girl who was standing before him with a smile on her lips.

Never had Javotte looked prettier. Though a girl of the people, she had a refinement of her own; compared to Camille, she was the wild violet compared to the cultivated violet, the essential charm was the same; but to Rochefort, suddenly disillusioned, she had neither charm nor grace.

"You!" said he, drawing back and walking towards the window.

The smile vanished from her lips, they trembled, and then, just as if it had started from her lips, a little shiver went all through her.

In a flash, she understood all; he had not discovered her window by some miraculous means, he had not come to see her, he did not care for her. It was her mistress for whom this visit was intended. Ever since he had kissed her in the corridor of the Hôtel Dubarry, she had dreamed of him, looked for him, fancied that he would come to seek her. He had come, but not for her.

The blow to her love, her pride, and her life was brutal in its directness, yet she took it standing, and after the first moment almost without flinching. She had come of a race to whom pride had been denied, a race accustomed to the *Droit de Seigneur*, the whip of the noble and the disdain of the aristocrat, yet the woman in her found the pride that hides suffering, and can find and place its hand even on disdain.

"Monsieur," said Javotte, "I am sorry, but my mistress is from home."

Rochefort, standing by the window, had recovered himself. He guessed quite well that little Javotte had a more than kindly feeling for him, that at a look or a touch she would be his, body and soul, and that she had led him upstairs thinking that his visit was to her. But he was moving under the dominion of a passion that held his mind from Javotte as steadily as centrifugal force holds the moon from the earth.

"From home?" said he. "Has she not been here, then, to-night?"

"Yes, monsieur, she was here till half-past twelve, then she left for the Rue de Valois with Mademoiselle Chon Dubarry."

"Mademoiselle Dubarry was with her here, then?"

"Yes, monsieur, and they left together."

He saw at once that the appointment Camille had given him was no lover's tryst—or, at least, a lover's tryst with a chaperon attached to it. This pleased him, somehow. Despite the fact that his heart had leaped in him whilst under the dominion of the thought that Camille had flung all discretion to the winds, the revelation of the truth that it was Javotte who was flinging discretion to the winds came to him as a satisfaction, despite the check to his animal nature. Camille was not to be conquered as easily as that.

She had waited for him till half-past twelve, there was some comfort in that thought; the question now arose as to what he should do. It was clearly impossible to knock the Dubarrys up at that hour in the morning. He must wait, and where better than here; he wanted a friend to talk to, and whom could he find better than Javotte?

There was a chair by the bed, and he sat down on the chair, and then what did he do but take Javotte on his knee.

He told her to come and sit on his knee whilst he explained all his worries and troubles, and she came and sat on his knee like a child. She would have resisted him now as a lover, yet there in that bedroom, in that deserted house, she let him caress her without fear and without thought. There was something great about Rochefort at times, when he forgot Rochefort the *flaneur* and Rochefort the libertine, or perhaps it would be nearer the mark to say there was nothing little about him, and nothing base.

"It is this way, Javotte," said he. "Monsieur le Duc de Choiseul, of whom you have no doubt heard, is pursuing me, and I am running away from Monsieur le Duc de Choiseul, and as I am not used to running away, I run very badly, but still I do my best. Now, you remember the other night when those bad men attacked you?—well, when I chased them away, I followed one of them and he threw a knife at me and I killed him. He was an agent of Monsieur de Choiseul, who, having discovered that I killed his agent, would like very much to kill me. He tried to arrest me at the Palace of Versailles some hours ago, and the agent he employed was Monsieur Camus, the same man whose face I smacked before you——"

"Oh, monsieur," said Javotte, "that is an evil man; his face, his very glance, took the life away from me."

"Just so," said Rochefort; "and I struck that evil man in the stomach, and left him kicking his heels on the steps of his Majesty's palace, whilst I made my escape. I got a horse and came to Paris, but I cannot stay in Paris. To-morrow I am going to the Rue de Valois to keep that appointment with your mistress, which I failed to keep to-night. Well, I may be taken prisoner or killed before I reach the Hôtel Dubarry. In that case, you will tell your mistress all, and that the fault was not mine, in that I did not arrive here in time. You will be my friend in this, Javotte?"

"Yes, monsieur," replied Javotte, "I will, indeed, be your friend."

She who had hoped only to be his lover cast away that hope, or imagined that she cast away that hope, in taking up the reality of friendship.

"I trust you," he said; "and now to another thing. I have here a letter belonging to Monsieur le Duc de Choiseul; it is addressed to a lady at Compiègne, it was in the saddle-bag of the horse which I took to carry me to Paris, and it must be delivered to the lady it is intended for."

He took the letter from his pocket and gave it to Javotte, who had now risen and was standing before him.

"You must find someone to take it for me, and that someone will expect to be paid for his trouble, so here are two louis——"

"Monsieur," said Javotte, "I do not need money."

Rochefort returned the coins to his pocket and stood up. He had not offered Javotte money for herself, but he should not have offered it at all. The brutality that spoils a butterfly's wing may be a touch that would not injure a rose-leaf.

"Nor did I offer it to you," said he, placing his hand on her shoulder. "One does not offer money to a friend—or only as a loan—I meant you to give it to some footman or other as a reward for his services. But should you ever need a loan, my little Javotte, why, then, Rochefort will be your banker, offering you his life and his services without interest. But there is one thing he will never lend you—and can you guess what that thing is?"

"No, monsieur."

"His friendship—for it is yours, now and always."

Javotte bowed her pretty head as if in confirmation and acknowledgment. Still holding the letter in her hand, she turned it over, glancing now at the superscription, now at the seals. Then, moving towards the chair, she sat down. Rochefort watched her, wondering what was in her mind, and waiting for her to speak.

"Monsieur," said Javotte at last, "you ask me to take this letter to its destination. To do so, I must first read the address, and I find it is addressed to Mademoiselle La Bruyère. You say Monsieur de Choiseul is the writer of it. You say Monsieur de Choiseul is pursuing you. Well, monsieur, is it not possible that, in parting with this letter, you are parting with a weapon that may be very useful to you?"

"Oho!" said Rochefort, laughing, amused at Javotte's seriousness and her air of subtlety and intrigue, as though some dove were suddenly to assume the garb of a serpent's wisdom. "What is this you say?"

"Simply, monsieur, that Mademoiselle La Bruyère is one of the greatest enemies of Madame la Comtesse Dubarry. I have heard my mistress say that she obtained her place in the entourage of the Dauphiness In order to poison the mind of the Dauphiness against her. Here is Monsieur de Choiseul writing to Mademoiselle La Bruyère——"

"Ah!" cried Rochefort, striking himself on the forehead, and speaking as though oblivious of Javotte's presence, "I see. Choiseul writes a despatch to Mademoiselle La Bruyère—and last night of all nights, immediately after the presentation, to tell her, without doubt, of the plan and its failure—and the plan was directed against his Majesty as well as against the Countess. Certainly, that letter may prove a very terrible weapon against Choiseul."

"And you will use it, monsieur?"

"The letter?"

"Yes, monsieur, the letter."

"I—no, I cannot use it. I do not even know that it would help me. I may be wrong even in my suspicion. The thing may have no value at all; how do I know that it is not a love-letter?"—he laughed at the idea of Love coupled with the idea of Choiseul—"or about some private matter? No, it is impossible. I cannot open Monsieur de Choiseul's letter to see if it concerns me, and even were I to open it, and were I to find the blackest conspiracy under the handwriting of Choiseul, I could not use it against him."

"Monsieur," said Javotte, "I am only a poor girl, but I have seen much in the service of Madame la Comtesse. I have kept my mind about me, and I have been employed in many things that have taught me many things. Living at Luciennes and Versailles, I have observed Monsieur de Choiseul—Look at the affair of yesterday—and there are other things—— Well, I know that if you were Monsieur de Choiseul, you would open this letter."

Rochefort laughed.

"You have touched the spot," said he. "If I were Monsieur de Choiseul, I would do as you say, but since I am Monsieur de Rochefort, I cannot. I am only a poor gentleman of Auvergne, without any head for political intrigue or any hand for political matters, and were I to open that letter, I would do the business so badly, that my unaccustomed hand would betray itself."

"Monsieur, I did not ask you to open this letter."

"Mademoiselle, had you done so, I would have obeyed you without murmur, for your lightest request would be for me a command. And now put the accursed thing away that it may not tempt us any more, and if you will show me to some room where I may snatch a couple of hours' sleep, I will lie down, for I have a heavy day before me if I am not very greatly mistaken."

Javotte rose up and placed the letter in the drawer of a bureau by the door. Then she ran out of the room and returned with a rug of marten skin, which she spread on the bed; she turned the rug back and arranged the pillows. She was offering him her bed.

"I will call you at six o'clock," said she.

She glanced round the room like a careful housewife who wishes to see that everything is in order, smiled at Rochefort, nodded, and vanished, closing the door behind her.

Rochefort removed his coat and sword-belt, got under the rug, rested his head on the pillow and in five minutes was snoring.

Javotte, crossing the landing, entered her mistress's bedroom, where a lamp was burning.

She turned the lamp full on and sat down in a chair by the fire-place. She was in love and her love was hopeless, and her power of love may be gauged from the fact that she was thinking less of herself than of Rochefort, and less of Rochefort than his position.

She knew Camille Fontrailles as only a woman can know a woman. That beautiful face, those eyes so capable of betraying interest and love, that charm, that grace—all these had no influence with Javotte. She guessed Camille to be heartless, not cruel, but acardiac, if one may use the expression, without impulse, negative towards men, yet exacting towards them, requiring their homage, yet giving in return no pay—or only promissory notes; capable of real friendship towards women, and more than friendship—absolute devotion to a chosen woman friend. This type of woman is exceedingly common in all high civilizations; it is the stand of the ego against the Race instinct, a refusal of the animal by the sensibilities, a development of the finer feelings at the expense of the natural passions— who knows——— Javotte reasoned only by instinct, and it was instinct that made her guess Rochefort's passion for Camille to be a hopeless passion, and it was this guess that now brought some trace of comfort to her human and wicked heart.

She was capable of dying for Rochefort, of sacrificing all comfort in life for his comfort, yet of treasuring the thought of his discomfiture at the hands of Camille.

She rose up, and, taking the lamp, stood before the mirror that had so often reflected the beauty of her mistress.

What she saw was charming, yet she saw it through the magic of disenchantment.

It was the wild flower gazing at her reflection in the brook where the lordly dragon-fly pauses for a second, heedless of her, on his way towards the garden of the roses.

Then she placed the lamp on the table again, and went downstairs to make coffee for the dragon-fly, to give him strength on his journey.

CHAPTER II

THE GRATITUDE OF THE DUBARRYS

ROCHEFORT was pursuing Camus through Dreamland, when the touch of a hand upon his shoulder brought him wide awake. It was Javotte. She had placed the tray with the coffee on a table by the window, and was standing beside him. He sat up, rubbed his eyes, burst out laughing as though the world he had awakened to was a huge joke, and, casting the marten-skin rug aside, rose to his feet.

"*Ma foi*," said he, "I was chasing a man through the palace of Versailles, when Monsieur de Choiseul laid his hand on my shoulder—and the hand was yours. It is a good omen."

He kissed the hand that had brought him the coffee, slipped on his coat and sword-belt, laughing and talking all the time, and then, coffee-cup in hand, stood still talking and at the same time glancing out of the window every now and then.

He had remembered, a most important fact, that he owed his valet a month's wages.

Javotte at once offered to take it for him, and placing five louis in a piece of paper, he gave them to her for the purpose.

"That will keep him going till things clear up," said Rochefort. "He is faithful enough, but without money he would be driven to seek another master. And now good-bye, little one, nay, not good-bye—*au revoir*. We will meet soon again, of that I am sure, and in happier circumstances."

"Are you going to the Rue de Valois, monsieur?"

"I am going to the Rue de Valois, and that as quick as my feet can take me."

"But, monsieur, have you not thought of the danger?"

"What danger?"

"Oh, *ma foi!* What danger? If Monsieur de Choiseul is pursuing you, will he not have the streets watched?"

"Undoubtedly; but as Paris is under Monsieur de Sartines, Monsieur de Choiseul must first put Monsieur de Sartines in motion. Now, Monsieur de Sartines is my friend and he will delay, I am perfectly sure; he will be bound to act, but he will not be bound to break his neck running after me. So I feel pretty safe till noon."

Javotte sighed. She said nothing more, but accompanied him down the stairs to the door, which she unlatched for him. The *concierge*, a discreet person, no doubt observed this letting out of a man whom he had not let in. However, that was nothing to him, and as for Javotte, she did not think of the matter, so filled was her mind with other things.

Having closed the door on Rochefort, she came up again to her room, and taking the letter from the drawer in the bureau looked at it long and attentively. Rochefort had refused to open it, but Javotte had no scruples at all on the matter. She argued with herself thus: "If I were to open this from curiosity, I would be on the level with those spying servants whom I detest, like Madame Scudery's maid or the maid of Madame du Close. But I am not doing it from curiosity. I am doing it for the sake of another person, who is too proud and too fine to take precautions for himself. And who is Monsieur de Choiseul that one should trouble about opening his letters? Does he not do the very same himself—and who is Mademoiselle La Bruyère that one should not open her letters? Does she not do much worse in many and many a way? And what are they writing to one another about, these two? Well, we will see."

She procured a knife and heated it over the still burning lamp in her mistress' bedroom. Then, with a dexterity which she had often seen exhibited in the Dubarry *ménage*, she slid the hot knife under the seals of the letter.

Meanwhile, Rochefort was walking briskly towards the Rue de Valois. It was a perfect morning, the sky was stainless and the new-risen sun was flooding the city with his level beams, pouring his light on the mansions and gardens of the Faubourg St. Honoré, on the churches and spires of the cité, on the Montagne Ste. Genevieve and on the grim, black towers of the Bastille.

His way lay through the Rue de Provençe, a street that might have been named after its inhabitants, for here, amidst the early morning stir of life, you might hear the Provençal patois, the explosive little oaths, the shrill tongues of the women of the Camargue; and here you might buy Arles sausages, and Brandade, from swarthy shopkeepers with red cotton handkerchiefs tied round their heads and with gold rings in their ears, and here you might see the Venus of Arles in the flesh at every corner.

He passed from here into the Rue d'Artois, and then into the Rue de Valois.

Yes, Monsieur le Vicomte was at home, and Rochefort, following the servant, passed into the hall and was shown into the identical room where, only the night before last, he had assisted at the council of war, and where the Countess had protested her devotion to him and the Vicomte Jean had sworn eternal friendship.

The servant had drawn the blinds, and the morning light entered, illuminating the place and striking the white and gold decorations, the painted ceiling and the crystal of the candelabrum. The chairs were set about just as they had been left by the last persons who had occupied the place, and on one of the chairs was lying a woman's glove.

From the next room could be heard voices; men's voices, laughter and the clink of money. The Vicomte Jean and some of his disreputable companions were, no doubt, playing at cards, had been playing, most likely, all night, or, at all events, since news came that the presentation was a success, for the Vicomte had not turned up at Versailles, he had been too busy in Paris arranging matters.

Now, as Rochefort listened, he heard the servant entering to announce a visitor; the voices of the card-players ceased, then came the sounds of voices grumbling. A minute later, and the door giving on the corridor opened, and Jean Dubarry made his appearance.

He had never looked worse. His face was stiff from drink and sleeplessness, his coat was stained with wine, and one stocking was slipping down and wrinkled. He had been taking huge pinches of snuff to pull himself together, and the evidence of it was upon him.

"Ha, Rochefort," cried the man of pleasure. "You are early, hey! You see me—I have not been to bed—when the good news came by special messenger, I had some friends here, they are here still——" He yawned and flung himself on a couch, stretched out his legs, put his hands in his pockets, and yawned again.

"Your special messenger did not come quicker from Versailles than I did," said Rochefort. "Dubarry, I'm in the pot this time. I have always avoided politics, but they have got me at last, it seems."

"What are you saying?" asked Dubarry.

"I am saying that Choiseul is after me."

"Choiseul after you!" echoed Dubarry, rousing himself. "What is this you say? What has he found out? *Dame!* I thought all this business was happily ended, and now you come and disturb me with this news—what is it?"

"Oh, *ma foi*, you may well ask what is it!" replied Rochefort, irritated by the manner of the other. "It is this precious business of yours that has fallen on me, and it seems to me now that I am the only one to pay. Choiseul has discovered my part in it; he tried to arrest me at Versailles last night, he failed and I am here. I am pursued—that is all."

Dubarry rose to his feet thoroughly sobered; he walked a few steps up and down the room, as if trying to pull his thoughts together. Then he turned to Rochefort.

"You will excuse me for saying it, my dear Rochefort, but, considering the delicate position of the Comtesse and the fact that Choiseul is in pursuit of you—it would have been wiser of you to have sought shelter elsewhere. We are quite ready to help, but it is imperative now that this affair has blown over that we should resume friendly relationship with Choiseul. Of course, we are not friends, still, you can very well understand the necessity of our keeping up an appearance of friendship with the man who is the first man in France after his Majesty. It is diplomacy—that is all."

"Excuse me," said Rochefort, "I don't know what you are talking about."

"In what way?"

"I did not come here to take shelter."

"You came, then, to see me?"

Rochefort looked Dubarry up and down, then he broke into a laugh.

"No, my dear man, I did not come here to see you. I came here to see Mademoiselle Fontrailles, and to take my leave of her before I leave France or enter the Bastille."

"To see Mademoiselle Fontrailles?"

"Precisely."

"At this hour?"

"The matter is urgent."

"But it is impossible. She is not up yet."

"She will get up when she learns that I am here."

"You think so. Well, I tell you no. Put off your visit to her, for she came back last night not well disposed towards you; you kept her waiting, it seems, and then you did not arrive."

"I wish to explain all that."

"Wait, then," said Jean.

He left the room in an irritable manner, and returned in a minute or two.

"Mademoiselle Fontrailles is unable to see you; she will not be visible before noon."

"Ah, then at noon she will not be visible to me, for at noon I must be out of Paris. You did not give her my message."

"Oh, *ma foi!*" cried Jean, swelling like a turkey-cock. "You say that to my face! You give me the lie direct!"

"I give you nothing. I say you did not explain to her fully my position."

"Explain to her your position? *Mon Dieu!* I explained it as well as I could, shouting through her closed bedroom door, and her reply was, 'Tell Monsieur Rochefort I am unable to see him, and in any event I will not come down till noon.' So you see, she did not even say she would see you at noon."

"The devil!" said Rochefort. "I don't know what to make of you all. I say nothing about any help I have given you, but I will say this, the man I have pitted myself against, Monsieur de Choiseul, is at least a gentleman who looks after the interests of his friends. Good-day."

He turned to the door.

"Where are you going to?" asked Jean.

"I am going to breakfast at the Café de Régence."

"In your position?"

"Precisely. What do I care? I will leave Paris at my own time, and in my own way."

"But, my dear Rochefort," cried Jean, now very eager and friendly, "if you are pursued by Choiseul, and if you do not leave Paris at once, you will be simply playing into his hands; you will be caught, imprisoned, they may even torture you to make you tell."

"About the presentation?"

"About anything—everything. You know Choiseul, he is pitiless."

"Make your mind easy," said Rochefort, "I will tell without letting them torture me. What are you all to me that I should care? Now you have used me, you have done with me, and you are anxious that I should escape, not because you care a *denier* for my safety, but because you fear that they may extract the story of Ferminard from me———. That is what I think of you, Monsieur le Vicomte, what I think of Madame la Comtesse, what I think of Mademoiselle Fontrailles; you can tell them so with my regards."

He turned on his heel, pushed the door open and walked out.

He was furious. Certain that Jean had told him the truth as to Camille's message—for Jean had indeed told the truth, and his sincerity was patent—he could have pulled the house of Dubarry down on the heads of its inmates.

Instead, however, of making such an attempt, he walked into the street and strode off without looking back.

Jean, left alone, rushed back to the room where the gamblers were still playing, drank off a glass of wine, excused himself, and then went to the servants' quarters, ordered a carriage to be brought at once to the door, rushed upstairs, changed his clothes, and the carriage being ready, drove to the Hôtel de Sartines.

CHAPTER III

THE PAIR OF SPECTACLES

THE Hôtel de Sartines was situated in the Faubourg St. Germain. Jean Dubarry's carriage drove into the courtyard as half-past eight was striking, he descended, went up the steps, and entered the great hall, where already the bustle and the business of the day was in full swing.

The door was guarded by soldiers, a Suisse stood as sentry at the foot of the great staircase, and soldiers sat about on the benches, whilst crossing the hall from department to department went clerks, and men with papers in their hands, messengers and agents.

Dubarry gave his name to the usher on duty, and asked him to take it to the Comte de Sartines, with a message that his business was urgent. In less than five minutes, the man reappeared and asked the visitor to follow him.

He led the way up the broad staircase to the first floor, past the entrance of the famous octagon chamber, down a corridor to the bedroom of his Excellency, who was at that moment being finished off by his valet, Gaussard, the same who, though a valet, claimed the right to wear a sword by virtue of the fact that he was also a hairdresser.

Sartines, released from the valet's hands, was in the act of rising from his chair, when Dubarry was announced.

The Minister of Police was in an ill temper that morning, and as the cause of his bad humour has an important bearing on our story, we will refer to it.

Briefly, then, some days ago a tragedy had occurred at Luciennes. Atalanta, the King's favourite hound, had been poisoned. Louis XV., to give him his due, had a not unkindly feeling for animals. He tolerated Mizapouff, the little dog of Madame Dubarry, that cut such quaint capers at a celebrated dinner-party, he fed the carp in the pond at Luciennes with his own royal hand—when he could find no better amusement, and he was fond of Atalanta. Besides, she was his dog, the only dog of all the dogs in France who had the entrée of his private apartments. She was on a footing with the Duc de la Vrillière, her coat had the royal arms embroidered on it, and she knew it; she was fed with minced chicken, and she had her own personal attendant.

Some days ago, this aristocrat had been found in the courtyard at Luciennes, stiff and stark, poisoned by some miscreant or some mischance. The King was furious. He took it as a personal matter. Sartines was fetched over from Versailles, where he was on a visit of inspection, and Sartines had the unpleasant task of inspecting the corpse and questioning the cooks, the scullions, the chambermaids, the grooms, the gardeners—everyone, in short, who might have had a hand in the business, or who might have been able to cast some light on the affair. The result was absolute darkness and much worry for the unfortunate Sartines. The matter had become a joke at Court, and Sartines might have measured the extent to which he was hated by the way in which he was tormented.

Everyone asked him about the dog, and whether he had made any further advance into the mystery; a ballad was written about it, and he received a copy. The whole business gave him more worry and caused him more irritation than any other of the numerous affairs that were always annoying and irritating him, and, to cap the business, he had received this morning a neat little parcel containing a pair of spectacles. Nothing more.

The Vicomte bowed to Sartines and then, when the valet had taken his departure, plunged into the business at hand:

"My dear Sartines, that fool of a Rochefort has complicated matters in the most vile way; he called an hour ago and knocked me up to tell me the pleasant news that Choiseul is in pursuit of him. More than that, he has taken a grudge against us. He is in love with the Fontrailles, she refused to see him. I advised him to leave Paris at once, and all I got for my advice was an accusation of ingratitude. He is against us now; he knows all about the Ferminard affair, and he frankly threatened me that, were Choiseul to capture him and question him in any unpleasant way, he would tell all he knew. Even were Choiseul simply to imprison him, he would most likely tell, just from spite against us and to obtain his release."

"The devil!" said Sartines. "Things seem to have a habit of going wrong these days—but he would not tell. I have great faith in Rochefort, though I am not given to having faith in people. He is a very proud man. He would not betray us."

"Has he promised secrecy?"

"No, he has promised nothing."

"There you are. He may be a proud man, an honourable man—what you will, but he fancies we have used him and cast him away. There is the Fontrailles business as well. He is angry, and I tell you, when Rochefort is like that, he cares for nothing. He said Choiseul was at least a gentleman who could look after his friends. He will join arms with Choiseul."

"Well, suppose he does?"

"Then Choiseul will be in power for ever. Once he gets hold of the true tale of the Ferminard business, he will flatten us out. I will be exiled, for one, his Majesty could never allow such an affront to the Monarchy to go unpunished; and you, Sartines, what will become of you? Who originated the whole idea but you, yourself?"

Sartines produced his snuff-box and took a pinch. Then he turned to the window and looked out on the courtyard.

He felt himself badly placed.

He had guarded against everything but this—Rochefort turned an enemy.

He knew quite well that the Dubarrys had used Rochefort just as they had used the old Comtesse de Béarn, for their own ends, and would throw him away when used; what angered him was the fact that this fool of a Vicomte Jean had clearly let Rochefort perceive this; there was the business of the girl, too. Rochefort had promised no secrecy.

"Before we talk of Rochefort," said he, "how about Madame de Béarn?"

"We have nothing to fear from her," said Jean. "She was furious, but the thing is over, and were she to make a fuss, she would gain nothing and lose a good deal. She has come in, and her price, between you and me, was not a low price. She has cost us two hundred thousand francs. By the way, I suppose Ferminard is safe?"

"Yes; when his work was done, he was driven to Vincennes very securely guarded. When Choiseul is gone from the Ministry, we will let him out. Now, as to Rochefort, we must deal with that gentleman in a drastic way. That is to say, we must save him from Choiseul. For, if Choiseul once takes him into his hands, we are lost."

"How do you propose to act?"

"Very simply. I shall arrest him and hide him in Vincennes."

"And Choiseul, when he hears the news, will visit him in Vincennes."

"Choiseul will not hear the news. We will pretend he has escaped. Early this morning I had a letter from Choiseul, asking me to drag Paris with a seine net for Rochefort. He is accused of having killed a man. Well, I will drag Paris with a seine net, imprison Rochefort, under the name of Bonhomme, or any name you please, and once we have him tightly tucked away in Vincennes, all will be smooth. Captain Pierre Cousin, the governor of Vincennes, is entirely mine."

"It is a good idea," said Jean; "and really, seeing how Rochefort is placed as regards Choiseul, it would be the best act we could do for him."

"It's the best we can do for ourselves," said Sartines. "Has Rochefort gone back to his rooms, do you think?"

"I don't know. He told me he would go to the Café de Régence for breakfast."

"If he said that, he will be there, it's just like his bravado, and there I shall arrest him."

"He will resist, and he will be surrounded by friends."

"Dubarry," said Sartines, "you talk as though you were talking to a police agent. If you had been with me the other night, you would have heard me giving Rochefort a little lecture on my ways and methods; you would have heard me say, amongst other things, that I hold my position not by cleverness—though, indeed, perhaps I am not a fool—but by my knowledge of men and how they reason and think and act. Of course, if I were to arrest Rochefort in the ordinary way, he would resist; his friends would help him, blood would be spilt, and the Parisians would cry out, 'Ah! there is that cursed de Sartines again.' Rochefort is a popular figure, and a popular figure only requires to be arrested to make it a popular idol. I do not intend to make an idol of Rochefort."

He went to the table by the window, and struck a bell.

"Send Lavenne to me," said he, when the servant answered the summons. "Has he arrived yet?"

"Yes, monsieur, he is here."

"Then send him up."

CHAPTER IV

THE ARREST OF ROCHEFORT

ROCHEFORT, when he left the Hôtel Dubarry, reached the Rue St. Honoré and walked up it, past the Hôtel de Noailles, and in the direction of the Palais Royal.

The Rue St. Honoré is the old main artery of the business and social world of Paris on the right bank of the Seine. In one direction, it led to the palaces of the Faubourg St. Honoré, in the other to the Bastille. In the eighteenth century it was as bustling and alive with business as it is now, and its side streets led even to more important places. Walking up it from the Faubourg St. Honoré, you had the Place Vendôme opening from it on the left, beyond the Place Vendôme the great door giving entrance to the Jacobins, beyond that, as you advanced, the Rue de l'Échelle, on the right, leading to the Place de Carrousel and the Tuileries; on the left, further along, the Rue de Richelieu, and on the right three streets leading directly to the Louvre. Beyond that the Rue de Poulies leading to St. Germain l'Auxerrois, and much further on, the Halles to the left. The river was much less accessible from the Rue St. Honoré than it is to-day, being barred off by the Tuileries, the buildings on the Quai des Galeries du Louvre, and the Louvre itself. Nothing was more remarkable in this old Paris than the way in which public convenience was sacrificed to the convenience of the King, the nobles and the religious orders. You entered a street and found yourself face to face with a barrier—as in that street where Rochefort encountered and killed de Choiseul's agent; a way that ought to have led you to the river, brought you to the back door of a monastery; a road that ought to have been a short cut, such as the Court St. Vincent, landed you to the gateway of Le Manége. Streets like the Rue du Brave led you into culs-de-sac like the Foire St. Germain.

The religious orders showed large over the city. One might say that it was a city of churches, monasteries, convents and religious houses, palaces and royal residences. If every religious house had offered sanctuary to the unfortunates pursued by the King or the nobles, then Paris would have been the best city in the world for a man who was trying to escape; this not being so, it was the worst, as Rochefort would have found to his cost had he been on that business. But M. de Rochefort was not making his escape. He was going to breakfast at the Café de Régence, despite Choiseul and the world, or rather because of them.

Anger had worked him up into a mood of absolute recklessness. He had never been famed for carefulness; wine made him mad—reckless; but anger and thwarted desire were to prove themselves even more potent than wine. As he went on his way, he expected arrest at each street corner, or rather attempted arrest; for, in his present temper, he would have resisted all of Choiseul's agents and all de Sartines' guards, even had they been led by Choiseul and Sartines in person.

He wanted to hit the Dubarrys, he wanted to strike at Camille Fontrailles; failing them, it would content him to hit Choiseul or his creatures should he come across them, or Sartines—or even his best friend.

Of course, the whole centre of this passionate fury was Camille Fontrailles. She would not see him; very well, he would see what he would not do.

As he walked along the Rue St. Honoré, he glanced from right to left, after the manner of a man who seeks to pick a quarrel even if he has to pick it with a stranger. But at that comparatively early hour, the Rue St. Honoré was not the place for a bully's business. People were too busy to give cause for offence, and too lowly to take it with a nobleman, and Rochefort, if the matter had been an absolute necessity with him, would have been condemned to skewer a shopboy, a market porter, or a water-carrier.

But at the Café de Régence, when he reached it, he found what he imagined to be the *hors-d'œuvre* for a regular banquet.

The Café de Régence, at that period, was the meeting-place of the intellectuals, and at the same time the meeting-place of the bloods. Rousseau might have been seen there of an evening, Jean Dubarry took breakfast there sometimes, Rochefort, and many others like him, frequented the place. At this hour, that is to say about ten o'clock, Rochefort found a couple of bald-headed men and several rather seedy ones sipping coffee and discussing the news of the day. They were Philosophers—Intellectuals, and like all Philosophers and Intellectuals of all ages, untidy, shabby, and making a great noise.

Rochefort, drinking the wine he had ordered and talking to the waiter who had served it, spoke in so loud a voice and made such free remarks about things in general, and the habitués of the café in particular, that faces were turned to him from the surrounding tables and then turned away again. No one wished to pick a quarrel with M. de Rochefort, his character was too well known, and his tongue.

He ordered *déjeuner* for half-past eleven, and then he sat drinking his wine, his virulence, like a sheathed sword, only waiting to be drawn. But no one came to draw it. People entered and spoke to him, but they were all Amiables. There was M. de Duras, rubicund and portly, with whom one could no more quarrel than with a cask of port; there was M. de Jussieu, the botanist and friend of Rousseau, beautifully dressed and carrying a book, his head full of flowers and roots, long Latin terms and platitudes; there was M. de Champfleuri, eighty years old, yet with all his teeth, dressed like a May morning, and fragile-looking as a Dresden china figure. He would damn your soul for the least trifle, but you could not quarrel with him for fear of breaking him. There was Monsieur Müller, who was finding his way in Paris as an exponent—by means of a translator—of the theories of Mesmer. You could not quarrel with him, as he only knew three words of French. There were others equally impossible. Ah! if only M. d'Estouteville had turned up, or Monpavon; Camus or Coigny!

Rochefort turned to the breakfast that was now served to him, and as he ate continued to grumble. If only some of these people whom he hated would come, that he might insult them; if only one of Choiseul's agents, or even a dozen of them, would come to arrest him, so that he might fight his way to the door and fight his way out of Paris; but no one came, till—as he was in the middle of his meal—an inconspicuous and quietly-dressed man entered, looked round, saw M. de Rochefort sitting at his breakfast, and came towards him.

It was Lavenne.

Lavenne came up to the table, bowed, and taking an empty chair at the opposite side of the table, sat down.

"Monsieur de Rochefort," said Lavenne, "I have come to arrest you."

He spoke with a friendly smile, and in a manner so urbane, and even deferential, that Rochefort was quite disarmed. He broke into a laugh as though someone had told him a good joke, refilled his glass, took a sip, and placed the glass down again.

"Oh, you have come to arrest me, Monsieur Lavenne; good. But where is your sword, and where are your assistants?"

"Monsieur," said Lavenne, "I never carry a sword, and I always act single-handed."

"Ah, you always act single-handed—So do I. *Mordieu!* Monsieur Lavenne, it is a coincidence."

"Call it a happy accident, monsieur."

"As how?"

"Simply because, monsieur, that as I come to do you a service, and to do it single-handed, your thanks will be all mine and I shall not have to divide it with others."

"Now, upon my faith," cried Rochefort, laughing and filling a glass with wine, "you have a way of putting things which is entirely new; and what I have observed in you before does not lose in value at all, I assure you, on further acquaintance. May I offer you this glass of wine? To your health—a strange wish enough, as I believe before many minutes are over—as many minutes, in fact, as I take in finishing my breakfast and rising from this table—I shall have the honour of spitting you on my sword."

"To your health, monsieur," replied Lavenne, perfectly unmoved and raising the glass to his lips. "One can only do one's duty, and as it is my duty to arrest you, I must take the risk of your sword, which I believe, monsieur, not to be sharper than your tongue to those who have offended you; a risk which I reckon as slight, inasmuch as I have no intention of offending you."

"Eh! no intention of offending me, and yet you talk of arrest!"

"That is the fault of our language, monsieur, which compels us sometimes to use words which carry unpleasant meanings to express our thoughts. Now the word Arrest is not a pleasant word, yet in my mouth and used at this table, it is not unpleasant—It means, in fact, Protection."

"And how?"

"It is necessary for you to leave Paris immediately, monsieur—is that not so?"

"I am going."

"No, monsieur, you are not. It is absolutely impossible to leave the walls of Paris, and were you by some miracle to do so, Monsieur de Choiseul would place his hand on you before you left France."

"I will risk it."

"You cannot—It is not a question of risk, it is a question of certainty. Now, monsieur, you are young, you have forty years more of good life before you, and you are in great danger of losing them."

"I do not fear death."

"Everyone knows that, but it is not death that you have to fear at the hands of Monsieur de Choiseul; it is something much worse."

"And that?"

"La Bastille, monsieur. She is a terrible person, who rarely lets go what she once lays a hold on. You say to yourself, 'Bah! I will fight my way from Paris, I will escape somehow.' Well, I tell you, you will not. I will prove it to you. Last night, you ordered a horse to be kept waiting for you at noon to-day a quarter of a mile beyond the Porte St. Antoine."

"How do you know that?"

"The Hôtel de Sartines knows everything, monsieur—— Well, Monsieur de Sartines would be very happy not to interfere with this way of escape for you, were it not that he knows Monsieur de Choiseul's plans as well as yours. In short, monsieur, the Porte St. Antoine is guarded so well by Monsieur de Choiseul's orders, that no one can leave Paris even in disguise; every other gate is guarded as strictly."

"*Diable!*" said Rochefort. "It seems, then, that I must convert myself into a bird to fly over the walls."

"Monsieur de Choiseul would set his falcons on you, monsieur."

"Into a rat, then, to crawl out through the sewers."

"The Hôtel de Choiseul contains many cats, monsieur."

"My faith, that's true," cried Rochefort, with a laugh, "since it contains Madame de Choiseul and her friend, Madame la Princesse de Guemenée. Well, then, I must stay in Paris. I will go and live with Monsieur Rousseau and help him to write poetry—or is it music that he writes?"

"Neither, monsieur—but time is passing, and my business is urgent. I am here to arrest you, and I call on you, monsieur, to follow me."

"And where?—to the Bastille?"

"No, monsieur, to Vincennes, where we will hide you away from Monsieur de Choiseul till this business has blown over, and where you will be treated as a prisoner, but as a gentleman."

"But were I to fall in with this mad plan of yours, Monsieur Lavenne, I would simply be running down Choiseul's throat, it seems to me. As the first Minister of France, he will easily find me in Vincennes."

"No, monsieur, he will not hunt in the prisons for a man whom he fancies to be running on the roads. Monsieur de Sartines, even, will have no official knowledge of your arrest. I am not arresting you under your own name. I have, in fact, mistaken you for one Justin La Porte, a gentleman under suspicion of conspiracy and of being a frequenter of certain political clubs. Should Monsieur de Choiseul, by some ill chance, find you at

Vincennes, the whole blame would fall on me. I would be dismissed the service for my 'mistake.'"

Rochefort, as he listened to all this, began to take counsel with himself. His madness and anger against the world had received a check under the hand of Lavenne. Lavenne was perhaps the only person in the world who had ever called him to order, thwarted his will without raising his anger, and made him think. Lavenne himself, in his person, his manner and his life was a criticism on Rochefort. This man who never drank—or only sipped half a glass of wine as a matter of ceremony—who belonged to the people, who dressed soberly, and whose life was very evidently one of hard work and devotion to duty, commanded respect just as he commanded confidence. But there was more than that. Lavenne had about him something of Fate, and an Authority beyond even that of the Hôtel de Sartines. One could never imagine this man reasoning wildly or acting foolishly, nor could one very well imagine him allowing a personal motive to rule his line of action. There was something disturbing in his calmness, as though one discerned beneath everything a mechanism moving with the unswerving aim of a mechanism towards the goal appointed by its constructor.

"Even now, monsieur," continued Lavenne, "you would have Monsieur de Choiseul's hand upon your shoulder had you not, urged by some good fairy, taken refuge in the very last place where his agents and spies would look for you; they are ransacking the streets, they are posted at the gates, they are all hunting for a man who is running away, and you have outwitted them simply by not running away, but coming to breakfast at the Café de Régence."

"And yet you found me," said Rochefort.

"Because, monsieur, I belong to the Hôtel de Sartines, not to the Hôtel de Choiseul."

"Let us be perfectly clear," said Rochefort. "The agents of Choiseul are hunting for me, the agents of Sartines are trying to hide me."

"Not quite so, monsieur: the agents of Choiseul are hunting for you, and all the agents of the Hôtel de Sartines must assist the agents of Choiseul if they are called upon by them to arrest Monsieur de Rochefort. But *one* agent of the Hôtel de Sartines, that is to say I, myself, is trying to hide Monsieur de Rochefort, and he is doing so at the instigation of Monsieur de Sartines."

"I see," said Rochefort. "The matter is of such a delicate nature, that Sartines dare not give a general order to his police to thwart Choiseul's men and to hide me, so he entrusts it to one man, and that man is Monsieur Lavenne."

"Precisely, monsieur. You have put the whole thing in a nutshell."

"Well, Monsieur Lavenne, the last time I played chess, it was with Monsieur de Gondy. I was stalemated by the move of a bishop. To-day, playing chess with Monsieur de Sartines, I am stalemated by the move of a knight. You are the knight, Monsieur Lavenne. You have closed in on me and shown me my position, and I do not kick the board over in a temper, simply because you have come to me as a gentleman comes to a gentleman, and spoken to me as a gentleman speaks to a gentleman. I cannot move, it seems, without being taken by either you or Choiseul. I prefer you to Choiseul, not so much because you offer me Vincennes in exchange for La Bastille, but because you are the better gentleman. Monsieur Lavenne, I place myself and my sword in your hands. Arrest me."

He rose from the table, flung a louis on the cloth to pay his score. Then, taking his hat, he left the café with his captor.

In this fashion did de Sartines rope in and tame without resistance a man whose capture, by Choiseul, might have involved his—Sartines'—destruction. For Rochefort, angry with the Dubarrys and incensed against Camille Fontrailles, was now the danger spot in the surroundings of the Minister of Police, Rochefort and Ferminard—who was already in the safe custody of Captain Pierre Cousin, the governor of Vincennes.

CHAPTER V

CAPTAIN ROUX

LAVENNE left the café, followed by Rochefort. They passed down the street to the corner, where, drawn up at the pavement, stood a closed carriage.

"Monsieur," said Lavenne, "this is a police carriage, and as such will be able to leave the Porte St. Antoine—which, as you know, is the gate leading to Vincennes—without question or examination."

"So I am to make my escape from the Bastille in a police carriage," laughed Rochefort. "Well, let us enter."

"Pardon me, monsieur, but I cannot go with you. I have to go to your rooms and make a perquisition, an examination for papers, and so on. Were I not to do this in person, it would be done by some fool, perhaps, who might find undesirable things and talk, or play in some other way into the hands of Monsieur de Choiseul. As for me, you may trust that I will respect all your private correspondence."

"It is all burnt, my dear Monsieur Lavenne. However, make what search you will. But am I to go alone to Vincennes—and what shall I say to this charming governor you spoke of?"

"No, monsieur, you are to go under strict arrest and masked. Captain Roux is in the carriage; he is rather dull-witted, but has no tongue, so he will not bore you."

"And will I see you at Vincennes?"

"Possibly, monsieur. And now let me say at once that my advice to you is patience. I do not hide at all from you, monsieur, that I am your friend. That morning when you invited me to drink wine with you whilst you breakfasted, showed me a gentleman, whom I am delighted to be of service to, always remembering that my first services are due to Monsieur de Sartines, my master. I will look after your interests whilst not disregarding his. And now, monsieur, into the carriage, quick, for delay is full of danger here in the open street."

"I thank you," said Rochefort, "I have absolute confidence in all you do and say. Well, *au revoir*, Monsieur Lavenne, and now for the acquaintance of Monsieur le Capitaine Roux."

He entered the carriage, the door of which Lavenne had opened.

"Captain Roux," said Lavenne, "this is the prisoner, La Porte. Whilst using him as a gentleman, keep him strictly guarded; and, above all, let no man see his face till he is safely at Vincennes. You have the mask. Monsieur La Porte will not object to your putting it upon him for the journey."

He shut the door and called to the driver, "Vincennes."

Rochefort, face to face with the redoubtable Captain Roux, broke into a laugh, which found no echo from the other.

Roux was a stout man who never laughed, an earnest-minded machine, if I may be allowed the term; he had also, to use Lavenne's expression, no tongue. The genius of de Sartines was never better shown than in his selection of these two men for the arrest of Rochefort—Lavenne to persuade him to accept arrest and be conveyed to Vincennes, Roux to convey him.

"Well, Monsieur le Capitaine," said Rochefort, as the carriage started, "it seems that we are to make a little journey together."

"Monsieur," replied the other, "I wish to be in every way agreeable to you and so fulfil my orders in that respect, but I am forbidden to talk to you."

"And yet you are talking to me, my dear sir."

"I was only making a statement of my orders, monsieur. And now, if you will permit me, this is the mask."

Rochefort took the grey silk mask and examined it, then, with a laugh, he put it on. It was fixed with strings which tied behind the head, and he had good reason to thank de Sartines' forethought in supplying it; for at the Porte St. Antoine, when the carriage stopped for a moment, one of the guards, despite the warning of the coachman, pushed aside the curtain of the window and popped his head in.

"Whom have we here?" said he.

Roux, in reply, struck the man a blow on the face with his clenched fist.

Then, leaning out of the window, he talked to the guards. He asked them did they not know a carriage of the Hôtel de Sartines when they saw it, and spoke to them about their intelligence, questioned their ancestry and ordered the arrest of the unfortunate, whose nose was streaming blood. Then he sank back, and the carriage drove on.

"Ah, monsieur," cried the delighted Rochefort, from behind his mask, "I have never heard anything quite like that before. I would give the liberty which I do not possess to be able to curse like that—and they said you had no tongue! Tell me, was it by training you arrived at this perfection, or was it a natural gift?"

"Monsieur," said Roux, "I am forbidden to speak to you."

The carriage rolled on, leaving the old Hôtel of the Black Musketeers on the right, and the Bastille and the Porte St. Antoine safely behind. Rochefort, seated beside his silent companion, said nothing more, at least with his tongue. The silence of Captain Roux might be a check to conversation, but it lent itself completely to that form of mental conversation which Villon has so well exemplified in the Debate between his heart and body.

Commonsense and M. de Rochefort were having a few words together, and commonsense was doing most of the talking.

"Well, Monsieur de Rochefort," said Commonsense, "and here we are in a police carriage, at last, being driven to his Majesty's fortress of Vincennes; and all on account of Politics—that is to say, a woman. You have known a hundred women, yet they have never succeeded in dragging you into Politics. How did this one manage it? You lost your heart to her. That is precisely what happened, and now you have lost your liberty as well as your heart; next thing, you will lose your estates, then you will take this Choiseul by the neck and strangle him, and then you will lose your head—and all through a woman.

"You have made a fool of yourself, Monsieur de Rochefort. Yesterday, you were free as a butterfly, the whole world lay before you, you did not know the meaning of the word Liberty. Well, you are to learn the meaning of that word, and the lesson promises to be a curious one. You are not Choiseul's prisoner, you are not Sartines' prisoner, you are not even yourself. You are Monsieur La Porte, and you are being tucked away in Vincennes, hidden, just as a man might hide an incriminating letter in a desk. Why is Sartines so anxious to hide you? Is it not that he fears that you may be found, and if this fear does not fade away in his mind, it is quite on the cards that you may never be found.

"And you can do nothing as yet, only wait. Monsieur Lavenne is your friend, and it seems to me he is the only friend you have got in the world."

Commonsense is sometimes wrong, as in this instance.

It had forgotten Javotte.

Rochefort was aroused from his reverie by the stoppage of the carriage. They had arrived at the main gate of Vincennes. The great fortress towered above them, the battlements cutting the sky and showing the silhouette of a passing sentry against the free blue of heaven.

Rochefort heard the harsh voices of the guards interrogating the coachman. Then the carriage passed on, rumbling across the drawbridge, and drew up in the courtyard before the door of the entrance for prisoners.

Rochefort got out and, following Captain Roux and being followed in turn by a soldier, passed through the doorway down a corridor to the reception-room. This was a bleak and formal place, the old guard-room of the fortress, where the stands for pikes still remained and the slings for arquebuses; but of pikes and pikemen, arquebuses or arbalètes, nothing now remained, their places being taken by desks, books and manuscripts, and a clerk dry as parchment, who was seated behind one of the desks, and who, having entered all particulars in a book, handed Captain Roux a receipt for Monsieur de Rochefort, as though that gentleman had been a bundle of goods.

Roux, having put the receipt in his belt, turned on his heel and, without a word, left the room. Rochefort, left alone with the clerk and the soldier, turned to the clerk.

"Well, monsieur," said Rochefort, "it seems to me that Monsieur le Capitaine Roux has left his good manners with his tongue at the Hôtel de Sartines; and he is in such a hurry back to find them that he has forgotten to introduce us properly. I do not even know your name."

The clerk wrote something on a piece of paper, and handed it to the soldier.

"Come, monsieur," said the soldier, touching Rochefort on the arm.

"Monsieur," said Rochefort, still addressing the clerk, "there is a mistake somewhere."

"In what way?"

"In this way, monsieur. When I consented to come here as the guest of Monsieur de Sartines, I did so on the understanding that I was to be treated as a gentleman. I demand to see Captain Pierre Cousin, the governor of Vincennes."

"He is absent."

"When does he return?"

"Monsieur," said the clerk, "it is not for a prisoner to ask questions."

"But it is for a clerk to reply. *Mordieu!* it seems to me you do not know to whom you are talking. Come, your master, when does he return?"

The man of parchment half rose from his chair. Then he sat down again. He had, in fact, a special despatch from Sartines on his table giving instructions as to Rochefort's treatment. He swallowed his anger, and took a different tone.

"The governor of Vincennes returns this evening; he will be informed that you wish to see him. And now, monsieur, our interview is ended. I am busy."

"Good," said Rochefort, turning on his heel. Following the soldier, he left the room.

This same soldier was the gaoler on duty by day, whose business it was to receive prisoners, accompany them before the governor or clerk, and then to see them safely incarcerated according to the orders of the governor. Vincennes was much more of a military prison than the Bastille. Soldiers were the gaolers, and the day went to the roll of drums and the blare of bugles, rather than to the clang of bells. Vincennes was more cheerful than the Bastille, but was reckoned less healthy. Madame de Rambouillet it was who said that the cell in which Marshal Ornano died was worth its weight in arsenic; yet of the two prisons, Vincennes was preferable, if there can be such a thing as choice between prisons.

Rochefort followed his guide down the corridor, and then up a circular stone staircase to the floor above. Here they passed down another corridor, till they reached a door on the right which the sergeant opened, disclosing a room, barely furnished, yet not altogether cheerless.

The grated window gave a sweeping view of the country; to the left, pressing one's nose against the glass, one could get a glimpse of the outskirts of Paris; immediately below lay the castle moat, and running past the moat, the Paris road bordered with poplar trees.

Rochefort went to the window and looked out, whilst Sergeant Bonvallot, for that was the name of his guardian, dismissed the soldier who had followed them, closed the door, and began to make arrangements for the comfort of his visitor.

He inspected the water-pitcher to see if it were filled, the bed coverings to see if they were thick enough, and the sheets to see if they were clean. He knew perfectly well that all was in order, but Rochefort had the appearance of a man who would pay for little attentions, and they were cheap.

"There, monsieur," said Bonvallot, when he had finished, "I have made you as comfortable as I can. Your dinner will be served at five o'clock, your supper at nine, and should you feel cold a fire is permitted, also writing materials, should you need them—but for those you will have to pay."

Rochefort turned from the window and contemplated his gaoler fully, and for the first time.

Bonvallot was a large man, with small eyes and a face that suggested good-humour. He would have made a capital innkeeper.

"Why, upon my word," said Rochefort, who knew at once how to tackle his man, "you seem to me an admirable fellow. My own servant could not have done better, and when I come to leave here, you will not have cause to regret your efforts on my behalf. Your name?"

"Bonvallot, monsieur."

"Well, Monsieur Bonvallot, here is a half louis to drink my health, and when my dinner is served, let me have a bottle of your best Beaune, and a fire, certainly, there is no companion like a fire, and as for writing materials, we will see about that to-morrow. Should there be any books in this old inn of yours, Monsieur Bonvallot, you may bring them to me. I am not a great reader, but who knows what one may become with so much time on one's hands, as it is likely I may have here—Is your inn pretty full?"

"Fairly so, monsieur," replied Bonvallot, falling into the vein of the other. "Though no guests have arrived for some days, still, those who are here remain a long time."

"Ah! they could not pay any better compliment to the house. Am I alone on this corridor?"

"No, monsieur, in the room next to yours there is another guest. *Ma foi!* he is not difficult to feed either; he seems to live on pens, ink and paper."

"He must suffer from indigestion, this guest of yours."

"I do not know what he suffers from, monsieur, but this I do know: when I bring him his food he makes me listen to what he has written, which I cannot understand in the least."

"Ah, he must be a philosopher, then."

"I do not know, monsieur. I only know that I do not understand him."

"Then he is most certainly a philosopher. Well, Monsieur Bonvallot, I will not keep you from your duties. Do not forget the Beaune; and presently, perhaps, you will be able to assist me in getting clean linen and so forth, for I came here in such a hurry, that I forgot to order my valet to pack my valise."

"We will arrange about that, monsieur," replied Bonvallot.

He went out, shutting and locking the door, and Rochefort was left alone with his thoughts. He walked to the window again and looked out. Then he opened the glass sash. The walls at the openings of these upper windows were bevelled, else each window would have been but the opening of a tunnel six feet long. They were guarded each by a single iron bar, and the glass sash opened inwardly. Rochefort had as yet no idea of flight, and he was, perhaps, the only prisoner who had ever looked through that window without measuring the thickness of the bar, or estimating the height of the window from the ground.

He was quite content with his position for the moment. Lavenne's words were still ringing in his ears, and Lavenne's face was still before him. Rochefort had never feared a man in his life, yet Lavenne had brought him almost to the point of fearing Choiseul.

At bottom, M. de Rochefort was not a fool, and he recognized that whilst Life and Death are simply toys for a brave man to play with, imprisonment for life is a thing for the bravest man to dread. Vincennes was saving him from Choiseul, and as he stood at the window whistling a tune of the day, he followed Choiseul with his mind's eye, Choiseul ransacking Paris, Choiseul posting spies on all the roads, Choiseul urging on the imperturbable and sphinx-like de Sartines, and Sartines receiving Choiseul's messages without a smile.

He was standing like this, when a voice made him start and turn round.

"Monsieur de Rochefort," said the voice, which sounded as though the speaker were in the same room as the prisoner.

"*Mon Dieu!*" cried Rochefort. "Who is that speaking, and where are you?"

"Here, Monsieur de Rochefort, in the next chamber to yours. I heard your voice and recognized it talking to that fat-headed Bonvallot, and I said there must be a hole in the wall somewhere to let a voice come through like that; so I searched for it and found it. The hole is under my bed. A large stone has been removed, evidently by some industrious rat of a prisoner, who never could complete his business. Search for the hole on your side, Monsieur de Rochefort."

Rochefort pulled his bed out from the wall, and there, surely enough, was a hole about a foot square in the wainscoting. He lay down on his face and tried to look through into the next chamber, but the wall was three feet thick and the head of his interlocutor on the other side blocked the light, so that he could see nothing.

"Here is the hole," said he, "but I can see nothing. Who are you?"

"Who am I? Did you not recognize my voice? *Hé, pardieu*, I am Ferminard. Who else would I be?"

"Ferminard! Just heaven! and what on earth are you doing here?"

"Doing here? I am hiding from Monsieur de Choiseul. What else would I be doing here?"

"Hiding from Choiseul! Explain yourself, Monsieur Ferminard."

"Well, Monsieur Rochefort, it was this way. After that confounded presentation, I had an interview with Monsieur Lavenne, one of Monsieur de Sartines' agents, and as a result of that interview, I consented to place myself under the protection of Monsieur de Sartines for a short time. You can very well guess, monsieur, the reason why, especially as it was brought to my knowledge that Monsieur de Choiseul had wind of my hand in that affair, and was about to search for me."

"Oho!" said Rochefort. "That is why you are here."

"Yes, monsieur, and now in return for my confidence, may I ask why you are in the same position and under the same roof?"

"Well, I am here for just the same reason, Monsieur Ferminard."

"You are hiding from Monsieur de Choiseul."

"Precisely."

"*Mordieu*, that is droll."

"You think so?"

"It is more than droll. For, see here, Monsieur de Rochefort, we are two prisoners, we neither of us wish to escape, yet we have the means."

"Explain yourself."

"Well, monsieur, I have only been here a very short time, yet, being an indefatigable worker, the moment I arrived I demanded writing materials and set to work upon a drama that has long been in my mind. Now it is my habit when working to walk to and fro and to act, as it were, my work even before it is on paper."

"Yes," said Rochefort, laughing, "I heard you once; go on."

"Well, monsieur, I chanced to stamp upon the floor whilst impersonating the character of Raymond, the villain of my piece, and the floor, where I stamped upon it, sounded hollow. 'Ah ha!' said I, 'what is this?' I found a flag loose and raised it, and what did I find there but a hole."

"Yes?"

"And in the hole, a knotted rope some forty feet long, a staple, and a big sou."

"*Ma foi!* But what do you mean by a big sou?"

"Why, monsieur, a big sou is a sou that has been split in two pieces and hollowed out, then a thread is made round the edges so that the two halves can be screwed together, so as to form a little box."

"And what can be held in a box so small?"

"A saw, monsieur, made from a watch-spring, a little thing enough, but able to cut through the thickest bar of iron."

"And does your big sou hold such a saw?"

"It does, monsieur."

"*Ciel!* what a marvel, what industry; and to think that some poor devil of a prisoner made all that, and got his rope ready, and then perhaps died or was removed before he could use it!"

"Yes, monsieur, he had everything ready. The thing is a little tragedy in itself, and is even completed by this hole."

Rochefort laughed.

"And how can a hole complete a tragedy, Monsieur Ferminard?"

"Why, quite simply, Monsieur de Rochefort. The window in this chamber is too narrow to permit the passage of a man's body, so, doubtless, the prisoner was anxious to reach your chamber. Of what dimensions is your window?"

"Large enough to get through for an ordinary-sized man."

"There, you see that the unfortunate was justified, and we may even say that the unfortunate must have had some knowledge of your chamber and the dimensions of your window. Well, Monsieur de Rochefort, his labour was not all lost, for though neither of us wish to escape, we both wish to talk to the other. We will have much pleasant conversation together, you and I. Up to this, I have had no one to speak to but that fat-head of a Bonvallot, a man absolutely destitute of parts, who does not know the difference, it seems to me, between a tragedy and a comedy, and to whom a strophe of poetry and the creaking of a cart-wheel amount to the same thing."

"I assure you, Monsieur Ferminard, the good Bonvallot and I are much in the same case. I know nothing about poetry, and I cannot tell a stage-play from a washing-bill. So in whatever conversations we have together, let us talk of anything but the theatre."

"On the contrary, Monsieur de Rochefort, since you confess yourself ignorant of one of the most sublime branches of art, it will be my pleasure to open for you the doors of a Paradise where all may enter, so be that they are properly led. But, hush! I hear a sound in the corridor. Replace your bed."

Rochefort rose to his feet and replaced the bed. Scarcely had he done so, when the door opened, and Bonvallot appeared, bearing some clean linen, two towels, and some toilet necessaries.

"Here, monsieur," said Bonvallot, "are several shirts new laundered, and other articles, which I have scraped together for your comfort. Half a louis will pay for them."

"Thanks, put them on the bed; and now tell me, which of the guests of your precious inn occupied my chamber last."

"Why, monsieur, this chamber has not had a tenant for two years and a half. Then it was occupied by Monsieur de Thumery."

"And what became of Monsieur de Thumery?"

"He was removed to the next chamber, monsieur."

"Ah, and is he there still?"

"No, monsieur, he died a month ago."

"What sort of man was he, this Monsieur de Thumery?"

"A very delicate man, monsieur, and very pious—one who scarcely ever spoke."

"He never tried to escape, I suppose."

"Oh, *mon Dieu!* no, Monsieur, he was as gentle as a lamb. He did nothing but read the lives of the saints."

"Thank you, and here is your half louis. And what is that book on the bed?"

"Why, I brought it with the clothes, monsieur, as you said you wished for books. It belonged to Monsieur de Thumery. It is not much, some religious book or other—still, it is a book."

He went off, and Rochefort picked up M. de Thumery's religious book. It was the works of François Rabelais, printed by Tollard of the Rue de la Harpe, in the year 1723.

BOOK III

CHAPTER I

THE POISONING OF ATALANTA

MEANWHILE, Lavenne, having watched the carriage containing Rochefort and Captain Roux taking its departure, turned and took his way to Rochefort's rooms in the Rue de Longueville. The Rochefort affair was only an incident in his busy profession, yet whilst he was upon it, it held his whole life and ambition in life. He was made in such a manner, that the moment filled all his purview without blinding him. He could see the moment, yet he could also see consequences—that is to say, the future, and causes—that is to say, the past.

In his seven years' work under Sartines, he had learned the fact that these social and political cases like that of Rochefort almost invariably produce, or are allied to, other cases, either engaging or soon to engage the attention of the police. Even in the spacious Court of France, people were too tightly packed for one to move in an eccentric manner without producing far-reaching disturbances, and he was soon to prove this fact in the case of M. de Rochefort.

Having reached Rochefort's house, he was admitted by the concierge. He passed upstairs to the rooms occupied by the Count, ordered the valet to take his place on the stairs, and should any callers arrive, to show them up. Then, having shown his credentials as an agent of the Hôtel de Sartines, he began his perquisition.

There was nothing to find and he expected nothing, yet he proceeded on his business with the utmost care and the most painstaking minuteness.

In the middle of his work, he was interrupted by the valet, who knocked at the door.

"Monsieur," said the valet, "there is a young girl who has called. She is waiting outside."

"Ah, she is waiting—well, show her in."

The man disappeared, and returned in a moment ushering in Javotte.

Lavenne looked up from some papers which he was examining. Javotte's appearance rather astonished him. Young, fresh, and evidently respectable, he could not for a moment place her among possible visitors to Rochefort. Then it occurred to him that she might be the maid of some society woman sent with a message, and, without rising from his seat, he pointed to a chair.

"What is your business here, mademoiselle?" asked Lavenne.

"My business, monsieur, is to pay the last month's wages of Monsieur de Rochefort's valet. I have the money here with me. May I ask whom I have the pleasure of addressing?"

"You are addressing an agent of the Hôtel de Sartines. Place the money on the table, mademoiselle, and it shall be handed to the valet. And now a moment's conversation with you, please. Who, may I ask, entrusted you with this commission?"

"Monsieur," replied Javotte, "that is my business entirely."

Lavenne leaned back in his chair.

"Mademoiselle, I am going to ask you a question. Are you a friend of Monsieur de Rochefort?"

"Indeed, I am, monsieur."

"Well, then, if you are a friend of his, I may tell you that I also am his friend, though I am, at the present moment, making an examination of his effects. So in his interests please be frank with me."

Javotte looked at the quiet and self-contained man before her. Youth and Innocence, those two great geniuses, proclaimed him trustworthy, and she cast away her reserve.

"Well, monsieur, what do you want me to say?"

"Just this, I want you to tell me what you know of this gentleman. What you say may not be worth a *denier* to me, or it may be useful. You need say, moreover, nothing to his disadvantage, if you choose. Well?"

"I know nothing to his disadvantage, monsieur. He is the bravest man in the world, the most kind, and he saved me but the other night from two men who would have done me an injury——" Then catching fire, she told volubly the whole story of the occurrence on the night of the Duc de Choiseul's ball.

Lavenne listened attentively.

Sartines had already given him Camus' story of the killing of Choiseul's agent. Javotte was now giving him the true story. He instantly saw the facts of the case, and the character of Camus.

"And you say, mademoiselle, that Monsieur de Rochefort, returning from the chase of those ruffians, one of whom he killed, by the way, found Monsieur Camus offering you an insult and struck him to the ground. Did Monsieur Camus not resent that action?"

"Monsieur, he did nothing, but he turned when he was going away and shook his finger at Monsieur de Rochefort."

"Well, Mademoiselle Javotte, one question more: on whose service were you carrying that letter of which the robbers wished to relieve you? Speak without fear, whatever you say will do Monsieur de Rochefort no harm."

"Monsieur, it was a letter addressed to Madame Dubarry."

"Ah ha! That is all I wish to know. Well, say nothing of all this to anyone else, and should you have anything more to communicate to me, come to my private address, No. 10, Rue Picpus; ask for Monsieur Lavenne. That is my name. And remember this, as far as it is in my power, I am the friend of Monsieur de Rochefort."

"Thank you, monsieur—and may I ask one question? Do you know where Monsieur de Rochefort is now, and is he safe?"

"I cannot tell you where he is, but I believe he is safe. In fact, I may be as frank with you as you have been with me, and say he is safe."

"Thank you, monsieur."

"One moment," said Lavenne, as she rose to go. "May I ask your address, should I by any possibility need it?"

"I am in the service of Mademoiselle Fontrailles, monsieur."

"Ah, you are in the service of Mademoiselle Fontrailles. Well, Mademoiselle Javotte, say nothing to anyone of our meeting, say nothing of our conversation, say nothing of Monsieur de Rochefort; but keep your eyes and ears open, and if you wish to serve Monsieur de Rochefort, let me have any news you may be able to bring me concerning him."

"Now, I will swear that girl is in love with the Count," said Lavenne to himself, when she had departed, "and the Count, according to my master, is in love with Mademoiselle Fontrailles, who has the reputation of being incapable of love. Mademoiselle Fontrailles is a bosom friend of Madame Dubarry, and Madame Dubarry's letter it was which caused the agents of Monsieur de Choiseul to attack Mademoiselle Javotte, and Monsieur de Rochefort to kill one of those precious agents. Mademoiselle Javotte has already proved to me that Monsieur le Comte Camus has lied in giving his evidence against Monsieur de Rochefort. The case widens, like those circles that form when one throws a stone into a pond. Well, let it continue to widen, and we will see what we will see."

He finished his examination of Rochefort's rooms, paid the valet off, locked the place up and started for the Hôtel de Sartines.

Monsieur de Sartines was seated in the octagon chamber on the first floor; he was busy writing at the famous bureau of a hundred drawers, which contained in its recesses half the secrets of France, and which had belonged to his predecessor, Monsieur D'Ombreval.

He looked up when Lavenne was announced, finished the letter on which he was engaged, and then turned to the agent.

"Well," said de Sartines, "what about Monsieur de Rochefort?"

"He is at Vincennes by this time, monsieur. The affair was a little difficult, but I made him see reason, and he made no objection to accompanying Captain Roux. I have examined his rooms and found nothing. I have also discovered that the evidence given against him by Count Camus is far from being truthful."

He told of Javotte and her story in a few words.

"Quite so," replied Sartines; "and you know perfectly well that it does not matter a button whether this agent was killed by foul or fair play, or whether Count Camus has lied or not. The case is just as bad against Monsieur Rochefort from Monsieur de Choiseul's point of view, and that is everything. No matter, we have Rochefort in safe keeping.

"Now to another business. Prepare to start at once for Versailles. You will inquire into the poisoning of this dog, which has given me more trouble and annoyance than the poisoning of Monsieur de Choiseul himself would have given me. I have inquired into it personally. I have put Valjean on the affair; the matter is as dark as ever, so just see what you can make of it. Here are all the papers relating to the business, reports and so forth, study them on the way and use expedition."

"Monsieur will give me a free hand in the matter?"

"Absolutely. And here is a thousand francs in gold; you may need money. Order a carriage for the journey, and tell them not to spare the horses. I am in a hurry for your report, find wings; but, above all, find the criminal."

"Yes, monsieur. It will be a difficult matter. The poisoning of a man is a simple affair, the evidence simply shouts round it for the person who has ears to hear. A dog is different. But I will find the criminal—unless——"

"Unless?"

"Unless, monsieur, the dog poisoned itself by eating some garbage."

"Oh, no. Atalanta was very delicate in her feeding. No, it was the work of some scoundrel, of that I am sure."

"Well, monsieur, we will see," said Lavenne.

He bowed to the Minister of Police, and left the room.

CHAPTER II

MONSIEUR BROMMARD

DE SARTINES had no need to urge expedition on Lavenne. Lavenne always moved as quickly as possible between two points. After the King and de Sartines, Lavenne was perhaps the best and most quickly served man in France. The carriages of the Hôtel de Sartines were always ready and never broke down, the horses of the Hôtel de Sartines never went lame, the grooms, the veterinary surgeons, and the coachmen employed by the Ministry of Police, were men who had been tried and tested, men, moreover, who knew that drunkenness, insubordination or neglect would be visited by imprisonment, not dismissal.

The Minister of Police knew the value of speed, and since the safety of France might depend upon the horses of the Minister of Police, he did not boast when he made the statement that his horses were the swiftest in France.

In five minutes' time, after giving the order, Lavenne was seated in a closed carriage drawn by two powerful Mecklenburg horses, and the carriage was leaving the courtyard of the Hôtel de Sartines and taking its way towards the Faubourg St. Honoré. During the journey, Lavenne studied the papers given to him by his master, pages and pages of reports. One might have fancied that the matter had to do with the assassination of an emperor, rather than the poisoning of a dog.

Lavenne read the whole of these papers and reports carefully, and then, folding them, placed them in his pocket.

According to them, everyone possible in connection with Versailles, the Trianons, and even with Luciennes, had been questioned and examined without result. The whole thing seemed to Lavenne rather clumsy. This questioning of individuals could bring little result. To the question, "Did you poison the dog?" could come but one answer, "No." And the poisoner was unlikely to have acted in the presence of a witness. The thing that did strike Lavenne as peculiar, was the fact that there had been no accusations; it was just the case for false accusations, yet there were none.

At Versailles, having ordered the carriage to be kept in waiting, he crossed the park to the Trianons. Arrived at the Grand Trianon, he walked round to the kitchen entrance. Here there was great bustle and movement, goods arriving from tradesmen in Versailles and being received by the steward, scullions darting hither and thither, and everyone talking. In the kitchen, it was the same.

Lavenne knew everyone, or at least was known by everyone, especially by Brommard, the master cook, who, magnificent in paper cap and white apron, was directing operations.

"Ah, Monsieur Lavenne," said Brommard, "and what happy chance brings you here to-day?"

"Why, I had some business at the Petit Trianon, and I just walked across to see if you were alive and well. *Ma foi!* Monsieur Brommard, but you are not growing thinner these days."

Brommard heaved a sigh.

"No, Monsieur Lavenne, I am not growing thinner, though if worry made a man thin, I would be a rake, what between tradesmen who do not send provisions in time and cooks who spoil them when they arrive. I have to supervise everything, and I have only two eyes instead of the two hundred that I require."

"Well, Monsieur Brommard, we all have our worries, even his Majesty, who, I fear, is in trouble over the death of his favourite hound, Atalanta."

Brommard made a motion with his hand.

"Oh, *ma foi!* don't speak to me about that business. Why, Monsieur Lavenne, I was had up myself and questioned on the matter by Monsieur de Sartines. As though I had poisoned the brute! I said to him, 'I know nothing of the matter, but since Atalanta was served every day at the King's table when he was at Versailles, she may have died of Ribot's cookery'; for Ribot, as you know, is now the chef at Versailles, a gentleman who stole the recipe of my Sauce Noailles and gave it forth under the name of Sauce à la Ribot. Put his name to my sauce! God's death, Monsieur Lavenne, a man who will steal another man's sauce is not above poisoning another man's dog. Not that I accuse Ribot, poor fool; he has not the spirit to poison a louse, and they say his wife beats him with his own rolling-pin. I accuse him of nothing but theft and stupidity, certainly not of poisoning his Majesty's dog wilfully. Besides, Monsieur Lavenne, the dog was not poisoned, in my opinion."

"Give us your opinion, Monsieur Brommard."

"Well, it is this way, Monsieur Lavenne—What does all cookery rest on?"

"I am sure I don't know, unless it is the shoulders of the chef."

"No, Monsieur Lavenne, all cookery rests on an egg. The egg is the atlas that supports the world of gastronomy, the chef is the slave of the egg. Think, Monsieur Lavenne, what is the masterpiece of French cookery, the dish that outlives all other dishes, the thing that is found on his Majesty's table no less than upon the tables of the Bourgeoisie, the thing that is as French as a Frenchman, and which expresses the spirit of our people as no other article of food could express it—the Omelette. Could you make an Omelette without breaking eggs? Aha! tell me that. Then cast your mind's eye over this extraordinary Monsieur Egg and all his antics and evolutions. Now he permits himself to be boiled plain, and even like that, without frills, naked and in a state of nature, he is excellent, for you will remember that the Marquis de Noailles, when he was dying and almost past food, called for what?—an egg, plainly boiled.

"Now he consents to appear in all ways from poached to *perdu*—an excellent recipe for which is to be found in my early edition of the works of Taillevent, who, as you know, was master-cook to his Majesty King Charles V.

"Now he is the soul of a *vol-au-vent*, now of a sauce; not a pie-crust fit to eat but stands by virtue of my lord the egg, and should all the hens in the world commit suicide, to-morrow every chef in France worthy of the name would fall on his spit, as Vatel fell on his sword, and with more reason, for fish is but a course in a dinner, whereas the egg is the cement that holds all the castle of cookery together."

"*Pardieu*, Monsieur Brommard," said Lavenne, laughing, "you are quite a philosopher, and I shall certainly take off my hat to the next hen I meet. But, tell me, what has an egg to do with the poisoning of Atalanta?"

"Nothing, Monsieur Lavenne; God forbid that it should. I was about to say that, just as all cookery stands on an egg, so does the whole world stand on commonsense; and it is not commonsense to think that any man would poison Atalanta, who was a gentle beast, on purpose to spite his Majesty. Atalanta, in my opinion, poisoned herself. Dogs are not like cats. If you will observe, a cat is very nice in her feeding. Offer her even a piece of fish, and she will sniff it to make sure that it is in good condition and not poisonous, before she will touch it. Whereas dogs eat everything."

"Dogs eat roses," said a small voice.

It was Brommard's little son, who, dressed in a white cap and apron, was serving his apprenticeship as a scullion. He had drawn close to his father, and had listened solemnly to the discourse about eggs.

Brommard glanced down and laughed, then he excused himself for a moment to supervise the work of one of the under-cooks, who was larding a fowl.

"Oh," said Lavenne, "dogs eat roses, do they? And how do you know?"

"Monsieur," said the child, "I have seen Atalanta, the beautiful dog of his Majesty, snap at a rose. I told my father when they were saying that Atalanta was poisoned, and I said that I had seen Atalanta eat a rose, and that perhaps the rose had killed her, and he laughed. But dogs do eat roses."

"And where did you see Atalanta eat this rose?"

"It was near Les Onze Arpents, monsieur. A gentleman and a lady were walking together, and he was holding a rose in his hand. The rose was hanging down, so, and the dog, who was following them, sniffed at the rose and then bit it."

"Yes—yes?"

"Well, monsieur, the gentleman, when he saw what the dog had done, threw the rose away behind his back into some bushes; the lady did not see, she was talking and laughing."

"What day was this?"

"The day before Atalanta died, monsieur."

"What was the gentleman like?"

"Very ugly, monsieur, and pitted with the smallpox."

"And the lady?"

"Oh, I don't know, monsieur, but she walked with a limp."

"Ah, well," said Lavenne, "dogs may eat roses, but roses do not poison dogs; so I would advise you to forget what you saw, or the ugly gentleman may be angry with you. You seem a bright boy, and here is something to buy sweets with. You are learning to be a cook, I suppose?"

"Monsieur," said the child, gravely, "I am a cook. I can lard a fowl and make an omelette and a mayonnaise, and I have committed to memory the rules and recipes of twenty-three sauces out of the two hundred and twenty-three that my father knows. Yet, all the same, I must serve my apprenticeship as a scullion, cleaning pots and pans and preparing vegetables and fish and game. But I do not grumble."

Little Brommard—destined to be the cook of Napoleon—put the coin Lavenne had given him in his pocket, and, thanking the latter, went off to supervise another scullion who was at work on some vegetables, whilst Lavenne, bidding good-bye to Brommard *père*, took his departure.

He took a side-path that led to the cottage of the chief gardener of Trianon.

That official happened to be in, and Lavenne invited him to put on his hat and to come out for a moment's conversation.

"Well, Monsieur Lavenne, what can I do for you?" said the man, putting on his coat as he came out, and latching the door behind him.

"You can get a spade and take me to the place where you buried the dog belonging to his Majesty. I see by the report that you were ordered to bury it."

"You mean Atalanta, monsieur?"

"The same."

The gardener, without a word, went to the tool-house by the cottage and took out a spade, then, shouldering the spade, he led the way to a clear space amidst some bushes.

"Now," said Lavenne, "dig me up the remains of the animal. I wish to examine them."

The gardener did as he was told, and Lavenne, on his knees, made a minute examination of the mouth of the dog. The body of the animal, lying in a light, dry soil, showed no trace of putrefaction, being, so the gardener said, as fresh as when he buried it.

Lavenne, having finished his inspection, rose to his feet, dusted the soil from his knees, and having paid the man liberally for his trouble, took his way to where the carriage was waiting to convey him back to Paris. On the journey, he made some notes with a pencil in his pocket-book.

He had discovered the poisoner of Atalanta. Led by the luck that sometimes attends genius, or perhaps by the commonsense which made him conduct his inquiry, not by direct interrogation, but by conversation on things in general, he had accomplished in a few hours what Sartines had failed to accomplish in several days.

Arrived at the Hôtel de Sartines, he found his master absent and Monsieur Beauregard acting in his stead. Beauregard was a big, fine-looking man, one of the best swordsmen in France, fearless and honest, but not of the highest intelligence as far as detective work was concerned. Nor did Sartines use him for that business. Sartines had made Beauregard his chief of staff because the latter had all the qualities of a good organizer, the fidelity of a hound, and the rigid business methods in which Sartines was lacking. He was also a fine figure of a man, and so upheld the dignity of his position in the eyes of the Court and the populace.

Beauregard was a great friend of Lavenne.

"So his Excellency is out," said Lavenne. "Well, that is a pity, as I have some news for him, and a request to make."

"And the news?" said Beauregard.

"The news is, simply that I have found an indication as to the poisoner of Atalanta."

"Oh, *mon Dieu!* My dear Lavenne, if you can only put your finger on that person, you will own the thanks of the entire staff. It is not that a dog has been poisoned, or that the dog is the favourite dog of the King, or rather, I should say, was the favourite dog of the King. It is that the Hôtel de Sartines has been put to shame by a small matter like this. Other failures one can hush up; other failures, though, indeed, we make few enough, are forgotten; but the smell of this business seems to permeate everywhere; and the thing will not be forgotten, simply because it is so small that it gives such a splendid field for the little wits of Paris and the Court to exercise themselves in."

"Well, Captain Beauregard," said Lavenne, "the poisoning of Atalanta, though seemingly a small enough affair, will, if I am not greatly mistaken, be the centre of an affair big enough to satisfy even the Hôtel de Sartines. I hope to put my hand on the poisoner, and in doing so to clear Monsieur de Rochefort from the charge of being an assassin, and also I hope to save a woman's life."

"*Mordieu!*" said Beauregard, "you are going to do a great many clever things, then—— Tell me, am I in your secret?"

"Why, yes, I don't mind letting you know what is in my mind, though you know how I hate telling of what I propose to do or propose to find. As a matter of fact, you are the only man in France to whom I can talk, and yet feel that I have not lost energy in so doing; for it is a strange thing, but once one opens one's mind to an ordinary person, a blight seems to creep in on the precious thoughts, hopes or ambitions that one cherishes in darkness. And I will tell you why it is different with you. You do not criticize or throw doubts upon budding fancies. Were I to open my mind to Monsieur de Sartines quite fully, he would put his hand in and take out my most precious thoughts, turn them over, criticize them, throw cold water upon them, perhaps, and put them back—then they would be dying—or dead."

"I do not criticize you, Lavenne, because I have a lively feeling that any criticism of mine would be an impertinence, at least on the work of so close a reasoner as you are. Tell me, then, and I will repeat nothing—Who was the poisoner of Atalanta?"

"Count Camus."

Beauregard whistled.

"And who is the lady whose life you are going to save?"

"The Comtesse Camus."

"The man's wife?"

"Precisely."

"Good God!—and how is it threatened?"

"By poison."

"And who is the prospective poisoner?"

"Count Camus."

"Just heavens! Tell me, for I am vastly interested, how you found this out?"

"A few days ago—or, to be more precise, the day after Count Camus had returned from a hunting expedition with Monsieur de Rochefort, he was walking with his wife in the grounds of Trianon. He had brought with him a prepared rose."

"A prepared rose?"

"A rose poisoned with one of those subtle poisons, whose secret was brought to France by the Italians in the time of King Charles IX. Once prepared, these roses have to be kept under cover, enclosed in a box. So kept, their virtue, or rather their vice, remains unimpaired for a considerable time, but once removed from the box, it disappears in the course of a few hours."

"Yes, yes, but what is their power, and how is it used?"

"Quite simply. The person who smells the perfume of the rose dies."

"Dies, simply from the perfume?"

"Absolutely, and as certainly as though he had drunk the Aqua Tofana of the Florentines."

"Go on."

"Well, our man, walking with his wife in the grounds of the Trianon close to Les Onze Arpents, took this rose from its box unseen by his companion, and carrying it very gingerly, you may be sure, by the tip of the stalk with the flower hanging downwards, was about to present it laughingly to her, when Atalanta, who was following them, out of caprice, or playfulness, or perhaps attracted by something in the scent of the flower, made a snap at it. Camus, on feeling what had happened, threw the ruined flower away behind his back into some bushes—and Atalanta paid the penalty instead of the lady."

"You are sure of this?"

"Absolutely."

"Can you prove it against the Count?"

"Not in the least. Or, that is to say, not effectually. I could cover him with suspicion, but that is useless."

"How, then, do you propose to proceed?"

"Ah, my dear captain, if I were to tell you that, I would tell you what I don't exactly know."

"You don't know what you are going to do?"

"Pardon me. I do, but not in an exact manner. But I will tell you this. My first move is to get into the house of Count Camus."

"On a warrant from de Sartines?"

"Heavens, no, as a servant. We have a man in all the important houses, and I believe one in the house of the Count."

"Certainly we have. You know that Sartines suspects him, and where suspicion goes there our servants go also. Stay." He rang a bell.

When a clerk answered the summons, he gave him an order, and the clerk returned in a few minutes with a huge book, bound in vellum and with a brass lock.

Beauregard took a bunch of keys from his pocket, selected one and opened the book.

He turned to the pages marked C, and ran his finger down the first column for the space of three inches.

"Yes. Jumeau is acting as pantry-man in the service of the Count."

"He is almost useless," said Lavenne; "but let us be thankful that he is there. Now let us send at once, and tell him that his mother is dying and that he must come at once; his cousin—that is to say, myself—is ready to take on his duties. As the cousin, I will take the message myself. I have just left the service of Monsieur—shall we say, Monsieur Gaston Le Roux?—he belongs to us. You will send a man round to him at once for a testimonial. The pantry-man's duty is to look after the plate, to clean it, keep it in order, be responsible for it, and to do a few light duties."

"Very well," said Beauregard, "all that shall be done."

"And now," said Lavenne, "I must go and dress for the part, and in an hour, when the testimonial arrives, I will be ready. Let it be dated last month, and let it be for two years' service. I may not even want it at all; they will be very glad, I should think, to accept Jumeau's cousin's service whilst Jumeau is seeing after his sick mother, and so save themselves the trouble of doing without a servant or hunting for one. Still, it is as well to be prepared at all points."

"Yes, you are right," said Beauregard. "Well, good luck to you."

Lavenne took his departure and hurried round to his rooms in the Rue Picpus. It was now seven o'clock in the evening. It had been a busy day for him, but the work of that day was not over yet. When he arrived at the house in the Rue Picpus, he found someone waiting for him. It was Javotte.

"Monsieur," said Javotte, "when I spoke to you this morning, I did not tell you quite all that I knew about the affairs of Monsieur de Rochefort. There was something I held back, and I would like to tell you it now."

"Come in," said Lavenne, with a smile. The eternal feminine was the same in his day as ours—that is to say, it might be summed up in the same words: "The animal with a postscript."

CHAPTER III

CHOISEUL'S LETTER

LAVENNE inhabited very modest apartments in the Rue Picpus, a street of that old Paris which, always dying and vanishing, never seems quite to die, which showed the towers of Philip Augustus to the people who lived in the time of Charles V. and the old houses of Louis XI. to the subjects of Louis XV., which shows, even to-day, glimpses of the remotest past in odd corners left unswept by the tide of Time.

The room into which he ushered Javotte was as old as the street and house that contained it. Beamed and wainscoted, its only furniture a few chairs, a table, a stove and a number of volumes piled on a shelf, it had, still, a fairly comfortable appearance. Rooms have personalities, and there are some rooms tolerable to live in even when stripped almost bare of furniture, others intolerable, furnish them how you please. Lavenne's belonged to the first order.

He took his seat at the table, pointed out a chair to Javotte, and ordered her in a good-humoured way to be quick with her business, as he had a pressing matter on hand.

"It is this way, monsieur," said Javotte. "I did not tell you all this morning, simply because what I left untold relates to an affair of which I am rather ashamed in one way, and not the least ashamed of in another."

"And this affair?"

"Relates to the opening of a letter addressed by Monsieur de Choiseul to a lady in Compiègne."

"And who opened the letter?"

"I did, monsieur."

"And how did it fall into your hands?"

Javotte explained how Rochefort had found it in the saddle-bag of the horse he had used in his escape from Versailles.

"He would not open it himself, monsieur. He gave it to me to deliver to the lady at Compiègne; when I said to him, 'Monsieur de Choiseul would open the letter were it one of yours,' he only replied—'You see, I am not Monsieur de Choiseul, but simply Monsieur de Rochefort.' That was the reply of a great noble; but I, monsieur, am simply a servant, and, what is more, the servant of Monsieur de Rochefort's interests, seeing that he saved me from those men of Monsieur de Choiseul, who might have killed me. I do not love Monsieur de Choiseul and———"

"You do love Monsieur de Rochefort," finished Lavenne, with a laugh.

Javotte flushed, her eyes sparkled, as though the words had been an insult, then she calmed down.

"Perhaps you are right, monsieur, perhaps you are wrong. In any case, my feelings have nothing to do with the matter."

"Pardon me," said Lavenne, "you are right. I have been indiscreet. Let us forget it—and accept my apology. Now, as to this letter. May I ask you to tell me its contents?"

"I can do better, monsieur, I can show you the letter itself."

She took the letter from her breast and handed it to Lavenne, who spread it open on the table before him and began to read, his elbows upon the table and his head between the palms of his hands.

It was a terrible document for Choiseul to have put his name to. Written in a moment of fury immediately after the presentation of Madame Dubarry, it consisted of only twelve lines. Yet it told of the failure of his plot against Dubarry, and it spoke of the King in a sentence that was at once indecent and almost treasonable.

"*Mordieu!*" said Lavenne. "What a letter! What a letter! What a letter!" He glanced at the back of it, then he cast his eyes again over the contents.

It will be remembered that Choiseul was the enemy of Sartines, and that the overthrow of Choiseul was, at that moment, the central desire of the heart of Sartines. Lavenne knew this fact, and he knew that the weapon lying before him on the table was of so deadly a nature, that were he to hand it to his master, both honour and money would be handed to him in return; he was no opportunist, however, nor could the prospects of personal advantage blind him to the fact that the weapon before him on the table was not his to sell. It belonged to Javotte. To serve Rochefort, she had sullied her integrity by opening Choiseul's letter; trusting to Lavenne, she had brought him the letter, and not a man, perhaps, in the Hôtel de Sartines other than Lavenne but would have put her off with promises or threats and carried the letter to his master, after the fashion of a dog retrieving game.

But Lavenne was not a common man. With a villain, he would use every art and subtlety; but with the straightforward and simple, he was always honest and straightforward. Your modern police or political agent is supposed to be a man who excels in his profession according to his capacity for the detection of crime; this is but a half truth, for the detection of innocence is just as important to the police agent, and to feel the innocence in others one requires a mind that can attune itself to innocence as well as to villainy. A mind, in other words, that can keep its freshness, even though its possessor dwells on the dust-heap of crime.

Lavenne could not betray Javotte over this matter without running contrary to his nature. He recognized at once that this weapon, when it was used, would have to be used in defence of Rochefort, not in furtherance of the desires of Sartines. He recognized, also, that with this weapon both purposes might be served; Rochefort might be defended and Sartines' ambition furthered at the same stroke. But the time had not yet come, and even when it did arrive, this lethal instrument would require to be used by a master hand. Turning to Javotte, he gave her, in the course of five minutes, his whole opinion on the business, showing her his whole mind on the matter with a frankness which she knew by instinct to be genuine.

"And you will keep that letter, then, monsieur?"

"With your permission, I will keep it, and I will use it, if use it I must, to further the interests both of Monsieur de Rochefort and of my master. But I promise you, it shall be used in Monsieur de Rochefort's interests first."

"Very well, then, monsieur," replied Javotte. "I will leave it with you."

Then she took her departure, and Lavenne, placing the letter in a secret compartment of the panelling, began to dress for the part he was to play in the household of Count Camus.

CHAPTER IV

THE DECLARATION OF CAMUS

JAVOTTE, when she left the Rue Picpus, took her way to the Rue de Valois. It will be remembered that Camille Fontrailles had slept at the Dubarrys' house in the Rue de Valois, and as Javotte was now in her service, she had to follow her mistress.

Immediately on Rochefort quitting her that morning, she had gone to the Rue de Valois, helped her mistress to dress, and then slipped out on her mission to Rochefort's rooms, where she had first met Lavenne.

Troubled in mind at not having made a clear breast of the affair about Choiseul's letter, and feeling sure that Lavenne would be the best person to help Rochefort in that matter, she had slipped out again at half-past six. She was now returning to help her mistress to dress for the evening.

An ordinary girl, knowing that the Dubarrys were the enemies of Choiseul, would have put the letter in their hands; but Javotte had a mind of her own, and a knowledge of Court life, and the Dubarrys in particular, which prevented her from putting the slightest trust in any person belonging to the Court, and more especially in the Dubarrys.

She knew that were they to use the letter against Choiseul, they would do so in their own interests, not in the interests of Rochefort. How right she was in this, we shall presently see.

When she arrived at the Hôtel Dubarry, she found the house *en fête*. The Countess was not there, she was still at Versailles, but Chon and Jean were in evidence, and they were receiving friends to supper; and amongst those friends, who should be first and foremost but Count Camus. The man who had engineered, or partly engineered, the plot against the presentation was among the first to call on Jean that day to congratulate him on the success of the Countess. Jean had received him with open arms. Nothing pleased Jean better now than to smooth things over, and make up to the Choiseul faction. The Countess had triumphed; she had beaten Choiseul, and she would break him. The duel was not over by any means, but she had scored the first hit, and it was politic to smile on Choiseul and his followers, just as Choiseul and his followers had found it politic to kiss her hand on the night of her triumph.

"Come to supper this evening, my dear fellow," said Jean. "I am expecting one or two people. Madame de Duras and a few others. Have I heard about Rochefort?—no, what about him?"

Camus told, in a few words, of Rochefort's crimes, and of how he had escaped the night before just as he, Camus, had laid his hand upon him in the name of Choiseul.

"I always said he was a mad fool," replied Jean; "and has he escaped for good?"

"Oh, *mon Dieu*, no," said Camus, "not whilst there is a frontier. Choiseul is scouring the roads, Paris is watched, and a reward of a thousand louis is offered for him, dead or alive."

"Well, if he is taken dead, we will be saved from his future *gasconades*," said Jean.

"I would sooner he were taken alive," replied Camus, "for I have a very particular desire to see that gentleman hanged; and hanged he will be, if I know anything of the mind of Choiseul."

Jean Dubarry showed Camus out, and opened the door for him with his own hand. He would not have minded the hanging of Rochefort in the least, if Rochefort could only be hanged before he could speak his mind and tell his tale; but he greatly dreaded the catching of Rochefort by Choiseul, and comforted himself with the thought that Rochefort must now be in the safe custody of the governor of Vincennes.

At eight o'clock, the first of the guests arrived in the person of Madame de Duras. Chon Dubarry and Camille Fontrailles were waiting to receive her, and Jean entered just as Camus was announced; on the heels of Camus came M. de Joyeuse, a young fop and spendthrift, and scarcely had he entered when the wheels of Madame d'Harlancourt's carriage were heard in the courtyard. She came in with M. d'Estouteville, whom she had brought with her.

Jean Dubarry was as pleased to receive d'Estouteville as he had been to welcome Camus. Nothing could underscore the Countess's success more deeply than the evident anxiety of these members of the Choiseul faction to be well with her.

"*Mordieu!*" said Jean to himself, "Choiseul himself will be coming next—well, let us wait and see."

He was in the highest spirits, complimenting Madame d'Harlancourt on her appearance, jesting with Joyeuse, with a word for everyone except Camus, who was deep in conversation with Camille Fontrailles.

"Ah, mademoiselle," Camus was saying, "it seems an age since I met you at Monsieur de Choiseul's, and yet, by the almanac, it was only the other night."

"Why, monsieur, since that night so many things have happened, that the time may well seem long—the Presentation, for instance."

"Ah, yes, the Presentation," said Camus, with a laugh. "We have all been deeply absorbed by that event."

"Deeply," said Camille.

"You are a friend of the Countess, mademoiselle?"

"Absolutely, monsieur."

"Well," said Camus, with an air of the greatest ingenuousness, "I have not been her friend. I have never been her enemy, still, I must confess I have not been her friend in the strict sense of the word. Court life is like a game of chess, and I daresay you are aware that, during the last few days, a great game of chess has been going forward between my friend Choiseul and the Countess. I was on Choiseul's side all through it; I even helped in some of the moves. She won, and I must say her courage has made me her admirer."

"And not her friend?"

"Mademoiselle, I am the friend of Monsieur de Choiseul, and I do not easily separate myself from my friends. Still, I am content to remain his friend, and yet to stand aside and take no part in any further move that he may make against the Countess."

"And why, monsieur, do you impose this inaction upon yourself?"

"Simply for this reason. I cannot take an active part in any move against a person who is a friend of yours."

"And why not, monsieur?"

"Ah, you ask me a question now that is very difficult to answer."

"How so?"

"Because the reply may make you angry."

"Then you had better not answer the question, monsieur."

"On the contrary, it is better to say what is in my mind, since to leave it unsaid would be an act of cowardice, and it is better that we should both know a secret that is tormenting me like fire. I cannot act against a friend of yours, simply for this reason—I have learned to love you."

He had risen before finishing the sentence, and at the last word, bowing profoundly, he moved away to where Jean, de Joyeuse and Madame d'Harlancourt were talking together, and joined in their conversation. Camille followed him with her eyes. He had attracted her at the ball, his action against Madame Dubarry had turned her against him, his frank confession of the part he had taken had somewhat modified her resentment, his declaration that in future he would remain neutral had modified it still more; his declaration of love had stunned her.

He was a married man.

The thing amounted to an insult, yet she did not feel insulted, nor did she feel angry; her being was stirred to its depths for the first time in her life. Unconscious of the fact that a declaration of love from Camus had about as much meaning as a declaration of pity from a tiger, or perhaps half-conscious of it, she was held now by the mesmerism of the man, and sat watching him as he conversed with the others; till Madame de Duras, coming up to her, broke the spell.

At supper, her eyes kept continually meeting those of Camus, and she was half conscious of the fact that a wordless conversation was going on between her almost unwilling mind and the mind of the Count.

Men like Camus do most of their murderous work against women without speech. They have the art of making women think about them, and they know that they have the art.

Camus all that evening kept aloof from the girl to whom he had made his declaration of love. He wore a brooding and meditative air at times. He knew that she was observing him closely, and he acted the part of the eternal lover to perfection.

Yet, despite his acting, he was desperately in earnest.

When the card-tables were being set out, it was found that Camille had vanished from the room. She did not appear again that night.

CHAPTER V

THE HOUSE OF COUNT CAMUS

MEANWHILE, Lavenne, when Javotte had taken her departure, set out on the business of dressing himself for the part he was about to perform. In a cupboard opening off his bedroom he had all sorts of disguises, from the dress of an abbé to the rags of a beggar-man. He was a master in the art of disguise, and knew quite well that every profession and station in life has its voice and manner and walk, as well as its dress; that dress, in fact, is only part of the business of disguise, deportment, manner and voice being equally essential, and even perhaps more so.

In fifteen minutes, or less, he had converted himself into a perfect representation of a servant out of a place, slightly seedy, and seeking a situation. Then, having glanced round his rooms to see that all was in order, he locked his door, put the key in his pocket and started for the Hôtel de Sartines. Here he received the written character, which had been prepared for him under the name of Jouve, and he started for Camus' house in the Rue du Trône.

It was a large house, decorated in the Italian style, and the *concierge*, who opened to Lavenne's ring, did not receive him too civilly; but he passed him on to the kitchen premises, and here Lavenne, finding Jumeau, gave him the news of his mother's mortal illness; and the distress of Jumeau was so well done and so natural, that Lavenne formed a better opinion of his capabilities than he had hitherto held, and made a mental note of the fact, afterwards to be incorporated in a report to de Sartines.

Jumeau, having dried his eyes, took Lavenne down a passage and, lighting a candle, drew him into the small bedroom which he occupied, and which was situated immediately beside the plate pantry. Jumeau had not only to clean the plate, but to act as a watchdog at night in case of thieves.

When the bedroom door was closed, Lavenne turned to Jumeau:

"Have you anything to report?"

"No, Monsieur Lavenne, nothing political at all has taken place in the house. Monsieur de Sartines told me to be especially watchful of any friends of Monsieur de Choiseul, or messengers, and to do my utmost to intercept any letter from the Duc. Not a scrap of paper of that description have I seen."

"Well, you have done your duty evidently with care, and I shall note that in my report. I have come to take your place, as you guessed by this; so now take yourself off to the major-domo, get leave of absence to see your mother, and say that your cousin, Charles Jouve, is prepared to take your place, that he is an excellent servant, and has the highest testimonials; then come back here and tell me what he says."

"Yes, Monsieur Lavenne."

"What sort of a man is this major-domo, and what is his name?"

"His name is Brujon, Monsieur Lavenne, and he is rather stupid, fond of talk, and very fond of his glass of wine."

"Good! He is a gossip?"

"You may say that."

"Well, off you go; and use all your wits, now, so that he may accept me in your place."

Jumeau left the bedroom, closing the door behind him, and Lavenne sat on the bed waiting his return, and glancing about him at the poorly furnished room, dimly lit by a candle tufted with a "letter," like a miniature cauliflower.

In five minutes, Jumeau returned.

"Well," said Lavenne, "what luck?"

"The best, Monsieur Lavenne. He is in a good humour. He asked me all sorts of questions as to my mother, spoke of filial duty and gave me leave of absence for three days. He wishes to see you."

Lavenne rose from the bed.

"Let us go at once, then," said he, "before his good-humour changes. Lead the way, introduce me to him, and then say nothing more. I will do the talking."

They left the room.

Monsieur Brujon's office was situated on the same floor, that is to say, the basement.

It was a fairly large room, with an old bureau in one corner, where Monsieur Brujon kept his receipted bills, his correspondence, his keys and a hundred odds and ends that had no place in a bureau; old playbills, ballades, wine labels, a questionable book or two, corks, shoe-buckles and so forth.

He was a character, Monsieur Brujon. Untidy as his bureau, stout, rubicund, with a fatherly manner and an eye for a pretty girl, he was a fine example of the old French servant that flourished in feudal times, the servant who became a part of the family, drank his master's wine, knew his master's secrets, and through other servants of his kind the secrets of half the town or countryside where he lived.

"Ah," said Brujon, "this is the young man who has come to take your place. He has some knowledge of his work, then?"

"Yes, monsieur."

"In whose service did you say he was last?"

"Monsieur," said Lavenne, "I was in the service of Monsieur Le Roux, and to expedite matters, I have brought with me the testimonial that he gave me on my leaving him?"

"And why did you leave him?"

"Oh, monsieur," said Lavenne, remembering Monsieur Brujon's instinct for gossip, "it was not that he had any fault to find with me, or I with him; it was on account of madame."

"Eh, madame! Had she a temper, then?"

"It was not her temper so much as other things, monsieur."

Monsieur Brujon read the testimonial and expressed himself satisfied, told Jumeau that he might take his departure, and Lavenne that he might remain; then when the door was shut, he turned to the new-comer.

"Well," said he, "what was the matter with madame?"

When Lavenne had finished his revelations, M. Brujon, chuckling and gloating, rose to conduct the new-comer round the house, so that he might have the lie of the premises. He took him through the basement, showed him the kitchen, the plate pantry, the room he was to occupy by the pantry, and the other offices. Then upstairs, that the new servant might see the dining-room, to which it was his duty to convey the plate. As they went on their way, Brujon conversed, and Lavenne, who had already taken the measure of his man, led the talk to Camus.

"I need not hide it from you," said he, "that I look on it as a feather in my cap taking service, even for a short time, under your master. I have heard much about him; it is even said that his cleverness is so great that he knows Arabic and all the secrets of the East."

"You may well say that," replied Brujon, pompously, "not only is he of one of the oldest families, but he has here—" and he tapped his empty forehead—"what all the others have not got. I, who know him so well, and whom he trusts, can speak of that."

"*Ma foi!*" said Lavenne, in an awed voice, "is it a fact, then, that he is an alchemist?"

Brujon pursed out his lips as he closed the door of the dining-room, having shown the place to his companion. "It is not for me to say anything of his secrets, but I can tell you this, he is clever enough to put Monsieur Mesmer in his pocket."

"*Mon Dieu!* but he must be even a greater man than I thought, and to think that you have seen him at work, perhaps. Why, it would frighten me to death—and where does he do these wonderful things?"

"Come here," said Brujon.

He led the way down the corridor, leading from the dining-room, paused at a door, took a bunch of keys from his pocket, and, choosing a key, opened the door.

The lamp which he was carrying disclosed a room lined with shelves containing bottles, glass cupboards containing bottles and flasks stood in the corners, and in the centre, on a heavy bench-like table, were more bottles, some retorts, and a lamp. Heavy red curtains hung before the window.

It was a chemist's laboratory.

"This is the room where my master works," said Brujon, "he and I only have access to it. I am exceeding my duties, even, in showing it to you; though, indeed, he has never given me orders on that matter. Now you may see the truth of what I say—but never say that you have seen it."

"Oh, *mon Dieu*, no! The place frightens me. You see, I am not clever like you, Monsieur Brujon; indeed, all my schooling taught me was just to repeat the *Credo*, and to read a few words of print."

"Well, if it taught you also to hold your tongue," replied the most inveterate gossip in Paris, "it has taught you enough to make you a good servant. Well, it is now time for bed. You know your duties, and should any noise awaken you in the night, your first thought will be of the plate under your keeping. You will give the alarm, call me and hold the thief should you be able to seize him. But I may tell you at once that there is little need of fear. All the doors are impossible to open, there are no windows on the ground floor, and there is always a watchman in the courtyard. Still, it is your duty to be on the *qui vive*."

"You may trust that I will do my duty, Monsieur Brujon; and now, where is your bedroom, so that, in the event of anything happening, I may call you?"

"I will show you," replied Brujon.

He led the way downstairs and showed the room, which was situated off the same passage as that on which Lavenne's opened.

"The menservants sleep in the basement, the maids under the roof," said Brujon, with a fat smile.

He bade good-night to the new man and shuffled off to his office, whilst Lavenne retired to his room. Lavenne had a theory that every mind is like a safe in this particular: that the strongest safe can be picked if only the locksmith is clever enough. He knew that to get at a man's secrets all questioning is useless, unless you bring your mind in tune with his. He knew that men run in tribes, and that there is a quite unconscious freemasonry between members of the same tribe.

His instinct told him the tribe to which M. Brujon belonged, and his marvellous power of adaptability made him for the moment a member of the same tribe. In short, his scandalous stories about the unfortunate Madame Le Roux had put him at once *en rapport* with the jovial, easy-going, scandal-loving and eminently Gallic mind of M. Brujon.

That mind had opened without any difficulty to the skilful pick-lock, giving up the fact as to the situation of the room where his master busied himself with his strange chemistry.

Lavenne had captured the situation of the room; it was now his business, and a much more difficult business, to capture the key, or, failing that, to pick the lock. He had brought with him an instrument similar to the old *crochet* used by the burglars of France ever since the time of the Coquillards—the instrument that is used still under the name of the Nightingale. With this he could unlock and lock a door as easily as with a key. It remained to be seen whether the door of Camus' room could be opened by this means.

He blew out the candle, lay down on the bed, and closing his eyes began, as a pastime, to review the whole situation.

It was a difficult situation enough. If Camus caught him in the act of making an examination of his room, Camus would certainly kill him, unless he killed Camus. Even in the latter event he would almost certainly be lost, unless he could make his escape, which was very unlikely. For if he killed Count Camus in his own house, he would, if caught, be most certainly hanged by de Sartines; it being the unwritten law of the Hôtel de Sartines that an agent caught on a business of this sort must never reveal his identity, or seek protection from the Law which employed him, suffering even death, if necessary, in the execution of his duty.

But this consideration did not deflect our man a hair's-breadth from the course he had mapped out for himself. The thing that was now occupying his mind was the room itself, of which he had caught a glimpse, its contents and its possible secrets.

It was the dark centre of Camus' life, the depository, without doubt, of his secrets. What he would find there in the way of written or other evidence, Lavenne did not know; of how he would prosecute his search, he had no definite plan; yet he knew that here was the only place where Justice might rest her lever as on a fulcrum, and with one swift movement send the Poisoner crashing to the pit that awaited him.

As he lay in the darkness revolving these matters in his mind, he heard the great clock of the Hôtel chiming the hour of eleven. He determined to wait till midnight. Jumeau had told him that Camus had gone to the Hôtel Dubarry and would not be home, most likely, till the small hours, if then.

Lavenne felt that he had the whole night before him, unconscious of the fact that Camus' hour of return that night was not at all to be counted on, simply for the reason that Camus, when Camille Fontrailles left the party, had become restless, and though he had taken his place at the card-table, showed such absence of mind that Luck, who hates a cold lover, declared herself dead against him.

Meanwhile Monsieur Brujon retired to rest, but not before sending a special messenger to Monsieur Gaston Le Roux with a note, enclosing the testimonial, and an inquiry as to whether the man mentioned in it was to be trusted.

M. Le Roux's reply consisted of only one word, "Absolutely."

CHAPTER VI

THE LABORATORY

AT twelve o'clock, Lavenne, slipping from the bed, felt in his pockets to make sure that the *crochet*, the tinder-box and steel and the three special candles which he had brought with him, short and thick like modern nightlights, were to hand. Then he opened his door.

The passage was in black darkness, yet he felt sure of finding his way. He had noted the length of the passage, the position of the doors, and the position of the staircase leading to the upper floor; he had counted the number of steps in the stairs, the form of the landing to which they led was mapped in his mind, and also the point in the landing from which opened the passage leading to the dining-room corridor and to the laboratory of Camus.

He closed the door of the bedroom carefully, and groping his way, passed down the passage to the stairs. The stairs creaked under his foot, some stairways seem to creak the louder the more softly they are trodden on. Lavenne knew this idiosyncrasy and went boldly, reached the landing, found the passage to the dining-room corridor, and in a moment more was spreading his fingers on the door of Camus' private room in search of the key-hole.

Then, taking the *crochet* from his pocket, he inserted it in the lock.

Lavenne possessed a vast fund of special knowledge without which, despite his genius and fertility of resource, he would have been lost a hundred times in the course of a year. Not only had he a quick mind to receive knowledge, he had also a memory to retain it. Again, that kindness and rectitude of spirit which made so many men his friends, opened for him a living library in the Hôtel de Sartines. For instance, he had learned much of the science of Cryptography from Fremin. Jondret, who would certainly have been hanged some day as a housebreaker, had not de Sartines recognized his genius and drawn him into the police, had taught him the science of picking locks, whilst Cabuchon, a little old man, who in the year 1767 had placed his dirty forefinger on the poisoner of M. Terell, the haberdasher of the Rue St. Honoré, had taught him many of the tricks of poisoners.

The art of poisoning, first studied in Europe seriously by the Italians, had been imported into France in the days of the infamous Catherine de Medicis. The Revolution put its heel definitely on the last remnants of this fine product of the Middle Ages, but in the time of the fifteenth Louis there were still a few practitioners of the business, as witness the case of M. Terell poisoned by a candle.

Cabuchon had disclosed many of the secrets of this horrible science to the eager Lavenne. He had not only given him considerable knowledge of the methods used by the practitioners of the Italian art, such as the poisoning of gloves and flowers, but he had also given his pupil an insight into the psychology of the poisoner who uses recondite means, showing clearly and by instance that these people develop a passion for the business, and are sometimes held under the sway and fascination of the demon who presides over it so firmly that they will poison their fellow men and women for the slightest reason, and sometimes for no perceptible reason at all.

It was this knowledge derived from Cabuchon that disclosed to Lavenne at one stroke the poisoner of Atalanta, and the intending poisoner of Madame Camus.

It was the knowledge derived from Jondret that was now guiding his dexterous hand in the use of the *crochet*. Feeling and exploring the wards, examining the construction of the lock, using the delicacy and gentleness of a surgeon who is probing a wound, he worked, till, assured of the mechanism, with a powerful and sudden turn of the wrist he forced the bolt back and the door was open.

He entered the room, shut the door, and proceeded to examine the lock. The bolt was a spring bolt, that is to say, that whilst it required a key to open, it required none to lock it again. He pressed the door to, and it closed with a click scarcely audible and speaking well for the perfection of the mechanism.

Then he struck a spark from the tinder and steel, and lit one of his candles. The lamp was standing on the table, but he would have nothing to do with it. It was necessary to be prepared for instant concealment should anyone arrive to interrupt him, and a lamp takes a perceptible time to extinguish. He placed the lighted candle on the table, and turned to the curtains hiding the window. They were of heavy corded silk, and there was space enough behind them for a man to hide if necessary. Sure of the fact, he turned again to the table. He scarcely glanced at the bottles and retorts upon it; hastily, yet thoroughly, he examined it for drawers or secret compartments, but the table was solid throughout, made of English oak, roughly constructed and showing no sign of the French cabinet-makers' art.

Leaving the table, he examined the cabinets in the corners of the room. They held nothing but the bottles and retorts visible through their glass doors. He examined the walls for concealed cupboards and *caches*, auscultating them here and there, just as a physician sounds the chest of a patient nowadays. But the walls made no response, they were of solid stone behind the stucco. He turned his attention to the flooring, sounding the solid parquet here and there, and had reached to a spot halfway between the table and the window-curtains, when a hollow note gave answer to his knock, a deep, resonant note, showing that a fairly large area of floor space was involved. He was going on both knees to examine this space more carefully when a step sounded in the corridor outside, a key was put into the lock of the door; and Lavenne, who, at the first sound of the step had blown out the candle, placed it in his pocket and whipped behind the curtains veiling the window.

It was Camus. He entered, lamp in hand, closed the door, placed the lamp on the table, and from it lit the other lamp. The Count evidently required plenty of light this evening, either to assist his thoughts or his studies. Lavenne, behind the curtains, had a good view of the room, its occupant, the table, the walls leading to the door and the door itself.

Camus, turning from the table, began to pace the floor. He seemed plunged in deep thought as he walked up and down, his hands behind his back, his head bent, the light now striking his face, now his hands knotted together, delicate yet powerful hands, remarkable, had you examined them closely, for the size of the thumbs.

Could you imagine yourself in the room with a man-eating tiger, and nothing separating you in the way of barrier but a curtain, you would feel somewhat as Lavenne felt alone thus with Count Camus. Looking through the small space between the curtains, he noted for the first time fully the powerful build of the man.

Camus, unconscious that he was being watched, continued to pace the floor. Then, pausing before one of the corner cupboards, he took a key from his pocket, opened the cupboard and drew out a wooden stand, holding two narrow tubes shaped like test-tubes. The tubes were corked, and one was half-filled with a violet-coloured solution, the other with a crystal-clear white liquid.

Camus closed the cupboard door with his left hand, and carrying the tubes carefully placed them and the stand containing them on the table. Then going to another cupboard, he took from it an object which held the watcher behind the curtain fascinated as he gazed on it. It was a mask made of glass, with black ribbons attached at the edge, so that it could be tied securely to the head of the wearer, the ribbons passing above and below the ears.

"Ah ha!" said Lavenne to himself, "we are going to see something now."

He watched whilst Camus, having placed the mask on the table, went to the cupboard and produced a glass slab, a rod of glass and a small brush of camel-hair, such as artists use for water-colour painting. Also, from the same cupboard, he produced a tiny bottle with a gold stopper; this bottle was not made of glass, but of metal.

Having arranged his materials on the table, the Count drew from his pocket an object which caused the watcher behind the curtain much searching of mind. The object was a dagger, or rather a sheath knife, small, of exquisite design, and with scabbard and pommel crusted with gems.

He drew the blade from the sheath, which he placed carefully on one side. The blade was of silver, double-edged and damascened, about an inch broad and four inches long.

He placed the blade by the sheath. Then he put on the mask, took the tube containing the violet liquor and poured a few drops on the glass slab, then, as swiftly as light, a few drops from the tube containing the crystal-clear liquid, stirring the two together with the point of the glass rod. He reached out his left hand for the small metal bottle, uncorked it, and poured a few drops on the slab.

Instantly a cloud of vapour rose up, the liquid on the slab seemed to boil; dipping the little brush in the seething fluid, he drew the dagger blade to him and began to paint the silver with swift strokes, reaching from the haft to the point.

He only painted one side of the blade, and when the business was completed, instead of returning the blade to the sheath, he laid it on the table as if to dry.

Then he rose from the chair and removed the mask from his face.

A faint sickly odour filled the room. Lavenne, who had a pretty intimate knowledge of most perfumes, pleasant or unpleasant, and who in the course of his duties in the old quarters of Paris had learned the art of possessing no nose, drew back slightly from this effluvium, the effect of which was mental rather than physical. It might have been likened to an essence distilled from an evil dream. But it did not seem to trouble Camus. He was now putting away the bottle and the tubes, the rod and the slab of glass. He returned the mask to the cabinet he had taken it from, and then, coming back to the table, he took up the dagger, examined it attentively and returned it to its sheath.

Going to the right-hand wall, he touched a spot about four feet from the ground; a tiny door, the existence of which Lavenne had failed to detect, flew open. He placed the dagger in the *cache* thus disclosed, shut the door, extinguished one of the lamps on the table, and carrying the other in his hand, left the room.

Lavenne drew a deep breath.

The situation was saved. Relieved of that terrible presence, his mind could now work freely. Up to this, he had been unable to guess the meaning of Camus' labours.

Why had Camus used this terrible fluid to poison the knife only on one side? Why had he used such immense precaution that the other side of the steel should remain untainted.

The answer came now in a flash. Cabuchon had told him of this old medieval trick, only Cabuchon had used the word knife, not dagger.

Camus would use his dagger in this way. Laughingly, at some festival or banquet, he would take out his beautiful dagger, and, cutting a pear or a peach or an apple in two, offer half to his companion, whoever he or she might be.

And the half offered to his companion would be poisoned, inasmuch as it would have come closely in contact with the poisoned side of the knife, whereas the half retained for himself would be innocuous.

And who could say to him, "Madame Camus died after eating that peach you offered her," considering the fact that he had also eaten of it?

CHAPTER VII

THE FAWN AND THE SERPENT

LAVENNE, considering this matter in his mind, still remained behind the curtain standing in absolute darkness and waiting so as to give Camus time to remember anything that he might possibly have forgotten.

After the lapse of ten minutes, fairly assured that the Count would not return, he pushed the curtains aside and struck a light.

This time, he boldly lit the lamp on the table and with it in his hand approached the wall on the right and began to hunt for the spring of the secret opening. He was not long in finding it; a tiny disc, the same colour as the wall and only revealed by its thread-like edge, showed itself to the light of the lamp. He pressed on it, the door of the *cache* flew open, and in a moment the dagger was in his hand. There was nothing else in the *cache*. Already he had formulated a plan in his mind, a plan which at first sight might seem diabolical, but which he considered, and with justice, the only means with which to meet the case.

Camus was no ordinary villain. This room was evidently his stronghold and the *cache* was evidently his most secret hiding-place. Yet there were no incriminating papers to be found in the room, no papers whatever; nor in the *cache*. This gentleman evidently kept his secrets in his soul. He made no mistakes. Justice, Lavenne felt, might search for ever without finding a tittle of evidence against him, and indeed this fact, de Sartines, who had long known his proclivities, had proved to the hilt. But there is such a thing as Retribution, and in the name of Retribution Lavenne had declared in his own mind that the knife of Camus should be Camus' undoing.

Lavenne, replacing the lamp on the table, examined the dagger minutely without drawing the blade. The design was different on the two sides of the sheath. On one side a fawn trod boldly on jewelled grapes, on the other a serpent of six curves extended itself from the blade-entrance to the point. The pommel on both its sides was of the same design.

Nothing could be more striking than the difference between the two sides of this dagger-sheath. One could have told them one from the other in the dark and just by the sense of touch.

Lavenne verified this fact with a grim pursing of his lips. The dagger and sheath had been constructed for a set purpose, so that the poisoner who had poisoned one side of the blade might know at once, and before drawing it from its sheath, which was the lethal side. A mistake on this point would have meant death to the poisoner instead of the intended victim. Now Lavenne did not know which side of the blade Camus had poisoned, for the sheath had been covered by the Count's hand when he put the blade back in it.

Lavenne, however, did not in the least require to know which was the poisoned side, or whether it faced to the serpent or the fawn. Camus knew this and that was sufficient.

To destroy Camus, Lavenne had only to draw the double-edged blade from the sheath and insert it again, the other way about.

That being done, this presenter of fruit to ladies would, when he cut his apple or pear in two, present himself with the poisoned half.

Lavenne drew the blade from the sheath, noticed that the poison, which doubtless was only soluble in an acid solution, like, for instance, the juice of a fruit, showed no sign of its presence on the silver, inserted the blade again in the sheath the other way about, and returned the dagger to the *cache*, which he then closed. His work was now done, there was nothing left but to extinguish the lamp and leave the room. He looked about to see that everything was in perfect order, and then, taking the *crochet* from his pocket, he approached the door.

The lock turned quite easily to the instrument, but the door did not open.

He withdrew the *crochet*, reinserted it, and made the turn with his wrist, and again with the same result.

The door was bolted now as well as locked. Lavenne drew the back of his hand across his forehead, which was covered with sweat. It was quite useless to try again. It was not the fault of the lock. He remembered now that Brujon, before he opened the door to show him the room, had placed one hand on the wall beside the door. Brujon was stout, and Lavenne had fancied that he leaned his hand on the wall to rest himself. He knew now that Brujon must have touched a spring withdrawing a secret bolt, without the release of which the door would not open.

When Brujon had closed the door, he must have forgotten to touch another spring which would have re-shot the bolt. Owing to this forgetfulness, Lavenne had been able to enter the room simply by picking the lock. But Camus, who seemed never to forget precaution, had not forgotten to touch the bolting spring, with the result that Lavenne was now a prisoner in a prison that threatened to be his tomb.

He knew that it was quite futile, with the means at his disposal, to make any further attempt upon the lock; even had he possessed a crow-bar and all the tools necessary, the noise of the breaking open of the door would arouse the house.

The doorway being impossible, he turned to the window, which he had not yet examined. The lamp held close to the window showed nothing of the dark world outside, but it showed very definitely strong iron bars almost touching the glass.

The window being impossible, he turned to the floor.

There was just a chance that the hollow-sounding portion of the parquet between the table and the window curtains might disclose a means of exit. There was, in fact, more than a chance, for a man like Camus, who forgot nothing, would be the least likely man to forget to provide a secret way of escape from this chamber of secrecy.

Lavenne was not wrong; the parquet on close examination showed the outline of a trap-door so well constructed as to be perfectly indistinguishable to the gaze of a person who was not searching for it.

In five minutes, or less, he had discovered the button of the opening spring. He pressed on it, and the flap, instead of rising, as in the ordinary trap-door, sank, disclosing a perpendicular ladder leading down into absolute darkness.

CHAPTER VIII

THE CATACOMBS OF PARIS

HERE was a way of escape, but escape to where? He did not consider the latter question for an instant. Replacing the lamp on the table, he glanced round to make sure that everything was in exact order, counted all the articles in his possession, the *crochet*, the two extra candles which he carried, etc., just as a surgeon counts the sponges which he has used during an operation, and having satisfied himself that he had disturbed nothing and left nothing behind, he extinguished the lamp, found the trap-door opening in the darkness and came down the ladder. It had fifteen rungs. When he felt the solid ground under his feet, he lit one of his candles and looked about him.

He was standing in a passage that led to a flight of steps descending into darkness, above was the square opening of the trap-door, and shining in the wall on his right, a brass handle. He guessed its use and pulling on it, the flap of the door above rose steadily and slowly and closed with a faint sucking sound like that of a piston driven home in a perfectly fitting cylinder.

It seemed to Lavenne that everything was favouring him, for had he been forced to leave the door open, his plan might have been ruined, as Camus would undoubtedly have suspected a spy on his movements.

With the lighted candle in his hand, he came towards the flight of steps. At the top of this stone stairway, he paused for a moment almost daunted. It seemed to have no end. The light of the candle became swallowed up in the darkness before revealing the last step. There were over a hundred of these steps leading to a passage, or rather a tunnel, which ended by opening into a corridor. The tunnel struck the corridor at right angles, and Lavenne, holding his light to the walls, looked in vain for an indication as to whether he should turn to the right or the left. Failing to find any, he turned to the right.

He had gone only a few yards when an opening in the corridor wall gave him a glimpse of something more daunting than the darkness. It was a skull resting on a heap of bones. The skull, from which the lower jaw was missing, was yet not wholly without speech. It told Lavenne at once where he was.

Pursuing his way and casting the light of the candle into several more of these lidless sarcophagi, he reached a large open space, where over the piles of bones heaped against the walls, the candle-light revealed a Latin inscription cut into the stone.

From this open space to the right, to left, in front and behind of the man who had just entered it, the candle-light showed four corridors each leading to darkness.

Lavenne had left the laboratory of Count Camus only to find himself entangled in the Catacombs of Paris.

Camus' house seemed built in conformity with his mind, secure, secret, containing many things unrevealable to the light of day, and based on a maze of dark passages offering a means of escape to the mind that knew them and bewilderment and despair to the mind that did not.

Lavenne knew something of the catacombs, but not much. They lay outside his province.

The Catacombs of Paris are to-day just as they were in the time of the fifteenth Louis, with this difference: they are more fully occupied, since they contain the bones of many of the victims of the Terror. This vast system of tunnelling which extends from the heart of Paris to the plain of Mont Souris is in reality a city where rock takes the place of houses, galleries the place of streets, dead men the place of citizens, and eternal darkness the place of day and night.

It has been closed now for some years on account of the danger to explorers arising from the huge army of rats that have made it their camping-ground. Some years ago a man was attacked and eaten by rats in one of the galleries.

Few inhabitants of the gay city of Paris ever give a thought to the city of Death that lies beneath their feet, and fewer still to the motto that is written on the walls of this vast tomb—just as it is written everywhere:

"Remember, Man, that thou art Dust, and that unto Dust thou shalt return."

It was in this terrific place that Lavenne found himself, with the choice of exploring it to find a way out or returning to encounter Camus.

BOOK IV

CHAPTER I

NEWS FROM VINCENNES

ONE morning, four days later, the Comte de Sartines, working in his official room in the Hôtel de Sartines, was informed that a person wished to see him on urgent business.

"What is the name?" asked he.

"Brujon, monsieur. It is the steward of M. le Comte Camus."

"Show him in," replied the Minister.

He continued writing; then, when the visitor was announced, he turned in his chair, pen in hand.

"Well, monsieur," said the Minister of Police, "you wish to see me? What is your business?"

"Monsieur," said Brujon, "I am in great perplexity and distress. For three nights I have not slept, and the thing has worked so on my mind that I said to myself, I will go to Monsieur de Sartines, who is all-powerful, and place this case before him."

"Yes?"

"Monsieur, four days ago, our pantry-man, Jumeau, who has charge of the silver belonging to my master, asked leave of absence on account of the illness of his mother; he introduced to me a young man, his cousin, named Jouve, in order that Jouve might take his place during the time of his absence. Jouve had an excellent reference, and I engaged him. Well, that night Jouve disappeared. At least, in the morning he was nowhere to be found. Yet he could not have left the house."

"And why could not he have left the house?"

"Because, monsieur, all the doors are locked, and, what is more, barred on the inside, yet no bar had been removed. My master, when he comes in late, is always admitted by the *concierge*, who re-bars the door, all the other doors are equally barred, and that night I examined the fastenings myself. If Jouve had left the house by any door, how could he have replaced the bars?"

"He may have had an accomplice in the house," replied de Sartines, deeply interested and wondering what new move of Lavenne's this might be, for Beauregard had told him of Lavenne's suspicions as to Camus, and the whole business, in fact.

"Yes, monsieur," replied Brujon. "But no silver was taken, no valuables of any sort, why should he have entered the house just to leave it in that manner? Monsieur, I have a feeling that he is still in the house, though, God knows, I have searched diligently enough to find him."

"Well," said de Sartines, "what can I do?"

"I do not know, monsieur, but I thought it my duty to consult you."

"Have you told your master of this affair?"

Brujon hesitated.

"No, monsieur, I have not—he is of such a violent temper——."

"Precisely. But the fact remains that you have hidden the thing from him, and that fact would not calm the violence of his temper should you disclose the affair now. He might even do you an injury, so, for the sake of peace and your own skin, I would advise you to say nothing, but keep a vigilant watch. Should Jouve turn up, hidden anywhere, lock him up in a room, and send here at once and I will send a man to arrest him."

"Thank you, monsieur," replied Brujon, who seemed relieved by Sartines' manner and advice. "I will do what you say. Good day, your Excellency."

When he was gone Sartines rang a bell and ordered Beauregard to be sent to him.

"*Ma foi!*" said Beauregard, "there is more in this than I can fathom. What can he be doing all these four days?"

"Who knows?" replied the Minister. "But I am quite confident he has not been idle. He will turn up, and I dare swear he will bring with him the rope to hang Monsieur Camus. It has been spinning for a long time and is overdue. Now here is a commission for you. Since I can't put hands on Lavenne for the business, go yourself to Vincennes and see how Rochefort is doing. They have had orders to make him comfortable, see that these orders have been carried out. We must keep him in a good temper."

"Yes, monsieur."

"Have a chat with him; and you might say that the Dubarrys are working in his interests to smooth matters with Choiseul—which, in fact, they are not."

"Yes, monsieur."

"See that he is allowed plenty of exercise—tennis and so forth, but always strictly guarded, for I know this devil of a Rochefort, one can't count on his whims, and should prison gall him he may, even against his own interests, try to break out and fly into the claws of Choiseul."

"Yes, monsieur."

Beauregard went off on his mission, and as he left the room, the Vicomte Jean Dubarry was announced.

"My dear Sartines," cried Jean as they shook hands, "I just called to see if you were going to Choiseul's reception to-night."

"I have been invited," replied Sartines.

"And you will go?"

"Yes, I think I will go—why are you so pressing?"

"Well, as a matter of fact," said Jean, "Choiseul asked me to make sure of your coming. He wishes peace all round now that the Dauphiness is to arrive so shortly."

"You are great friends with Choiseul now, you and Madame la Comtesse?"

"We are at peace, for the moment. I do not trust him one hair's breadth, but we are at peace."

"Just so," said Sartines; "and how is Mademoiselle Fontrailles?"

"As beautiful as ever."

"And as cold?"

"Oh, *ma foi!*" said Jean, laughing, "I think the ice is broken in that direction—Camus——"

"You mean to say she cares for Camus?"

Jean laughed. "I say nothing. I only know what the Countess told me this morning. Mind this is between ourselves—well, she is Camus', heart and soul."

"*Peste!* What does she see in that fellow?—Are you sure of what you say?"

"I am sure of nothing, but the Countess is. Camille has made her her confidante. I do not know what women see in Camus, but they seem to see something that attracts them."

"But he is married—Oh, *mon Dieu!*" cried Sartines, suddenly interrupting himself and breaking into a laugh. "What am I saying—it is well known that Madame Camus is delicate—and should she die——"

"Then our gentleman would be free to marry Camille," said Jean.

"No, monsieur," replied Sartines, "I doubt if it would all be as simple as that. However, we will not consider the question of Camus' marriage with this girl in any event. She is a fool."

"Why?"

"Why? Because if the Devil had allowed her to care for Rochefort, and she had thrown in her part with him, it would have assisted to smooth matters with Choiseul. The Countess would have worked more earnestly for a *démarche*, and the Fontrailles would have kept Rochefort contented in Vincennes with a few notes sent to him there— Well, one cannot make up a woman's mind for her and there is no use in trying. She is going to-night, I suppose, to this affair at Choiseul's?"

"Oh, you may be sure. Camus will be there."

The Vicomte went off and Sartines returned to his writing.

But this was to be an eventful morning with him. Five minutes had scarcely passed when the door burst open without knock or warning, and Beauregard, who by this ought to have been on the road to Vincennes, entered, flushed and breathing hard.

"Monsieur," cried Beauregard, "Rochefort has escaped."

"Escaped! *Mordieu!* When did he escape?"

"In the early hours of this morning or during the night. Here is Capitaine Pierre Cousin himself who has brought the story."

"Show him in," said Sartines.

CHAPTER II

THE TWO PRISONERS

SARTINES' uneasiness about Rochefort had arisen from an intuitive knowledge of that gentleman's character, and strange misdoubts as to how that character might develop under the double influence of Love and Prison.

As a matter of fact, no sooner had the excitement of his arrival at Vincennes passed off, no sooner had he dined that evening, cracked a bottle of Beaune, joked Bonvallot, and rubbed his hands at the discomfiture of Choiseul, than reaction took place accompanied by indigestion. He flung himself on the bed.

Monsieur de Rochefort was not made for a quiet life. If he could not be hunting or hawking he must be moving—moving on the pavements of Paris, talking, laughing, joking or quarrelling.

Here there was no one to laugh with, joke with, or quarrel with—nothing to walk on, except the floor of his cell. And it was now that he first became aware of a fact which he never knew before: that it was his habit to change about from room to room. He was one of those unfortunates who cannot endure to be long in one place. He never knew this till now.

It was now that he became aware for the first time of another fact unknown to him until this: that he was a great talker. And of another fact, more general in its application, that to enjoy talking one must be *en rapport* with the person to whom one is talking.

This latter fact was borne in upon him by the voice of Ferminard.

Ferminard, who had also finished his dinner, seemed now in a sprightly mood, to judge by the voice that came to Rochefort, a voice which came literally from under his bed.

"Monsieur de Rochefort," said the voice, "are you there, Monsieur de Rochefort?"

"Oh, *mon Dieu!*" cried Rochefort, who had started on his elbow at this sudden interruption of his thoughts. "Am I here? Where else would I be? Yes, I am here—what do you wish?"

"*Ma foi!* nothing but a little quiet conversation." Rochefort laughed.

"A little quiet conversation—why, your voice comes to me like the voice of a dog grumbling under my bed. How can one converse under such circumstances? But go on, talk as much as you please, I have nothing to do but listen."

"Well, Monsieur de Rochefort, you are not encouraging, but I will do my best; it is better to talk to a bad listener than to talk to no one, and it is better to talk to no one than not to talk at all. Let us talk, then, of Monsieur Rousseau's absurd comedy with music attached to it, which at the instigation of M. de Coigny he produced at Versailles."

"Good heavens, no! What do you take me for—a music-master? If you cannot talk on reasonable subjects, then be dumb. Let me talk of getting out of this infernal castle of Vincennes, which, it seems to me, I was a fool to have entered. Have you that big sou upon you, M. Ferminard?"

"Yes, M. de Rochefort, it is in my pocket."

"Well, then, if you wish to be agreeable to me, pass it through the hole to me. I wish to examine it. It, at all events, will speak to me of liberty."

"Monsieur," said Ferminard, "if my pockets were full of louis, I would pass them to you for the asking. But the big sou—no."

"And why not, may I ask?"

"Because, monsieur, it would, as you say, talk to you of liberty, and it might even tempt you to try and make your escape."

"And why should I not make my escape?"

"For two reasons, monsieur. First, you have forgotten that you are hiding from M. de Choiseul."

"Curse Choiseul!"

"I agree, yet still you are hiding from him. Secondly——"

"Well?"

"Secondly, monsieur, if you escaped, I would be left with no one to talk to."

"Have you not Bonvallot?"

"*Oh hé!* Bonvallot. A man without parts, without understanding, without knowledge of the world! A nice man to leave me in company with!"

"But I do not intend leaving you in his company. I ask you only for the big sou that I may look at it and see what another man has done so that he might obtain his liberty. If you refuse to gratify my curiosity, M. Ferminard,

I shall stuff up that hole with my blanket, and there will be an end of our pleasant conversations."

"Well, M. de Rochefort, here it is, pull your bed out and I will put it in your hand."

Rochefort arose and pulled his bed out and the hand of Ferminard came through the hole. Rochefort took the coin and approached the lamp with it.

It was indeed a marvel: in a moment he managed to unscrew the two surfaces and from the tiny box which they formed when in apposition leaped a little silvery saw, small as a watch-spring.

Rochefort, leaving the little saw on the table, refastened the box.

"*Mordieu!*" said he, "it is clever. What will you sell it to me for, Monsieur Ferminard?"

"You shall have it as a gift, M. Rochefort, when we are both breathing the free air of heaven, but only then."

"You think I will use it to make my escape?"

"No, monsieur, I think you might use it to break your neck, or to be re-captured by this horrible Choiseul whose very name gives me the nightmare."

"Well, you are wrong," replied the other. "Were I outside this place I would not be re-captured, simply because I would do what I ought to have done this morning."

"And what is that?"

"Go straight to his Majesty and tell him the whole of my story and ask him to be my judge—or better still, go straight to de Choiseul and talk to him as a man to a man."

"To M. de Choiseul?"

"Why, yes. I should never have run away from him. Nor would I, only that on the night of the Presentation I was in a hurry to go to Paris; he tried to stop me and I resisted arrest. And now it seems to me that I am in a hurry to go to Paris again and that de Sartines is trying to stop me, and that I am prepared to resist his hand."

He had almost forgotten Lavenne and his words, he had almost forgotten the presence of Ferminard on the other side of the wall, and he talked half to himself as he paced the floor uneasily, the big sou in his hand and his mind revolving this new idea that had only just occurred to him.

He should not have resisted arrest, even at the hands of Camus. Choiseul wanted him primarily for the killing of the agent. Had he gone straight to Choiseul and given him the whole truth, including Camus' conduct in the case of Javotte, whom he could have called as a witness, Choiseul would he now imagined have released him after inquiry. But he had resisted arrest, not because he felt guilty, but because he wanted to go to Paris to meet Camille Fontrailles. Choiseul did not know that.

It seemed to Rochefort, as his thoughts wandered back, that Camille Fontrailles had been his evil star. She it was who had made him join with the Dubarrys, she it was who had made him run away from Choiseul, she it was who, refusing to see him, had put him in such a temper with the world that his mind, unable to think for itself, had allowed other men to think for it.

It seemed to him now that Lavenne's advice, though it was the best that Lavenne could give, was not the best that Policy could devise. He—Rochefort—was saved from Choiseul for the moment; tucked away in Vincennes he might be saved from Choiseul as long as Choiseul remained in power—but how long would that be?

Choiseul might remain in power for years, and at this thought the sweat moistened M. de Rochefort's hands, wetting the big sou which he still held, and which, like some magician, whilst talking of Liberty to him, had shown him, as in a vision, his foolishness and his false position.

Sartines had put him under "protection" at Vincennes, not for his—Rochefort's—sake, but for his—Sartines'—convenience.

So many charming people in this world are wise after the event; it is chiefly the hard-headed and unpleasant and prosperous people whose wisdom, practical as themselves, saves them and makes them prosper. If Rochefort could only have gone back in his life; if he could only have carried his present wisdom back to the night of the Presentation, how differently things might have shaped themselves as regards his interests—or would he, in the face of everything, have pursued the path pointed out to him, as the old romance-writers would have said, "by Love and Folly"?

I believe he would, for M. de Rochefort had amongst his other qualities, good and bad, the persistence of a snail. Not only had Love urged him that night to strike Camus and escape on the horse of Choiseul's messenger, but Persistence had lent its powerful backing to Love. This gentleman hated to break his word with himself, and, as a matter of fact, he never did. If he had promised himself to repent of his sins and lead a virtuous life, I believe he would have done so.

He was longing to promise himself now to escape from this infernal prison into which Folly had led him.

"Well, M. de Rochefort," came the voice of Ferminard, "it is not for me to say whether you are right or wrong, but seeing that you are here, and safe under the protection of M. de Sartines, there is nothing to be done but have patience."

"*Mordieu*, patience! To be told that always makes me angry. Monsieur Ferminard, if you use that word again to me I will stuff up that hole with my blanket."

"Pardon," said Ferminard. "The word escaped from me, and now, monsieur, if you have done with that big sou."

"Here is your sou," replied the other, replacing the coin in the hand of Ferminard that was thrust through the opening, "and now, M. Ferminard, I am going to sit down on my bed and try if sleep will not help me to forget M. de Sartines, M. de Choiseul, myself, and this infernal castle where stupidity has brought me. *Bon soir*."

"*Bon soir*, monsieur," replied Ferminard.

Rochefort blew out his candle, and having replaced the bed, flung himself upon it, but not to sleep. Camille Fontrailles it was who now haunted him. The rapid events of the day had pushed her image to one side, and now in the darkness it reappeared to torment him. His passion for her, born of a moment, was by no means dead, but it had received a serious blow. At the crucial moment of his life she had refused to see him; after all that he had done for her friends, after all he had sacrificed for her, she had refused to see him, and not only that, she had sent a cold message, and also, she had sent it by the mouth of that fat-lipped libertine, Jean Dubarry.

Jean Dubarry could talk to her through her bedroom door, whilst he, Rochefort, had to remain downstairs, like a servant waiting for a message.

Yes, he would escape, if for no other object than to pull Jean Dubarry's nose. An intense hatred of the whole Dubarry faction surged up in his mind again. Jean, Chon, and the Countess, he did not know which was the more detestable. He rose from his bed. The moon, which was now near the full, was casting her light through the window, a ray fell on the little steel saw that was lying on the table. He picked it up and examined it again.

The window had only one bar, but the bar was fairly thick and it seemed impossible that he could ever cut through it with the instrument in his hand. Yet M. de Thumery had prepared to do so and would he be daunted by a business that an invalid had contemplated and would undoubtedly have carried out had not Death intervened?

He opened the sash of the window carefully and examined the bar. Then he brought his chair to the window, and, standing on the chair and holding either end of the saw between finger and thumb, drew its teeth against the iron of the bar.

It was one of those saws nicknamed "Dust of Iron," so wonderfully tempered and so keen that, properly used, no iron bar could stand before them. After five minutes' work Rochefort found that he could use the thing properly and with effect, and it seemed to him that with patience and diligence, working almost night and day, he could cut through the bar top and bottom—in about ten years' time.

In fact, though five minutes' work had produced a tiny furrow in the bar sufficient to be felt with his thumb-nail, the whole thing seemed hopeless. But only for a minute. He began to calculate. If five minutes' labour made a perceptible furrow in the iron of the bar, fifty minutes would give him ten times that result, and a hundred minutes twenty times. Two hours' labour, then, ought to start him well on his way through the business.

But even with this calculation fresh in his mind, his heart quailed before the thought of what he would have to do and to suffer before the last cut of the saw and the crowning of his efforts.

It was a life's work compressed into days. The labours of a Titan condensed and diminished, but not in the least lightened, and his heart quailed at the thought, not because he was a coward, but because he knew that if he once took the job in hand he would go through with it to the end.

He came from the window and putting the saw on the table, lay down on the bed. He lay for a few minutes without moving, like a man exhausted. Then all of a sudden, and as though some vital spring had been wound up and set going, he rose from the bed, snatched the saw from the table and approached the bar.

From the next cell he could hear a faint rhythmical sound. It was the sound of Ferminard snoring. Asleep and quite unconscious of the fact that his precious box which he had placed in his pocket after receiving it back, had been rifled of its contents.

CHAPTER III

THE TWO PRISONERS (continued)

NEXT morning, Rochefort awoke after five hours' sleep to find the daylight streaming into his cell and Bonvallot opening his door to bring him the early morning coffee that was served out to prisoners of the first class.

He had worked for three hours with the saw, and in his dreams he had been still at work, cutting his way through iron bars in a quite satisfactory manner, only to find that they joined together again when cut.

"Here is your coffee," said Bonvallot, "and a roll—*déjeuner* is served at noon—and the bed—have you found it comfortable?"

"*Mordieu!* Comfortable!" grumbled the prisoner, "it seems to me I have been sleeping on brickbats. Put the coffee on the table, Sergeant Bonvallot—that is right, and now tell me, has your Governor, M. le Capitaine Pierre Cousin, returned yet?"

"He has, monsieur."

"And when may I expect to see him?"

"Ah, when—that I cannot tell you. Maybe to-morrow, maybe the next day, maybe the day after, there are no fixed rules for the visits of the governor through the castle of Vincennes."

"Maybe to-morrow, maybe the next day—but I wish to see him to-day."

"Monsieur, that is what the prisoners are always saying. If the governor were to obey the requests of everyone he would be run off his legs."

"I do not wish to run him off his legs. I simply wish to see him."

"And what does monsieur wish to see him about?"

"*Ma foi!* what about, that is a secret. I wish to have a private talk with him."

"A private talk, why that is in any event impossible."

"Impossible, how do you mean?"

"When the governor visits the prisoners, monsieur, he is always accompanied by a soldier who remains in the room. That is one of the rules of Vincennes."

"Confound your rules—There, you can leave me, I am going to get up—and do not forget the writing materials when you come next. I will write the governor a letter—or will some soldier have to read it over his shoulder?"

Bonvallot went out grinning. Rochefort had paid him well for the clean linen and other attentions and he hoped for better payment still.

Then Rochefort got up, still grumbling. The labours of the night before at the bar, and his dreams in which those labours were continued, had not improved his temper. He drank his coffee and ate his roll and then turned to the window to see by daylight what progress he had made with the saw. He was more than satisfied; quite elated also to find that the top part of the bar, just where it entered the stone, had become spindled by rust. Were he to succeed in cutting through the lower part a vigorous wrench would, he felt assured, bring the whole thing away.

He took the little saw from the place where he had hidden it the night before, and, inspired with new energy, set to work.

He felt no fear of being caught; the size of the saw made it easily hidden, the cut in the bar would only be seen were a person to make a close inspection. The noise of the saw was negligible.

Whilst he was so engaged, Ferminard's voice broke in upon his labours.

"Good-morning, M. de Rochefort."

"Good-morning, M. Ferminard—what is it you want?"

"Only a little conversation, monsieur."

"Well, that is impossible as I am busy."

"*Oh hé*, busy! and what are you busy about?"

"I? I am writing letters."

"Pardon," said Ferminard. "I will call on you again."

As he laboured, pausing every five minutes for five minutes' rest, a necessity due to the cramped position in which he had to work, he heard vague sounds from Ferminard's cell, where that individual was also, it would seem, at work.

One might have fancied that two or three people were in there laughing and disputing and now quarrelling.

It was Ferminard at work on one of his infernal productions, tragedy or comedy, it would be impossible to say, but making more noise in the close confines of a prison cell than it was ever likely to make in the world.

After *déjeuner*, when Rochefort, tired out, was lying on his bed, the voice of Ferminard again made itself heard.

"M. de Rochefort—are you inclined for a little talk?"

"No," replied M. de Rochefort. "But you may talk as much as you like and I will promise not to interrupt—for I am going to sleep."

"Well, before you go to sleep let me tell you of my new design."

"Speak."

"I have torn up the play I was writing."

"Why, M. Ferminard, have you done that?"

"In order to write a better one."

"Ah, that is decidedly a good idea."

"A drama full of action."

"Hum-hum."

"M. de Rochefort, you are not listening to me."

"Eh—what! Where am I—ah, yes, go on, go on—you were saying that you had torn up a play."

"In order to write a better one, and I am introducing you as one of my characters."

"You are putting me in your play?"

"Yes, monsieur, I am putting you in my play."

"Well, M. Ferminard, I forbid it, that's all. I will not be put in a play."

"But I am putting myself in also, monsieur."

"*Bon Dieu!* what impudence!"

"It is not impudence, but gratitude, monsieur. I will not hide it from you that, despite what brains I have, I am of small extraction; one of the *rafataille*, as they say in the south. But you have always talked to me as your equal; and if I have put myself in the same piece as you it is only as your servant, imprisoned in the next cell to you in the dungeons of the castle of Pompadiglione."

"And where the devil is Pompadiglione?"

"It is the name of the castle in my play. Well, monsieur, the first scene is just as it is here, now. The count and his servant, imprisoned just as we are in adjoining cells, with a hole in the partition wall through which they can speak to one another, and the servant has discovered a knotted rope, a big sou and a staple just as I have discovered them. Well, monsieur, the count is to be beheaded, and his execution is fixed for the next day, but the faithful servant hands him through the hole in the wall the means for escape, the rope, the big sou containing a saw, and the staple. The count escapes that night."

"One moment, M. Ferminard, you say he escaped that night?"

"Yes, monsieur."

"How did he escape?"

"He escaped by cutting away the bar of his cell with the little saw contained in the sou."

"Oh. And do you fancy he could do that in one night?"

"Not in reality, monsieur, but on the stage he could."

"Ah, well, I know nothing of these things—well, he escapes, this count—what then?"

"Next morning his escape is discovered and the faithful servant—that is me—refuses to give any explanation, though the hole in the wall has been discovered—he is dumb."

"Dumb—good heavens, M. Ferminard—that part would never suit you."

"Pardon me, monsieur, but I believe it would—well, as I was saying, the count, who had indeed escaped by means of the rope from his cell, had not managed to escape from the precincts of the castle. The rope was not long enough and he had to take refuge on a ledge where he is shown in the next scene crouching and watching the faithful servant being led forth to execution in his place."

"Well?"

"That is as far as I have got, monsieur."

"Oh, you have not fixed on the end of your play yet?"

"No, monsieur."

"But surely, M. Ferminard, the end is the most important thing in a play?"

Ferminard coughed, irritated, as all geniuses are by criticism.

"Why," said he, "I thought monsieur said he could not tell a play from a washing-bill."

"Perhaps, yet even in a washing-bill, M. Ferminard, the end is the most important part, since it sums up the whole matter in francs and sous. But do not let me discourage you, for should you fail to find a good ending I will be able to supply you with one. An idea has occurred to me."

"And what is that idea, monsieur?"

"I have, yet, to think it out. However, go on with your business in your own way and we will talk of the matter when you have finished. I wish now to sleep."

He felt irritated with Ferminard. Ferminard was the man who possessed the rope which was the only means of escape, and Ferminard, he felt, would refuse the rope to him, just as he had refused the big sou. By using arguments, threats, or entreaties he might be able to make Ferminard give him the rope, but he was not the man to threaten, entreat, or argue with an inferior. Besides, he was too lazy. The cutting of the window-bar was absorbing all his energies.

Besides, why waste time and tongue-power to obtain a thing that could be obtained when desired by a little finesse. When the time came he would obtain the rope from Ferminard just as he had obtained the saw which Ferminard fancied still to be contained in the sou. Rochefort, whilst feeling friendly towards the dramatist, had very little respect for him; he might be a good actor, but it was evident that he was very much of a child. Besides, he was—as he himself confessed—one of the *rafataille*, a man of the people, and though M. de Rochefort was not in the least a snob, he looked upon the people from the viewpoint of his class. He was not in the least ashamed of the deception he had practiced on Ferminard. The little saw did not belong to Ferminard, he had found it by chance, and it was the property of the dead M. Thumery, or his heirs.

CHAPTER IV

THE TWO PRISONERS (continued)

THE next day passed without a visit from the governor, and the next. Rochefort ceased to ask about him; he resented this neglect, now, as a personal insult. He forgot that he was incarcerated under the name of La Porte, and that any neglect of M. La Porte, though unpleasant to M. de Rochefort, need not be taken as a personal affront.

He would have resented the thing more had it not been that he was very busy.

On the afternoon of the fourth day his work was complete. The bar was not quite divided, but sufficiently so to yield to a strong wrench. With his table-knife, which he had been allowed to keep, he had scraped away the rust where the upper part of the bar was mortised into the stone and had verified the weakness of this part of the attachment.

He had fixed upon midnight as the hour for his evasion, and nothing remained now but to obtain the rope from the unsuspecting Ferminard.

The latter had also not been idle during the last four days. Happy as a child with a toy, the ingenious Ferminard had not noticed the faint sound of the saw in the next cell. If it reached him at all at times, he no doubt put it down to the noise of a rat.

Never before in his life had he possessed so much paper, ink, and time to write in. Up to this his leisure had been mostly consumed by taverns, good companions, women, and the necessity of getting drunk which his unfortunate temperament imposed on him. Also, in hunting for loans. Now he found himself housed, fed, and cared for, protected from drink and supplied with all the materials his imagination required for the moment. So, for the moment, he was happy and busy, and his happiness would have been more complete had Rochefort been a better listener.

Towards dusk, Rochefort considered that the time had come to negotiate the business of the rope with M. Ferminard. Accordingly, he drew the bed away from the wall, and, kneeling down, approached his head to the opening.

"Monsieur Ferminard."

"Ho! M. de Rochefort, is that you?"

"Yes, it is I—let us talk for awhile."

"With pleasure, monsieur."

He heard Ferminard's bed being moved away from the wall. Then came the dramatist's voice.

"I am here, monsieur. I was asleep when you called me and I was dreaming that I was at the Maison Gambrinus drinking some Flemish beer that Turgis had just imported, and that there was a hole in the bottom of my mug, so that as fast as I drank so fast did the beer run out. I got nothing but froth, and even that froth had a taste of soap-suds. Now tell me one thing, M. de Rochefort."

"Yes?"

"Why is it that when one dreams, one's dreams are always so unsatisfactory? Whenever I meet a pretty girl in dreamland, she always turns into an old woman when I kiss her, and whenever I find myself in good company, I am either dressed in rags, or, what is worse, not dressed at all. If I go to collect money I always enter by mistake the house of some man to whom I owe a debt, and if I find myself on the stage I am always acting some part, the lines of which I have forgotten."

"The whole world is unsatisfactory, M. Ferminard, and as dreamland is part of the world, why, I suppose it is unsatisfactory too. Now as to that play of yours whose ending you insisted on describing to me this morning, that is like dreamland and the world—unsatisfactory. The ending does not satisfy me in the least."

"In what way?"

"I have thought of a better."

"Oh, you have. Well, please explain to me what you mean."

"I will, certainly. But first let me see that rope which you told me you had discovered, and the discovery of which gave you the idea for this play of yours."

"The rope, but what can you want with the rope?"

"I will show you when it is in my hands, or at least I will explain my meaning; come, M. Ferminard, the rope, for without it I cannot show you what I want."

"Wait, monsieur, and I will get it."

In a moment one end of the precious rope was in Rochefort's hands. He pulled it through into his cell, noted the length, the thickness and the knots upon it, and was satisfied.

"Well, monsieur?" said the impatient Ferminard.

"Well, M. Ferminard, now I have the rope in my hands I will tell you exactly how your play is going to end, in reality. The count—that is myself, for since you have put me into your play I feel myself justified in acting in it—the count is going to pull his bed to the window of his cell, tie this precious rope to the bedpost, and, crawling out of the window and dangling like a spider, he is going to descend to the ground. He will not remain stuck on a ledge, as in your version of the play, he will reach the ground—then he will pick up his heels and run to Paris, and there he will pull M. de Choiseul's nose—or make friends with him."

"But you cannot," replied Ferminard, not knowing exactly how to take the other.

"And why cannot I?"

"Because, monsieur, the bar of your window would permit you, perhaps, to lower your rope, but it would prevent you from following it."

"No, M. Ferminard, it would not."

"Ah, well, then, it must be a most accommodating bar and have altered considerably in strength since you spoke to me of it first."

"It has."

"In what way?"

"Why, it has been filed almost in two."

"Ah," cried Ferminard, "what is that you say? Filed in two—and since when?"

"Since we had our first talk together."

"You have cut it then—with what?"

"Heavens! can't you guess?"

"Your table-knife."

"Oaf!"

"You had, then, a knife, or file, or saw or something with you."

"M. Ferminard, prison does not seem to improve your intelligence. I cut it with the little saw contained in the big sou."

"But that is impossible, for you had not the sou two minutes in your possession."

Rochefort laughed. "Open your sou, then, and see what is in it."

Leaning on his elbow, he laughed to himself as he heard Ferminard moving so as to get the sou from his pocket to open it.

Then he heard the voice of Ferminard who was speaking to himself. "It is gone—he must have taken it—never!—yet it is gone."

The astonishment evident in Ferminard's voice at the trick that had been played on him acted upon Rochefort just as the sudden stripping of the bedclothes from a person asleep acts on the sleeper.

It was not stupidity on the part of Ferminard that had prevented him from guessing with what instrument the bar had been cut, it was his complete belief in Rochefort's honour. His mind, of its own accord, could not imagine the Comte de Rochefort playing him a trick like that, and his voice now betrayed what was passing in his mind.

Had Ferminard been a suspicious man, and had he discovered the abstraction of the saw on his own account, anything he might have said would not have shown Rochefort what he saw now.

He felt as though, by some horrible accident, he had shot and injured his own good faith, fair name and honour.

"*Mon Dieu!*" said he. "What have I done!"

CHAPTER V

M. DE ROCHEFORT REVIEWS HIMSELF

FOR a moment he said nothing more. And then: "M. Ferminard?"

"Yes, M. de Rochefort?"

"I have been a very great fool, it seems to me, for I did not in the least consider the fact, when I played that deception upon you, that it was an unworthy one. You believed in me. You had formed an opinion of me. You paid me the compliment of never imagining that I would deceive you. Well, honestly and as between man and man, I looked on the matter more in the light of a joke. I said to myself, 'How he will stare when he finds I have outwitted him.' It was the trick of a child, for it seems to me one grows childish in prison. Give me that big sou, M. Ferminard."

Ferminard passed the coin through the hole and Rochefort, rising, opened it, put the little saw in, closed it, and returned it to the other.

"And here is the rope," said he. "I have no more use for it."

"But, monsieur," said Ferminard. He paused, and for a moment said nothing more. Ferminard was, in fact, covered with confusion. Rochefort's unworthy trick had struck him on the cheek, so to say, and left it burning. He felt ashamed. Ashamed of Rochefort for playing the trick and ashamed of himself for having found it out, and ashamed of Rochefort knowing that he—Ferminard—thought less of him. Then, breaking silence:

"It is nothing, M. de Rochefort. If you are tired of prison why should you remain? It is true that there may be danger for you from M. de Choiseul, but one does nothing without danger threatening one in this world, it seems to me. Why, even walking across the street one may be run over by a carriage, as a friend of mine was some time ago."

"My good Ferminard," said Rochefort, dropping for the first time the prefix "monsieur," "you are talking for the sake of talking, and for the kind reason that you wish to hide from yourself and me what you are thinking. And you are thinking that the Comte de Rochefort is a man whom you trusted, but whom you do not trust any longer."

"Monsieur—monsieur!"

"Let me finish. If that is not what you are thinking you must be a fool, and as you are not a fool that is what is in your mind. Well, you are right and wrong. I do not know my own character entirely, but I do know that when I stop to think I am sometimes at a loss to imagine why I have committed certain actions; some of these actions that startle me are good, and some are bad; but they are not committed by the Comte de Rochefort so much as by something that urges the Comte de Rochefort to commit them. I fancy that some men always think before they act, and other men frequently act before they think, but I do know this, that once I am propelled on a course of action I don't stop to think at all till the business is over one way or another.

"Now, when I took that saw of yours, I said to myself, 'Here is a joke I will play on M. Ferminard. What a temper he will be in when he finds that I have outwitted him. He wishes to prevent my escape so that he may not be left in loneliness? We will see.' Well, M. Ferminard, embarked on that course of action, I never stopped to think that all the time I was cutting that bar I was violating your trust in me. When I found that you did not open the sou to examine whether its contents were safe, I should have paused to take counsel with myself and inquire if liberty were worth the deception of a good and honest mind which placed its faith in me. But I did not pause to take counsel with myself, and for two reasons. First, as I said before, I never stop to think when I am in action; secondly, I am so unused to meeting with good and honest minds that I did not suspect one was in the next cell to me. It is true, M. Ferminard. The men with whom I have always lived have been men very much like myself. Men who do not think much, and who, when they do think, are full of suspicion as a rule. We are robbed by our servants, our wives, and our mistresses. We cheat each other, not at cards, but with phrases and at the game of Love, and so forth. You said you were of small extraction and one of the *rafataille*—well, it is among the *rafataille*, among the People, during the last few days that I have met three individuals who have struck me as being the only worthy individuals it has been my lot to meet. They are yourself, Monsieur Lavenne, and little Javotte, a girl whom you do not know."

"Believe me, monsieur," said Ferminard, "I have no unworthy thought concerning you. At first, yes, but now after what you have said, no. I am like that myself, and had I been in your place, I would, I am very sure, have done as you did."

"Perhaps," replied Rochefort. "But I cannot use the rope, so here it is and I will leave my release from prison to God and M. de Sartines."

He began to push the rope through the hole. It would not go. Ferminard was pushing it back.

"No, M. de Rochefort—one moment till I speak—I have been blinded to my best interests by my desire to keep you as a companion. You must escape, you must do as Fate dictated to you, and to me, when she gave us the fruits of the labours of M. de Thumery. Honestly, now that I think of the matter, I do not trust M. de Sartines a whit. He put us here to keep us out of the way. Well, it seems to me that considering what we have done and what we know, it may be in his interest to keep us here always. Take the rope, M. de Rochefort, use it, follow the dictates of Fate, and don't forget Ferminard. You will be able to free me, perhaps, once you have gained freedom and the pardon of M. de Choiseul."

Rochefort said nothing for a moment. He was thinking.

"M. de Rochefort," went on the other, "the more I consider this matter, the more do I see the pointing of Fate. Take the rope and use it."

"Very well, then," said Rochefort. "I will use it for your freedom as well as mine. We will both escape."

"Impossible. How can I come through this hole?"

"I will find a means. It is now ten o'clock, or at least I heard the chime a moment ago when I was talking to you. Be prepared to leave your cell. Can you climb down a rope?"

"Yes, monsieur, I have done so once in my early days."

"Well, be prepared to do so again."

"But I do not see your meaning in the least."

"Never mind, you will soon."

"You frighten me."

"By my faith," said Rochefort, laughing, "I am not easily frightened, but if I were, I believe I should be frightened now. Put back your bed, M. Ferminard, and when Bonvallot visits you on his last round pretend to be asleep."

CHAPTER VI

THE ESCAPE

"VERY well, M. de Rochefort," replied Ferminard. "I will do as you tell me, though as I have just said, I do not know your meaning in the least."

Rochefort heard him putting his bed back in its place. Then he set about his preparations. He placed the rope under the mattress of his own bed, and stripping the coverlet off, took the upper sheet away. Having replaced the coverlet, he began tearing the sheet into long strips. The sheet was about four feet broad and it gave him eight strips, each about six inches broad by five feet in length. Four of these he placed under the coverlet of his bed just as he had placed the rope under the mattress, the other four he put in his pockets.

Then he sat down on his chair, and, placing his elbows on the table and his chin between his hands, began to review his plans, or rather the new modification of them which the inclusion of Ferminard in his flight necessitated.

When Bonvallot appeared at his door on his last round of inspection, Rochefort was seated like this.

"Ah, ha!" said he, turning his head, "you are earlier to-night, it seems to me."

"No, monsieur," replied Bonvallot, "I am not before my time, for the clock of the courtyard has struck eleven."

"Indeed. I did not hear it. Sound does not carry very well among these stone walls, and though the courtyard clock is close to this cell, and though it doesn't whisper over its work, the sound is scarcely perceptible. A man might shout in my cell, Monsieur Bonvallot, without being heard very far."

"My faith, you are right," said Bonvallot. "We had a lunatic of a prisoner in No. 32 down the corridor, and it seemed to me that he spent all his time shouting, but he disturbed no one. Our inn is well constructed, you see, monsieur, so that the guests may have a quiet time."

Rochefort rose from his chair, walked to the door, shut it, and put his back against it.

"Hi," said Bonvallot, who had been bending to see if the water-pitcher were empty. "What are you doing, monsieur?"

"Nothing. I wish to have a word with you. I am leaving your inn to-night and wish to settle my bill. Do not shout, you will not be heard, and if you move from the place where you are standing——"

Bonvallot, who had grown pale at the first words, suddenly, with head down and arms outstretched, made a dash at Rochefort. The Count, slipping aside, managed to trip him up, and next moment the gallant Bonvallot was on the floor, half-stunned, bleeding from a wound on his forehead, and with Rochefort kneeling across him, a knee on each arm so as to keep him still.

"Now see what you have done," said the victor. "You might have killed yourself. The wound is nothing, however, and you can charge for it in the bill."

Bonvallot heaved a few inches as though trying to rise, then lay still.

"There is no use in resisting," went on the Count, "you have no chance against me, Monsieur Bonvallot, nor have I any wish to harm you. Besides, you will be well paid by me and that wound on your forehead will prove that you did your duty like a man. Now turn on your face, I wish to tie your hands for appearance's sake."

Bonvallot in turning made an attempt to break loose and rise, but the Count's science was too much for him. Literally sitting on his back, or rather on his shoulder-blades, Rochefort, with a strip of the sheet which he took from his pocket, tied the captive's wrists together. Then he tied the ankles.

"Monsieur," said Bonvallot, craning his face round, "I make no further resistance, but for the love of the Virgin, bind my knees together and also gag me so that it may be seen that I did my duty."

"Rest assured," said Rochefort.

He bound the unfortunate's knees and elbows, made a gag out of a handkerchief and put it in his mouth. Then, taking ten louis from his pocket, he showed them to the trussed one, and dropped them one by one into the water-pitcher.

Then he took Bonvallot's keys, left the cell, opened the door of Ferminard's prison and found that gentleman seated on his bed, a vague figure in the light of the moon, a few stray beams of which were struggling through the window.

"*Mordieu!*" said Ferminard, "what has happened?"

Rochefort, instead of replying, seized him by the arm, and half pushing, half pulling him, led him into the corridor.

"Now," said he, "quick; we have no time to waste, I have tied up Bonvallot; but when he does not return to the guard-room they are sure to search. There he is. He is not hurt. Come, help me to pull the bed to the window."

Ferminard, after a glance at Bonvallot lying on the floor, obeyed mechanically. They got the bed close up with the head-rail under the window. Rochefort tied the rope to the head-rail, and, standing on the bed and opening the sash, seized the bar. It came away in his hands, and then, flinging it on the bed, he seized the rope which he had coiled and flung it out.

This done, he leaned out of the window-place and looked down.

The moonlight lit the castle wall and the dangling rope and showed the black shadow of the moat, a terrific sight that made Rochefort's stomach crawl and his throat close. This was no castle wall which he had to descend. It was like looking over the cliff at the world's end or one of those terrific bastions of cloud which one sees sometimes banking the sky before a storm. The moonlight it was that lent this touch of vastness to the prospect below, a prospect that made the sweat stand out on the palms of Rochefort's hands and his soul to contract on itself.

It was a prospect to be met by the unthinking end of man if one wished for any chance of success, so with a warning to Ferminard not to look before he came, and having wedged two pillows under the rope where it rested on the sill, Rochefort got one leg over the sill, straddled it, got the other leg out and then turned on his face. He was now lying on his stomach across the pillow that was forming a pad for the rope, and as bad luck would have it, a knot in the rope just at this point did not make the position any more comfortable. Then he slowly worked his body downwards till he was supported only by his elbows; supporting himself entirely with his left elbow, he seized with his right hand the rope where it rested on the cushion, gave up his elbow hold and with his left hand seized the sill.

He was hanging now with one hand grasping the sill, the other, the rope. The sill was no longer a window-sill, it was the tangible world, to release his hold upon it and to trust entirely to the rope required an effort of will far greater than one would think, so great that even the plucky mind of Rochefort refused the idea for a moment, but only for a moment, the next he was swinging loose.

But for the pad made by the pillow, the rope would have rested so close to the bevelled stone that he might not have been able to seize it. As it was, his knuckles were bruised and cut, and, as he swung in descending, now his shoulder, now his knee came in contact with the wall. As the pendulum lengthened, these oscillations became terrific. Then, all at once he recognized that the business was over; he was only fifteen feet or so from the ground.

The rope was some six feet short, and at the last few feet he dropped, landed safely and then looked up at the wall and the window from which he had come.

Looking up it seemed nothing, and as he stood watching, and just as the clock of Vincennes was chiming the quarter after eleven, he saw a leg protrude from the window, then the body of Ferminard appeared, and Rochefort held his breath as he watched the legs clutching themselves round the rope and the body swinging free. He seized the rope-end and held it to steady it. He had no reason at all, now, to fear; Ferminard seemed as cool and methodical as a spider in his movements, came down as calmly as a spider comes down its thread, released his hold at the proper moment and landed safely.

"*Mordieu!* but you did that easily," whispered Rochefort, filled with admiration and not knowing that Ferminard's courage was due mainly to an imagination that was not very keen and a head that vertigo did not easily affect. "Now let us keep to the shadow of the moat for a moment till that cloud comes over the moon. There are sentries on the battlements."

"Monsieur," whispered Ferminard, "it just occurred to me as I was coming down the rope that when our flight is discovered, they may hunt along the roads for us, but they will not warn the gates of Paris to be on the look-out for us, simply because, were we caught, some of M. de Choiseul's agents might be at the catching, there would be talk, and the discovery might be made that we had been imprisoned secretly to keep us out of M. de Choiseul's way."

"*Ma foi!*" said Rochefort, "there is truth in that—however, it remains to be seen. Ah, here comes the shadow."

A cloud was slowly drawing across the moon's face, and in the deep shadow that swept across castle and road and country, the two fugitives scrambled from the moat, found the road and started towards Paris.

CHAPTER VII

ROCHEFORT'S PLAN

THAT night, or, rather, early next morning, the Vicomte de Chartres was returning to his house in the Rue Malaquais and had just entered the street when, against the setting moon, he saw a form coming towards him which he thought he recognized.

It was Rochefort.

Chartres was one of the few men in Paris whom Rochefort numbered as his bosom friends. He could not believe his eyes at first, and when Rochefort spoke, Chartres scarcely believed his ears.

Rochefort, of whose flight all Paris was talking, Rochefort, the man who was supposed to be far beyond the frontier, Rochefort in the Rue Malaquais, walking along as calmly and jauntily as though nothing had happened.

"Ah, my dear fellow," said Rochefort as they shook hands, "what a fortunate meeting! Where have you sprung from?"

Chartres broke into a laugh.

"Where have I sprung from? You to ask that question! On the contrary, my dear fellow, it is for me to ask where you have sprung from?"

"Nowhere," replied Rochefort, also laughing, "or at least from a place I cannot talk of here in the street. I want shelter for the night and a change of clothes; here is your house and we are both about the same size, and I know you have always half a dozen new suits that you have never worn. So, if you want my story, take me and clothe me, and let me rest for a while before I set out on my mission to hunt for M. de Choiseul."

"To hunt for M. de Choiseul! *Bon Dieu!* Are not you aware that he is ransacking Paris and all France for you?"

"Then we are both on the same business, and that being so, I think it is highly probable we shall meet."

He followed Chartres into the house, where in the library and armoury his host lit lamps and produced wine.

The clock on the mantel pointed to two o'clock.

"And now, my dear fellow," said Chartres, "tell me all about yourself, where have you been, what have you been doing, and what is this nonsense you are saying about hunting for M. de Choiseul."

"Well, as to what I have been doing, I can answer you simply that I have been in retirement in the country."

"Where?"

"In the Castle of Vincennes."

"The Castle of Vincennes!"

"Precisely. Sartines put me there to hide me from Choiseul. I would not tell you this only that I know you are entirely to be trusted. He did not want Choiseul to lay his hands on me, so he arrested me under another name, but with my consent, and popped me into Vincennes, where I have been for the last few days."

"Yes?"

"Well, my dear Chartres, no sooner did I find myself in prison there than I found that I did not like it."

"I can understand that."

"And though Sartines had put me there for my own good—so he said—and to keep me from being imprisoned by Choiseul, it began to dawn on me that I had been a fool."

"Ah, that began to dawn on you."

"I said to myself, 'Sartines is no doubt the best soul in the world, but the best souls are sometimes selfish.' I said to myself, 'Sartines has compromised himself in a way by playing this game with Choiseul, and hiding me from him.' I said to myself, 'Sartines, however kind he may be, is not the man to compromise himself by letting me out whilst Choiseul has any power in France.' In fact, I felt that were I to remain passive, I would be saved from M. de Choiseul, but I would still be a prisoner, and that, perhaps, for years, so I determined to escape, to go straight to Choiseul and to tell him frankly the truth about the business for which he wished to apprehend me."

"I have heard that you killed a man," said Chartres.

"I did. And that man was one of Choiseul's agents, but he was a ruffian who was molesting a girl, and whom I caught in the act. I followed him, he attacked me and I killed him in fair fight."

"Can the girl give evidence?"

"Yes."

"Then why on earth, my dear fellow, did you resist arrest that night when M. Camus was deputed to arrest you? I had the whole story from Monpavon."

"I resisted arrest because I wanted to go to Paris to meet a woman who had given me an appointment."

The Vicomte de Chartres, who was five years older than Rochefort in time, and fifty in discretion, moved in his chair uneasily.

He was fond of Rochefort, and nothing had surprised him more in the last few days than the Rochefort episode. The fact that Rochefort had killed a man was easily understandable, but that Rochefort had evaded arrest instead of facing the business was an action that he could not understand, simply because it was an action unlike Rochefort.

Here had a man gone against his true nature and placed himself in the last position, that of a murderer flying from justice—for what reason? To keep an appointment with a woman.

Unhappily the reason cleared everything up.

It was exactly—arguing from the reason—the thing that Rochefort might be expected to do.

"But did you not consider that for the sake of keeping this confounded appointment you were risking everything—losing everything. *Mon Dieu!* it makes me shudder. Did you not think, my dear man, did you not think?"

"Ah, think!" said the other, "a lot you would think were you in that position. Had he deputed any man for the business but Camus, it might have been different; but to be told, in effect, by Camus, a man I despise, that I was not to go to Paris, but to remain at Versailles, a prisoner of Choiseul's, well, it was too much! No, I did not think. There is no use in saying to me what I ought to have done. I ought, of course, to have followed Camus like a lamb, faced Choiseul like a lion, and cleared the matter up. As it was, I showed the front of a lion to Camus and the tail of a fox to Choiseul. That was bad policy—but it was inevitable. It seems to me, Chartres, that the whole of this was like a play written by Fate for me to act in. Camus had been my friend. After I had rescued that girl, of whom I told you, from Choiseul's ruffianly agent, Camus tried to assault her and I struck him in the face. That was Fate. He did not return the blow or seek a duel, he wanted revenge, and behold, when Choiseul put out his hand for someone to arrest me, whom should he employ but Camus—that also was Fate. The girl I served is the servant of the woman I spoke of, and the woman was the friend of Choiseul's dearest enemy, the Comtesse Dubarry.

That was Fate. To serve the woman I mixed myself up with the business of the Presentation, and so have given Choiseul an extra grudge against me. That was Fate. And stay—just before my row with Camus, he had imparted to me a plot which Choiseul was preparing against the Dubarry, a plot which I refused to mix myself with and the gist of which I disclosed to the Dubarry. There again was Fate."

"*Mon Dieu!*" said Chartres, "what a tangle you have got yourself into. But tell me this, does Choiseul know that you disclosed this plot of his to the Dubarry?"

"He is sure to know. Camus is certain to have told him that he disclosed the business to me, and as I visited the Dubarry's house that same night, and as I believe his agents were watching the house—there you are."

"You visited the house of the Dubarry the same night that Camus told you of the plot—why did you do such a foolish thing?"

"Fate. I escorted the girl I had rescued home to see her safe—and what house did she bring me to but the house of the Dubarrys. I was giving her a kiss in the passage when Jean Dubarry appeared, he invited me in, I came, the woman I spoke of was there, and at the sight of her, knowing that she was the Countess' friend, I flung in my part with the Dubarrys and told of the plot. I was not breaking a trust, I had made no promise of secrecy, the thing had disgusted me—and I told."

"And the name of this woman for whose sake you have got yourself into this dreadful mess?"

"Ah, now you are asking me to tell something that I would not tell to anyone but yourself—it was Mademoiselle Fontrailles."

"Mademoiselle Fontrailles—why only yesterday——"

"Yes?"

"Well, I heard—it is said—but I don't know how much truth there is in the story, that she is in love with Camus."

Rochefort laughed.

"Camus again and Fate again."

"But there may be no truth in it. Some fool told me, I forget who, Joyeuse, I think. You know how stories run about Paris."

"It is true," said Rochefort, "it is the only thing wanting to make the business complete. Whilst I have been tucked away at Vincennes, Monsieur Camus has improved his time. You know the way he has with women.

Well, I do not care; that is to say about the girl, but I will make things even with Camus."

"First, my dear fellow, make things right with Choiseul, that is to say, if you can. And if I were you, I would not trouble about Camus or the girl. She will be punished enough if she has anything to do with him."

"Well, we will see," said Rochefort. "We will see, when I have finished with Choiseul. Is he in Paris?"

"No, he is at Versailles, but he is coming to Paris to-morrow, or rather to-day, since it is now nearly three o'clock in the morning. I know he is coming, simply because he has invited me to a reception at his house in the Faubourg St. Honoré."

"Ah, he is holding a reception. When?"

"This very day at nine o'clock in the evening."

"Good. I will go to it."

"You will go to it—but he will arrest you!"

"Not in his own house. I would be his guest."

"But you have not been invited, and so you would not be his guest."

"Well, my dear Chartres, you know how Choiseul always permits a friend of his to bring a friend to his receptions. You must take me with you."

"Take you with me! My dear fellow, you are asking what is quite impossible."

"Why?"

"Why—well, to be frank with you, it is necessary for me to stand well with Choiseul, and if I were to do that I would damage my position at Court."

"What I like about you," said Rochefort, "is your perfect frankness. Another man would have excused himself, said that he had already invited a friend, and so forth; but you state your own selfish reason, and that is precisely what I would have done in your place. Well, I can assure you that you will not damage your position in the least. First of all, I am going to make peace with Choiseul; secondly, if I fail, you can tell him that the whole fault was mine and that you understood from me that I had put myself right with him. I will bear you out in that. There is no danger to you, and think what fun it will be to see his face when I appear."

Chartres hung on this fascinating prospect for a moment.

"All the same," said he, "I think, in your own interests, you are wrong—the whole thing is mad."

"So is the whole situation, my dear man. I want to get a word alone with Choiseul. I cannot reach him in any other way. If I went to see him at Versailles I would be taken by the guards and I would only see him across drawn swords. If I went to interview him at his house the *concierge* would pass me to the major-domo, and the major-domo would show me into a waiting-room, and Choiseul, ten to one, when he heard I had called, would order my arrest without even seeing me. No. This reception of his was arranged by Fate for me, of that I feel sure, as sure as I am that I will make things even with Camus before to-morrow."

"You seem to count a good deal on Fate, yet it seems to me she has not treated you very kindly."

"Ah," said Rochefort, laughing, "that is because you do not know how she treated me in the Castle of Vincennes. I assure you, I have made entire friends with the lady———" He paused for a moment and then looked up at Chartres.

"When we talk of Fate, my friend, we always refer to our own persons and fortunes; when we receive a buffet in life we never consider that the shock may come to us, not directly from Fate, but indirectly as the result of a blow struck at some other person, just as at the Lycée Louis le Grand, one boy would strike another so that he would fall against the next, and he against the next. Well, Fate in this case is decidedly on my side, since she protected me till now at Vincennes and gave me my release on the day of Choiseul's reception, and threw me into your arms in the Rue Malaquais. If she is with me she cannot be with the persons who are against me, that is to say, Camus and the Fontrailles, if she cares for Camus.

"Fate, my dear Chartres, seems to me to be hitting at these two, and I reckon the blows I have received, not as blows aimed directly against me, but as blows I have received indirectly and by *contre coup*."

"You are becoming a philosopher," said Chartres, laughing.

"Well, we will see," replied Rochefort. "I believe I am on the winning side, the indications are with me—well, do you still refuse to take me with you to Choiseul's?"

"No, my dear Rochefort, I do not refuse, simply because I cannot—and for this reason: The thing you propose is distasteful to me, but it is a matter of urgency with you, and though you may be wrong, still, if the case was reversed, I know you would do for me what I am going to do for you. I will take you to Choiseul's."

"Thank you," said Rochefort. "I will never forget it to you. And now as to clothes. I am unable to go or send for anything to my place, can you dress me as well as take me to this pleasant party of Choiseul's?"

"Without doubt. My wardrobe is at your disposal—and now, if you will have no more wine, it is time to go to bed. I will have a bed made up for you."

He called a servant and gave instructions as to the preparation of a room. As they were going upstairs, Rochefort remembered Ferminard, with whom he had parted outside the walls of Paris.

Ferminard had refused to enter by the Porte St. Antoine, preferring to make his way round to the Maison Gambrinus and take shelter there. Rochefort had entered by the Porte St. Antoine, not on his legs, but by means of a market gardener's cart which they had overtaken. He had given the gardener a few francs for the lift, and, pretending intoxication, had entered Paris lying on some sacks of potatoes, presumably asleep and certainly snoring.

Having been shown to his bedroom, Rochefort undressed and went to bed, where he slept as soundly as a child till Germain, Chartres' valet, awoke him at nine o'clock.

CHAPTER VIII

THE HONOUR OF LAVENNE

THAT same morning, it will be remembered, Sartines received the visit of the Vicomte Jean, and also Captain Pierre Cousin, the governor of Vincennes, who came in person with the news of Rochefort's escape.

Having dismissed Cousin, Sartines, perplexed, distracted, furious with himself, Rochefort, Choiseul, and the world in general, put aside the letters on which he had been engaged and rising from his chair began to walk up and down the room.

Everything now depended on what Rochefort would do. With Rochefort and Ferminard safe in Vincennes, Sartines felt safe. He knew instinctively that Choiseul was deeply suspicious about the affair of the Presentation. He knew for a fact that Choiseul had, through an agent, questioned the Comtesse de Béarn before she left Paris, and that the Comtesse, like the firm old woman she was, had refused to say a single word on the matter. She had, in fact, refused for two reasons. First: she had the two hundred thousand francs which the Dubarrys had paid her tight clutched in her hand. Secondly: she was too proud to acknowledge to the world how she had been tricked. Such a scandal would become historical, but not if she could help it with a de Béarn in the chief part.

There was no one to talk, then, but Rochefort and Ferminard, the chief actor—and they who had been in safe keeping were now loose.

In the midst of his meditations, a knock came to the door and the usher announced that Lavenne had arrived and wished to speak to the Minister. Sartines ordered him to be sent up at once. No visitor would be more welcome. The absence of Lavenne had been disturbing him for the last few days, for this man so fruitful in advice and expedient had become as the right hand of the Minister. Of all the clever people about him, Lavenne was the man whom he felt to be absolutely essential.

"*Mordieu!*" cried de Sartines, when Lavenne entered. "What has happened to you?"

He drew back a step.

The man before him looked ten years older than when he had seen him last, his face was white and pinched, his eyes were bloodshot, and the pupils seemed unnaturally dilated.

"Monsieur," said Lavenne, resting his hand on a chair-back as if for support, "I have had a bad time, but I will soon get over it. Meanwhile, I have an important report to make."

"Sit down," said de Sartines.

He rang the bell and ordered some wine to be sent up immediately. "And now," said he, when the other had set down his glass, "tell me first where have you come from?"

"I have come from the Catacombs of Paris, monsieur, where I have been trapped and wandering since I don't know when."

"From the Catacombs?"

"Yes, monsieur, or rather from the plain of Mont Souris to which the gallery which I pursued led me."

"But what were you doing in the Catacombs?"

"Trying to escape, monsieur, and I can only say this, that I hope never to have a similar experience."

Then rapidly he began to tell of his visit to Camus' house, of the laboratory, of what he had seen, and of his escape.

"I had to choose between three corridors, monsieur, and the one I chose led me to a blank wall. I had to come back, which took me a day. I had to go most of the time in darkness to husband the candles I had with me.

"The new corridor I chose led me right at last, but the last was a long time coming. Several times I fell asleep and must have slept many hours. I would have died of exhaustion had I not found water. At several places I found water trickling through crevices of the rock and I had to cross one fairly big pool. I had to walk always, feeling my way with one foot. My progress was slow. At last I came to the old grating which guards the entrance to the Catacombs on the plain of Mont Souris. There I might have died had not my cries attracted the attention of a man, who, obtaining assistance, broke down the bars and freed me. That was yesterday evening. He took me to his cottage, and then after I had taken some food I fell into a sleep that lasted till late this morning."

Lavenne's story filled Sartines with such astonishment that he forgot for a moment the main business in hand, that is to say, Rochefort. It was Lavenne who recalled him to it.

"And now that I have told you my story, monsieur," said he, "let us forget it, for there are matters of much more importance to be considered.

I have been out of the world practically for four days. Is Count Camus still alive?"

He had told Sartines about the poisoning of the silver dagger, but he had not told him all.

"Alive," said the Minister, "oh, yes, he is very much alive, or was so late last night. Why do you ask?"

"Because, monsieur, before leaving the room I told you of, I drew that dagger from its sheath and inserted it again, but I took particular care to insert it the other way about."

"The other way about?"

"Yes, monsieur. It fitted the sheath either way."

"So that if Camus uses it," cried Sartines, starting from his chair, "if the gentleman of the Italian school uses his fruit knife in the way that the poisoning of the blade suggests, it is he himself who will suffer?"

"Precisely, monsieur; I had only a moment to think in. I said to myself, this wicked blade has been prepared for the slaying of an innocent woman, he has already tried to kill her with a prepared rose, he failed, he killed Atalanta instead, the death of his Majesty's favourite dog drew me into the business, and now I am made by God his judge. I said to myself—There is no use at all trying to bring this gentleman to justice by ordinary means, he is too clever, his poisons are too artfully prepared, he will surely give us the slip. Let his own hand deal him justice, and I reversed the dagger in its sheath."

"*Mordieu!*" said de Sartines, "that was at least a quick road. But the handle of the dagger, will he not notice that it has been reversed?"

"No, monsieur, for the pattern of the handle was the same on both sides, whereas the patterns on the sides of the sheath were widely different."

Sartines sat down again; for a moment he said nothing; he seemed plunged in thought.

"That was four days ago," said he at last, "yet nothing has happened. Both Camus and his wife are alive and very much in evidence."

"Have they met much, monsieur?"

"As far as I can say, no, for Madame Camus has been at Versailles for the last couple of days."

"When I asked had they met much, monsieur, I should have asked, have they met at any public entertainment or banquet, for it is then that the deed will be done, openly and before witnesses. For that is the essence of the whole business. It would be quite easy for Count Camus to poison his wife at home and in secret, but it is necessary for him to say, 'I only met her once in the last so many days, we were quite good friends, so much so, that we shared an apple together. Do you suggest that I poisoned the apple? Well, considering that I ate half of it and that I did not touch it beyond taking it from the dish and cutting it in two such a suggestion is absurd.—And here is the knife itself. I always use it for cutting fruit, see, the blade is silvered on purpose, take it, test it for poison——' So, monsieur, you see my drift. The deed will be done at some public entertainment, and I ask you, have they met at such an entertainment where the thing would be feasible?"

"No," said Sartines, speaking slowly and raising his eyes from the floor where they had been resting. "But they will to-night."

"To-night?"

"I believe so. M. de Choiseul is holding a reception at his house in the Rue Faubourg St. Honoré. Camus, who is in love with Mademoiselle Fontrailles, will surely be there, and the girl will surely be there, since the Dubarrys are now friends with Choiseul—for the moment—and since Madame Camus is a friend of Madame de Choiseul, she will be there."

"Then, monsieur," said Lavenne, "I will not give a *denier* for M. Camus' life after midnight to-night."

"He will save the hangman some trouble," said Sartines, taking a pinch of snuff. "And it will be interesting to watch—yes—very interesting to watch." Then suddenly his face changed in expression. "*Dame!* I forgot, all this put it out of my head. Rochefort has left Vincennes."

"M. de Rochefort left Vincennes!" cried Lavenne. "Since when, monsieur?"

"He escaped last night."

"But—but," said Lavenne. "He had agreed to stay. He quite understood his danger. This is strange news, monsieur."

"He must have got tired of prison," said Sartines. "That devil of a man never could be easy anywhere, and not only that, he has let out Ferminard."

"But how did they escape, monsieur?"

"How, by means of a rope which M. de Rochefort must have woven out of nothing in three days, by means of a file which he must have invented out of nothing for the purpose of cutting his window-bar, by half strangling the gaoler and leaving him tied up on the floor—I do not know, the thing was a miracle, but it was done."

"And you have heard nothing of him this morning?"

"Nothing."

"Now," said Lavenne, talking as if to himself, "I wonder what his motive was in doing that? I explained to him and he understood——"

"He had no motive, he is a man who acts on impulse."

"Has he been visited in prison, monsieur?"

"No. I was sending Captain Beauregard to see him this morning, but it was too late."

"Has he been treated well?"

"Excellently. Captain Pierre Cousin, who came to me with the news this morning, vouched for his good treatment."

"Did he say anything to Captain Cousin that might give a clue to his motive?"

"No, Captain Cousin never saw him."

"Never saw him?"

"Well, it seems that he has been very busy with the half-yearly reports and accounts of Vincennes, and the governor in any case does not visit new prisoners as a matter of routine."

"Ah," said Lavenne. "One can fancy M. de Rochefort imagining himself neglected and getting restive, but I cannot imagine where he could have got the means of escape."

"Nor can anyone else," replied de Sartines.

He looked up. The usher had knocked at the door and was entering the room, a letter in his hand.

"Who brought it?" asked Sartines, taking the letter.

"I don't know, monsieur, a man left it and went away saying that there was no answer."

He withdrew and the Minister opened the letter.

He cast his eyes over the contents and then handed it to Lavenne.

"Dear Sartines," ran this short and explicit communication, "I hope to have the pleasure of meeting you to-night at the Duc de Choiseul's reception. I have left Vincennes, it was too dull. Meanwhile, do not be troubled in the least. I hope to make everything right with Choiseul.

"Yours,
"De Rochefort."

"Well, monsieur," said Lavenne, returning the letter, which he had read with astonishment, but without the slightest alteration of expression, "we have now, at least, a clue to M. de Rochefort's plans."

Sartines was white with anger.

"A clue to M. de Rochefort's plans. Is the Hôtel de Sartines to sit down, then, and wait for M. de Rochefort to develop his plans?" He had taken his seat, but he rose again and began to walk up and down a few steps, his hands behind his back, his fingers twitching at his ruffles. "M. de Rochefort finds the Château de Vincennes too dull, he leaves it just as I would leave this room, he comes to Paris to amuse himself and he sends me a note that he hopes to meet me at M. de Choiseul's. Delightful. But since it is my wish that he should not have left the Château de Vincennes, that he should not be in Paris, that instead of visiting the Duc de Choiseul, he should be ten thousand leagues away from the Duc de Choiseul—it seems to me, considering all these things, that I have been ill-served by my servants, by my agents, and by the police who have the safe keeping of the order of his Majesty's city of Paris."

Lavenne looked on and listened. When Sartines was taken with anger in this particular way, he literally stood on his dignity, and seemed to be addressing the Parliament.

"What, then, has happened to us?" went on the Minister. "We have lost touch with our genius, it seems. Are we the Hôtel de Sartines or the Hospital of the Quinze-Vingts?" Then, blazing out, "By my name and the God above me, I will dismiss every man who has touched this business, from the gaoler at Vincennes to the man who received that letter and allowed the bearer to take his departure."

"Monsieur," said Lavenne, "it is less the fault of your servants than of events. M. de Rochefort is free, but you need have no fear of the consequences."

"Do you not understand," said Sartines, in an icy voice, speaking slowly, as though to let each word sink home to the mind of the listener, "that if M. le Duc de Choiseul takes this Rochefort in his net he will not be satisfied with imprisoning him. 'For the good of the State,' that will be his excuse—he will question him by means of the Rack and the Question by Water. Or rather, he will only have to mention their names and Rochefort will tell all. Why should he shelter the Dubarrys whom he hates? And once he tells, we are all lost. His Majesty would never forgive the affair of the Presentation—never—and now we have this precious Rochefort walking right into M. de Choiseul's arms."

"There is nothing to fear, monsieur, I have in my pocket something that will act on M. de Choiseul as a powerful bit acts on a restive horse. It is no less than a letter which M. de Choiseul wrote on the night of the Presentation."

He took Choiseul's letter from his pocket and handed it to Sartines.

"Where did you get this from?" asked Sartines when he had finished reading it.

Lavenne told.

"Ah," said the other. "Well, this simplifies everything indeed. This is the bowstring. *Mon Dieu!* was the man mad to write this? At once I shall take this to his Majesty and lay it before him with my own hands."

"No, monsieur," said Lavenne.

"Ah! What did you say?"

"I said no, monsieur. The letter is not mine, or at least only mine to hold as a means for the protection of M. de Rochefort. I promised the girl I told you of to keep it for that purpose."

"Why, *Mon Dieu!*" cried Sartines, "I believe you are dictating to me what course of action I should take!"

"No, monsieur, or only as regards that letter and—a thing which is very precious to me—my honour."

"Your honour. My faith! An agent of mine coming to me and talking of his honour where a business of State is concerned." Then, flying out, "What has that to do with me?"

"Oh, monsieur," said Lavenne coldly, and in a voice perfectly unshaken, "have you lived all these years in the world, and have you faced Paris and the Court so long in your capacity as Minister of Police that you set such a light price on honour. You value the keen sword of Verpellieux, the acuteness of Fremin, the cleverness of Jumeau, but what would all these men be worth to you if they could be bought? I have never spoken to you of the many times I could have accepted bribes in small matters, but the fact remains that without hurting you I could have accumulated fair sums of money. I did not, simply because something in me refused absolutely to play a double part. You know yourself how often I could have enriched myself by selling important secrets to your enemies. Where would you have been then? And the thing that saved you was not Lavenne, but the something that prevented Lavenne from betraying you. I call that something Honour. If it has another name it does not matter. The thing is the same. Well, I have pledged that something with regard to this letter, and if I do not redeem the pledge I will be no longer Lavenne, but a secret service agent of very little use to you, monsieur. That is all I wish to say."

De Sartines took a few turns up and down. Then he folded up the letter and handed it back to Lavenne. From de Sartines' point of view the word Honour belonged entirely to his own class. It was the name of a thing used among gentlemen, a thing appertaining to the higher orders. He had never considered it in relation to the *Rafataille*, had he done so he would have considered the relationship absurd.

According to his view of it, Honour, even amongst the nobility, was a very lean figure. Splendidly dressed, but very lean and capable of being doubled up and packed away without any injury to it.

A man must resent an insult sword in hand.

A man must not cheat at cards—or be caught cheating at cards.

A man may lie as much as he pleases, but he must kill another man who calls him a liar.

These were the chief articles in his code.

Sartines himself was almost destitute of the principles of Honour as we know it, just as he was almost wanting in the principles of Mercy as we know it. Witness that relative of his whom he had kept imprisoned in the Bastille for private ends and who was only released by the Revolutionaries of July.

Still, he had his code, and he talked of Honour and he considered it as an attribute of his station in life.

Lavenne just now had shown him a new side of the question, shown him in a flash that what he had always called the Fidelity of his subordinates was in reality a principle. He had always taken it as a personal tribute. He saw now that in the case of Lavenne, at least, it had to do with Lavenne himself, and secondarily only with de Sartines. And it was a principle that must not be tampered with, for on its integrity depended M. de Sartines' safety and welfare.

He knew, besides, that the letter was in safe hands and that the wise Lavenne, in using it for the protection of Rochefort, would use it also for the protection of de Sartines. And away at the back of his mind there was the ghost of an idea that this terrible letter was safest for all parties in the hands of Lavenne.

Therefore he returned it.

"What you say is just, here is the letter. I will trust you to use it not only for the protection of M. de Rochefort, but in my interests if necessary. That is to say, of course, the interest of the State."

"Thank you, monsieur," replied the other, rising from his chair. "And now I must find M. de Rochefort if possible—though I have very little hope of doing so before to-night."

CHAPTER IX

THE GATHERING STORM

LAVENNE, when he left the Hôtel de Sartines, made straight for the Rue St. Dominic. He wanted to find Rochefort and he fancied that Javotte might know of the Count's whereabouts.

He stopped at the door of the house where Camille Fontrailles' apartments were, rang and was admitted by the *concierge*.

Scarcely had he made the inquiry as to whether Mademoiselle Javotte were at home when Javotte herself appeared descending the stairs and ready dressed for the street.

"Why, monsieur," said Javotte, "it is strange that you have called at this moment, for in a very short time you would not have found me. I am leaving."

"Leaving?"

"Yes, monsieur, and at this moment I am going to call a *fiacre* to remove my things to a room I have taken in the Rue Jussac close to here."

He accompanied her into the street.

"And why are you leaving?" asked Lavenne. "Have you quarrelled with your mistress?"

"No, monsieur, she quarrelled with me."

"Well, well," said Lavenne, "these things will happen. I called to ask, did you know of the whereabouts of M. de Rochefort?"

"No, monsieur, I do not, and strangely enough, it was concerning M. de Rochefort that my quarrel arose with Mademoiselle Fontrailles."

"Aha! that is strange. Tell me about it."

"It was this way, monsieur. That night when M. de Rochefort had the dispute with M. de Choiseul, he took shelter here. He came to see Mademoiselle Fontrailles, she was not here, he asked for shelter and I gave it to him. He slept in my room, whilst I took the room of my mistress. Well, it appeared that the *concierge* talked, and yesterday Mademoiselle Fontrailles asked me what I meant by harbouring a man here for the night.

I was furious; before I could reply two gentlemen were announced, M. Dubarry and Count Camus.

"Count Camus was the man who insulted me that night when M. de Rochefort rescued me, and when the gentlemen were gone I said to Mademoiselle, 'I would sooner harbour a gentleman here for the night than allow a ruffian to kiss my hand.'

"She asked me what I meant. I told her, and I told her that M. de Rochefort had smacked Comte Camus' face.

"Her face fired up so that I knew the truth at once. She is in love with him, monsieur, and I was so furious at the false charge she had made about me that I lost all discretion. I said, 'It is easy to see your feelings for that man; as for me, though I am only a poor girl, I would choose for a lover, if not a gentleman, at least not a cur-dog who snaps at women's dresses and who runs away when kicked by a man.'"

"And what did she say to that?"

"She boxed my ears, monsieur. She is infatuated. Ah, monsieur, what is it that she can see in a man so horrible to look at, so evil, and so cruel; for he is cruel, and I swear to you the sight of him makes me shudder, and would make me shudder even if I had not personally experienced his baseness."

"I do not know," replied Lavenne; "nor can I possibly say why this man should affect two persons so differently. He is, as you say, a terrible man, and your innocence, or what is kindly in your nature, is revolted by him; as for your late mistress, why, we must suppose there is something in her nature that is attracted by him. But she is treading on dangerous ground, for should Madame Camus die and should she marry him, she would find herself under the thumb of a very strange master. Now, listen to me, Mademoiselle Javotte. I have still in my pocket that letter which you gave me, and I hope to make it useful to M. de Rochefort. What is the number of the house in the Rue Jussac which will be your new abode?"

"No. 3, monsieur."

"Well, it is important for me to know your address as I may want you. I may even want you to-night, so be at home."

"I will, monsieur—and M. de Rochefort?"

Lavenne smiled.

"Set your mind at rest. He is in danger, very great danger, but I hope to save him."

"In danger?"

"Yes, but I hope to save him. He is in Paris, I do not know his address, but I shall see him to-night."

"Ah—in danger—" said Javotte. "I shall not rest till I hear that he is safe."

"You care for him so much as that?"

"Oh, monsieur, I care for him much more."

Lavenne left her. "Now there is a faithful heart," said he. "Ah, if M. de Rochefort had only the genius to see that friend of all friends, the woman who loves him!—And why not. Madame la Comtesse Dubarry was a shopgirl. She had only a pretty face. And here we have the pretty face, but so much more also."

He dismissed Javotte from his mind, concentrating his attention on the events of the forthcoming evening, on the Duc de Choiseul's reception, which he felt to be the point towards which all these diverse fortunes were tending. Lavenne half divined the truth that the life of society is really the agglutination of a thousand stories, each story containing so many characters working out a definite plot towards a definite, and sometimes to an indefinite, *dénouement*. He felt that in this especial business in which he was engaged the story, beginning with the Presentation of the Comtesse Dubarry, was about to find its *dénouement* at the reception of the Duc de Choiseul, and he could not help contemplating all the complex interests involved, their reaction one on the other and the manner in which they were being drawn together towards one definite point. Sartines' fortune was at stake, Rochefort's liberty, Camus' life, Camille Fontrailles' future, Javotte's love and Choiseul's position as a Minister.

The thing seemed to have been arranged by some dramatist—or shall we say some chemist, who had slowly brought together, one by one, all these diverse elements that wanted now only the last touch, the last drop of acid or spark of fire to produce the culminating explosion.

CHAPTER X

THE DUC DE CHOISEUL'S RECEPTION

CHOISEUL'S position in the world was a doubly difficult one. He was continually fighting for his life, and he had to conduct the battle in a silk coat that must never be creased and ruffles that must ever be immaculate. He had to parry dagger thrusts with a smile, kiss hands whose owners he hated, laugh when most severely smitten and turn defeats into epigrams.

The Comte de Stainville, now Duc de Choiseul, was well qualified, however, by nature and by training for the difficult position that he held.

The genius that had prompted him, when Comte de Stainville, to make an ally of his enemy the Pompadour, did not desert him when, under the title of Duc de Choiseul, he was created Prime Minister in 1758.

Choiseul was the man who almost averted the French Revolution. He was the first of the real friends of Liberty not dressed as a Philosopher, and the greatest Minister after Colbert. He had his littlenesses, his weaknesses; he made great mistakes, allowed impulse to sway him occasionally, and could be extremely pitiless on occasion. He did not disdain to use the meanest weapons, yet he was great and far more human than the majority of the men of his time, than Terray, or de Maupeou, or de Sartines, or d'Aiguillon, or d'Argeson, more human even than the men who were beginning to babble about Humanity. He did not write "The Social Contract," but he destroyed the tyranny of the Jesuits in France. He did not profess to love his own family, but at least he did not desert his own children after the fashion of M. Jean Jacques.

To-night, as he stood to receive his guests, he looked precisely the same as on the last occasion, less than a week ago, when, standing in his own house, he had received his guests with the certainty in his mind that the Presentation would not take place. But he showed nothing of his defeat.

De Sartines was among the first to arrive. As Minister of Police it was his duty to guard the safety of the Prime Minister of France on all occasions, and more especially at State functions, balls, and receptions, even when these receptions, functions or balls took place at the Minister's own house.

There were always dangerous people ready for mischief—Damiens was an example of that—lunatics and fanatics, and to-night, as usual, several agents of the Hôtel de Sartines were among the servants of Choiseul and indistinguishable from them. But to-night, for certain reasons, the occasion was so especial that Lavenne was present, watchful, seeing all things, but unseen, or rather unnoticed, by everyone.

Sartines passed with the first of the crowd into the great *salon* where Madame de Choiseul was receiving. Here, when he had made his bow, he found himself buttonholed by M. de Duras, the old gentleman who knew everything about everyone and their affairs. The same, it will be remembered, who had explained Camille Fontrailles to Camus on that night of the ball.

"Ah, M. le Comte," cried this purveyor of news,

"I thought I was too early, but now that I see you, I feel my position more regular. I came here chiefly to-night to make sure that Madame la Princesse de Guemenée was not present. You have heard the news? No? Well, there has been a great quarrel. It is entirely between ourselves, but the Princesse de Guemenée and Madame de Choiseul have quarrelled, so much so that the Princesse has not been invited."

"Indeed!" said de Sartines, "I have heard nothing of it."

"All the same, it is a fact—and the fact is rather scandalous. It was this way——"

"Madame la Princesse de Guemenée," came the voice of the usher as the Princesse, smiling, entered and made her bow to Madame de Choiseul.

"Yes," said Sartines, "you were going to say?"

"Why, that is the lady herself. Yet the facts were given to me on unimpeachable authority. They must have made the matter up between them. *Ma foi!* women are adaptable creatures. One can never count on them—as, for instance, the Dubarry. She is hand in glove with the Choiseuls now, and that great fat Jean Dubarry swears by his friend Choiseul; one might fancy them brothers to hear Jean talking, but I would like to hear Choiseul's view of the matter. Ah, there is Count Camus, he seems quite recovered from the blow that M. de Rochefort gave him—what an affair!—a fine, open-hearted man, Camus, and only for that vile smallpox he would not be bad-looking, but beauty is only skin deep and it is the man who counts after all. Have you heard the news about Rochefort?"

"No," said Sartines with a little start. "Have you heard anything fresh?"

"Oh, *ma foi!* yes. He is in Germany. Managed to make his escape, fool. I always said he would make a mess of his affairs, but I never thought he would have gone the length he did."

"Oh, in Germany, is he?" said Sartines, wishing sincerely that the news was true.

"Yes. He made his escape from France in the disguise of a pedlar. I had the news only yesterday. Ah, there is Mademoiselle Fontrailles, with Mademoiselle Chon Dubarry and the Vicomte Jean. What did I tell you? Hand in glove, hand in glove. She looks well, the Fontrailles. Cold as an icicle, but beautiful. And they say she has a fortune of a million francs. Why, there is Madame Camus, she has come with Madame de Courcelles; and look at Camus, he seems to have no eyes but for his wife."

Sartines gazed in the direction of a group consisting of Camus, his wife, Camille Fontrailles and Jean Dubarry. They were all laughing and talking, and now, apropos of some remark, Camus, with a little bow, took his wife's hand and kissed the tips of her fingers. The others laughed at the joke, whatever it was.

"Look," said de Sartines, "what a charming husband. And yet it seemed to me, for I have been watching them all since they came in, that this charming husband slipped a little note behind his back to the Fontrailles, and that she took it quite in the orthodox way—that is to say, without being seen."

"Except by you."

"Except by me, but then, you see, I am the Minister of Police, and I am supposed to see what other people do not see, and know what other people do not know." De Sartines, as he finished speaking, turned again towards the group and contemplated them with a brooding eye, his hands behind his back, and his lips slightly thrust out.

"But she can have no hopes, since Madame Camus is alive and, despite her lameness, evidently in the best of health," said M. de Duras.

"My dear fellow," said de Sartines, "that is not a girl to build on hopes. If she cares for Camus, as I believe she does, he has only to wink and she will follow him. She is of that type. The type of the perverse prude. The creature who would refuse herself to an honest man, and yet is quite ready to roll in the gutter if the gutter pleases her. Here has this one refused a man whom she might have made something of—that is to say, Rochefort, and who has welcomed the advances of a speckled toad—that is to say, Camus. You say Camus is an open-hearted man, at least I fancy you made some curious remark of that sort; you are wrong, just as wrong as when you said Madame de Guemenée had quarrelled with Madame de Choiseul; just as wrong as when you said de Rochefort was in Germany. M. de Rochefort is in Paris—and there he is in the flesh."

"Monsieur le Vicomte de Chartres. Monsieur le Comte de Rochefort," came the usher's voice.

An earthquake would not have shaken de Choiseul more than that announcement, and just as he would have remained unmoved after the first shock of the earthquake, so did he now after the first shock of the announcement.

Rochefort, accompanying Chartres, advanced a hair's-breadth behind the Vicomte, and with that half-smiling, easy grace which was one of his attractions. He was beautifully dressed in a suit of Chartres' which a tailor had been half a day altering to suit his fastidious tastes. He bowed to his hostess and host.

Had de Choiseul changed colour or expression, Rochefort would have been far better pleased; but the Minister received him with absolute courtesy, as though they had parted in friendship but a few hours ago, and as though it were the most natural thing in the world for a man against whom he had issued a warrant, and for whom he was hunting throughout France, to appear as his guest. The appalling *sang-froid* of de Choiseul, who would have suffered anything rather than that a scene should be created in his house, disconcerted Rochefort. The idea clutched his mind that he had taken another false step. He had come to meet a man, he found himself face to face with etiquette. He had hoped, by an explosion, to create the warmth that would lead to a mutual understanding; he found no materials for an explosion—nothing but ice.

Against the faultless reception of de Choiseul, his intrusion now seemed bad taste.

All this passed through his mind, leaving no trace, however, on his manner or expression as he turned from his host and hostess and calmly surveyed the people in his immediate neighbourhood.

Not a person present that was not filled with astonishment, yet not a person betrayed his or her feelings. Rochefort had, then, made his position good again, and Choiseul had invited him to his reception. How had Rochefort worked this miracle? Impossible to say, yet there was the fact, and if Choiseul was satisfied it was nobody's business to grumble.

Camus was the most astonished of all, yet he said nothing, only turning to the Vicomte Jean Dubarry with eyebrows lifted as though to say, "Well, what do you think of that?"

Sartines alone knew the truth of the whole business and Sartines wished himself well away, for he knew that Rochefort would come and speak to him, Sartines—the man who ought to take M. de Rochefort by the arm and lead him out to arrest, an action that would have pleased his vexed soul, and which he would promptly have taken were it not impossible.

To arrest Rochefort now would mean simply to hand him over to the agents of Choiseul, to be questioned and to reveal to them everything he knew. He would sacrifice the Dubarrys most certainly rather than suffer for them, that was patently apparent now, for Rochefort, passing the Dubarry group, turned on Mademoiselle Fontrailles, on Chon, on Jean Dubarry and on Camus, a glance in which hatred was half veiled and contempt clearly manifested.

And the group did not fail to respond.

On the way towards Sartines, Rochefort was stopped by M. de Duras.

"Why, M. de Rochefort," said the old gentleman, "this is an unexpected pleasure."

"Which, monsieur?"

"Why, to meet you here to-night."

"Well, M. de Duras, unexpected pleasures are always the sweetest; but why should the pleasure be unexpected?"

"Why——?" stammered the old fellow—"Well, monsieur, it was rumoured that you were in Germany."

"Ah! it was rumoured that I was in Germany—well, Rumour has told a lie for the first time. Ah, Sartines, you see I have kept my promise; how are you this evening—charmingly, I hope?"

Rochefort had recovered his spirits. The sight of Camus, the Fontrailles, Chon, and Jean Dubarry all in one group laughing and talking together, had clinched the business with him and given the last blow to his half-dead passion for Camille Fontrailles. But a dead passion makes fine combustible material when it is bound together with wounded pride. This dead passion of Rochefort's burst into flame like a lit tar-barrel, and his anger against the Dubarry group became furiously alive and the next worse thing to hatred.

"Hush, my dear fellow," said de Sartines, drawing him aside. "I do not know what has driven you to this mad act, but at least remember that I am your friend. You have kept no promise to me. You have kept no promise to me. I could not help receiving your letter; had I been in communication with you, I would have been the first to warn you against what you have done."

"And you know perfectly well," replied Rochefort, "that I have never taken warnings—or at least only once, when I was foolish enough to take a cell in that rat-haunted old barrack of Vincennes at your advice, instead of facing Choiseul like a man."

"Facing Choiseul like a man! And what do you expect from that?"

"I expect that he will listen to reason, hear my story, which I would have told him had he not tried to arrest me as I was just starting to Paris to keep an appointment, and release me."

"You do not know Choiseul."

"Excuse me, but I believe I do. He is a gentleman, he knows that I am a gentleman and he will take my word."

"Choiseul will have you arrested the instant you leave this hôtel. He would arrest you now only he does not wish to make a scene."

"I am going to explain to him."

"Where?"

"Here."

"And how are you going to obtain an interview with him?"

"You must do that for me."

"I?"

"Yes, you are the proper person. Go to him and say, 'Rochefort wishes to speak to you on a matter of great importance.' You can say to him also if you like, 'He asked me to say that he came here to-night not as your guest, but as a gentleman who has been lied against and misunderstood and who wishes to lay his case before the first gentleman in France, after his Majesty.'"

"Words, words," said Sartines. "He will crumple them up and fling them in your face."

"He will not. Choiseul is a gentleman and will listen to me."

"Ay, he will listen to you—you are like a child with your talk of 'gentleman—gentleman.' However, you are not quite lost. You had a letter of Choiseul's."

"I?"

"Yes, you took it from the saddle-bag of a horse."

"Oh, that!"

"Yes. Well, I have that letter in my pocket."

"How did you get it?"

"You gave it to a girl—like a fool—to send back to Choiseul, and the girl, who seems to have cared for you a lot, opened it."

"Ah, Javotte! Little meddler——"

"Read it."

"Yes—yes!"

"And found that it was a—what shall I say?—a revelation of how Choiseul had plotted against the Dubarry and a libel on his Majesty. It was written in a moment of anger, it was one of the false steps men make who have not control of their temper. With this letter in your hand you are safe from Choiseul. He, of course, knows that the thing was taken from the saddle-bag of the horse, but I doubt if he suspects you as having taken it, simply because in the ordinary course you would have used it against him before this."

"How did you get this letter?"

"The girl gave it to my agent, Lavenne, making him promise that it was to be used only for your protection. Now we have some honour amongst us at the Hôtel de Sartines, otherwise this—um—treasonable document would have been laid by this before his Majesty for the good of the State. Lavenne, to-night, knowing that you would be here, gave it to me to give to you."

"Let me have it."

"Come into this corridor, then."

Sartines led the way between two curtains into a corridor giving entrance to the *salon* where to-night refreshments were being served.

He handed the letter to Rochefort, who hastily put it in his pocket.

"Thanks," said Rochefort. "This will make the matter easier for me. Or at least it will serve as an introduction to our business. And now, like a good fellow, obtain for me my interview with Choiseul."

They went back against a tide of people setting in the direction of the room where the buffet was laid out and where little tables were set about for the guests.

Rochefort waited in a corridor whilst Sartines advanced towards Choiseul and buttonholed him.

CHAPTER XI

ROCHEFORT AND CHOISEUL

ROCHEFORT watched the two men. One could make out absolutely nothing from their expressions or movements. Then they turned slowly and walked towards a door on the left of the *salon*.

Choiseul, with his hand on the door-handle, nodded slightly to his companion, passed through the door, shut it, and Sartines came hurrying towards Rochefort.

"Your interview has been granted. Remember that the letter in your pocket stands between you and social and bodily destruction. *Mordieu!* remember also your friends, Rochefort, for I will not hide it from you, that, should you fall into Choiseul's hands, things will go badly with us."

"Do not worry me with directions, my dear fellow," said Rochefort. "If I am to do this thing, I must do it in my own way—come."

He led the way through the door and into a passage leading to a room the door of which was ajar.

Rochefort knocked at this door and entered the room, followed by Sartines.

It was a small but beautifully furnished writing-room. Choiseul was standing before the fireplace, with his hands behind his back. He seemed in meditation, and raising his head, bowed slightly to the Count whilst Sartines closed the door and took a position on the right.

Sartines, as he came to a halt, produced his snuff-box, tapped it, opened it, and took a pinch.

"Well, Monsieur de Rochefort," said Choiseul, "you wish to speak to me?"

"Yes, monsieur," replied Rochefort, "I wish to make an explanation. Some days ago, at his Majesty's palace of Versailles, you in your discretion, and acting under your powers, thought fit to issue a warrant for the arrest of my person, and you entrusted this business to two of your gentlemen, M. le Comte Camus and M. d'Estouteville."

Choiseul nodded slightly.

"I resisted that arrest, monsieur, not because I was conscious of having done any wrong and not because I dreaded any consequences that might arise from false information given against me. I resisted arrest simply because I was going to Paris on important business and did not wish to be stopped."

"Oh!" said Choiseul, "you were going to Paris on important business and did not wish to be stopped. Indeed! And you have come here to tell me that you resisted an order of the State because you were going to Paris and did not wish to be stopped!"

Choiseul's voice would have frozen an ordinary man, and few men in Rochefort's position could have stood under the gaze of his cold grey eyes unmoved.

"I came to tell you absolutely the truth, monsieur. Yes, I resisted the order of the State for private reasons, but I will add this, my reasons were not entirely personal. I had to meet a lady——"

"Go on," said Choiseul, "I do not wish to pry into your personal affairs. Have you anything more to say?"

"Yes, monsieur. To make my escape, I had to take a horse that was standing in waiting. On it I reached Paris. In the saddle-bag I found a letter addressed by you to a lady—I have forgotten the name—I do not wish to pry into your private affairs."

Choiseul's face had changed slightly in colour, but otherwise he betrayed none of the emotion that filled him, except, Sartines noticed, by a slight twitching of his left shoulder.

"Ah!" said he, "you found a letter of mine!"

"Yes, monsieur, I entrusted it to a person, who is my very faithful servant, to take to the address upon it. Now, this person—knowing that I was in trouble with M. de Choiseul—thought fit to open the letter, an action most discreditable and only excusable inasmuch as it was prompted by an humble mind, blinded by devotion to my interests.

"The letter was put into my hands with a strong suggestion that the contents might be useful to me."

"Now, M. le Duc, you will at once understand that, so far from making use of this letter, I did not even read it. It is in my pocket now, perfectly safe, and I have the honour of returning it to you."

To Sartines' horror, Rochefort put his hand in his pocket, took out the letter and gave it to Choiseul, who opened it, glanced at the contents and placed it on the mantelpiece as though it were of no importance.

"I have only to add, monsieur," continued Rochefort, "that in Paris, instead of taking the wise course of returning to Versailles to seek re-arrest, I said to myself, 'M. Choiseul is against me. I had better make my escape or at least keep concealed until the storm blows over.' That was very foolish, but I was enraged about other matters and I did not think clearly, and now, monsieur, what is the charge against me?"

"You are charged, Monsieur de Rochefort, with the killing of a man in the streets of Paris on the very night upon which you were here as my guest last."

"The charge is perfectly correct, monsieur, but your informant did not tell all."

"Walking home with Comte Camus I rescued a woman from two men who were maltreating her. I pursued one of the men, he attacked me and I killed him. I returned only to find the unfortunate woman whom I had rescued being assaulted by Count Camus. I struck him in the face and rolled him in the gutter, and he has never yet sought redress for that assault which I made upon him."

"What is this you say?" asked Choiseul.

"The truth, monsieur," replied Rochefort proudly.

Now Lavenne that evening, on taking over the police arrangements for Choiseul's reception, had given special instructions to Vallone, one of his subordinates who had nothing to do with the policing of the reception, who, as a matter of fact, was a spy of the Hôtel de Sartines engaged in the service of Choiseul. It was Vallone, in fact, who had given Sartines the information that Choiseul had sent the note which the Comtesse de Béarn had received in the basket of flowers.

Lavenne had given the man instructions to watch Count Camus as a cat watches a mouse, and Lavenne, just at this moment, was standing unobserved watching the throng passing in and out of the *salon* where refreshments were served. He saw Vallone leave the *salon*. Vallone glanced about, saw Lavenne and came rapidly towards him.

"Well," said Lavenne, "what is it?"

"Monsieur, you told me to watch Count Camus, and more especially should he use a dagger to cut fruit with."

"Yes—yes?"

"He is seated at a small table with Madame Camus, Mademoiselle Fontrailles, and M. le Vicomte Jean Dubarry."

"Yes—yes?"

"He has just taken a peach from a dish of fruit handed to him by a servant, and producing a knife like that which you spoke of, he cut the peach in two."

"Quick—go on!"

"He handed one half of the peach to Madame Camus."

"Yes—and the other half he ate himself?"

"No, monsieur. The other half he handed on his plate to Mademoiselle Fontrailles."

"Did she eat it?"

"Yes, monsieur, she ate it, looking all the time at Monsieur Camus with a smile, and between you and me, monsieur, she seems to favour the Count more than a little."

Lavenne did not hear this last. Horrified at what he had heard, he felt as though some unseen hand had suddenly intervened in this game of life and death, dealing the cards in a reverse direction, and the ace of spades, not to Camus, but to Camille Fontrailles. He turned from Vallone and walked rapidly to the door of the supper-room.

He entered.

Dressed in a sober suit of black he had the appearance of a confidential servant, and no one noticed him, or, if they did, put him down as one of the stewards of the house superintending the service. Numerous small tables were spread about, the place was crowded and a band of violins in the gallery was playing, mixing its music with the sound of voices, laughter, and the tinkle of glass and silver.

Lavenne passed the table where the Dubarry group was seated. Camille Fontrailles was chatting and laughing with the others; she had never appeared more beautiful, she was seated opposite to Camus. Lavenne swept the room with his eyes, as though he were searching for some plan of action; then he hurriedly walked to the door, crossed the reception *salon* and passed through the door through which he had seen Sartines and Rochefort following Choiseul. He reached the door where the conference was going forward and knocked.

Choiseul paused for a moment without replying.

"Let us see," said he, "you accuse Monsieur Camus of having assaulted this girl, and you would add to that the suggestion that his accusation against you was prompted by anger at the blow you dealt him."

"I did not know that the accusation against me came from Comte Camus," replied Rochefort, "but I must say I suspected that he had a hand in the business. Now that you tell me, I would say that most certainly the accusation was prompted by spite."

"Well," said Choiseul, "I have listened to what you have said, and what you have said has impressed me, Monsieur de Rochefort. But I stand here to do justice, and for that purpose I must hear what Comte Camus has to say, for he distinctly told me that he had parted company with you, that he had started on his way home, that he altered his direction in order to call on a friend, and that by accident he had come upon the evidence which he disclosed to me. I shall call Comte Camus and you can confront him."

"Do so, monsieur," replied Rochefort, "and now one word first. I fell into politics by a false step, just as a man might fall into a well. I confess that I acted against you, monsieur, not from animosity, but simply because the party with which I momentarily allied myself was in opposition to you. I would ask you to forget all that and forgive an antagonist who is now well disposed towards you, should you decide that Monsieur Camus' story is a lie, and that I have spoken the truth. Monsieur, I am not fit for politics; I want to enjoy my life since I have only one to enjoy. I don't want to go into the Bastille on account of your anger, and I don't want to be hanged for having killed a ruffian who attempted my life. Therefore, Monsieur le Duc, should you think that I have acted as a straight man and a gentleman through all this, I would ask a clear forgiveness. Firstly, for ridding Paris of a rogue with my sword; secondly, for having been such a fool as to ally my life and my fortune to the fortune of those cursed Dubarrys."

The outward effect of this extraordinary speech on Choiseul was to make him turn half way in order to hide a smile. Then, stretching out his hand he rang a bell; with almost the same movement he casually took the letter lying on the mantelpiece and put it in his pocket.

Sartines knew from the expression on Choiseul's face that Rochefort was saved, unless Camus, by some trickery, were to turn the tables. Everything rested now with what Camus would do and say.

He was taking a pinch of snuff when Lavenne's knock came to the door.

Lavenne entered. His face was absolutely white.

"Monsieur," said he to Sartines, disregarding the other two, "send at once for Monsieur Camus. Mademoiselle Fontrailles has been poisoned—he may know some antidote, but it will have to be forced from him."

"Good God!" said Sartines, instantly guessing the truth. "He has given her the poison instead of his wife."

"Yes—yes, monsieur—but send quick."

"I will fetch him myself," cried Sartines, rushing from the room.

Choiseul, amazed, found his speech.

"What is this you say?" he asked. "Poisoned, in my house? Explain yourself!"

"Monsieur," said Lavenne, "Comte Camus has poisoned a lady at the supper-table—yes, in your house; he intended to poison his wife. I have been watching him for some time. He poisoned Atalanta, the King's hound, with poison which he had prepared for his wife, and which the dog ate by accident. Woe is me! I should have seized him to-day, but the evidence was not complete. I had arranged things otherwise, but God in His wisdom has brought my plans to nothing."

"*Bon Dieu!*" said Rochefort, all thoughts about himself swept away. There was something shocking in Lavenne's face and voice and words. Choiseul, mystified, understanding only half of what had happened, yet comprehending the depth of the tragedy of which his house had been chosen for the stage, stood waiting, half dreading the re-appearance of Sartines, too proud to cross-question a subordinate and at heart furious at this scandal which had thrust itself upon his hearth.

He had not to wait long.

Steps sounded outside, the door opened and Camus entered, closely followed by Sartines. Camus, not comprehending the urgent summons, was, still, pale about the lips, and his manner had lost its assurance.

Sartines shut the door.

"That is the man," said Lavenne, stepping forward and suddenly taking command of the situation.

Lavenne, in a flash, had altered. He seemed to have increased in size; something ferocious and bullying lying dormant in his nature broke loose; advancing swiftly on Camus he seized him by the collar as he would have seized the commonest criminal and absolutely shouting in his face, held him tight clutched the while:

"I arrest you, your game is lost. The antidote for the poison you have just given an unfortunate woman! Confess, save her, and you may yet save your neck. You refuse? You would struggle? Ah, there——"

He flung himself on Camus as if he would tear the secret from him, but he was not searching for the secret, but for the dagger, which he found and plucked from him, flinging it to Sartines.

Camus, who had not spoken a word, struggled furiously, white, gasping, terrific, proclaiming his infamy by his silence, knowing that all was over, and that this terrible man whom he had never seen before, this man who had lain hidden in his path and who had seized him like Fate, was his executioner.

The struggle lasted only half a minute, then Camus was on the floor and Lavenne, with the whipcord which he always carried, was fastening the wrists of his prisoner. There was no appeal, no defence, or questions or cross-questions. Just a prisoner bound on the floor, and Lavenne, now calm, rising to address his master.

"Shall I remove him, monsieur?"

"But the antidote," said Sartines.

"There is no antidote, monsieur," said Lavenne, "else he would have confessed to save his life." He gave a down glance at Camus. Camus, white and groaning, lay like a man stricken by a mortal blow, and then Choiseul, glaring at him, spoke.

Choiseul, who had not moved nor spoken, suddenly found speech. Filled with fury at the whole business, not caring who was poisoned as long as the affair did not occur in his house, stricken in his dignity and hating the idea of a scandal, he turned to Sartines.

"Take that carrion away," he burst out. "Away with him by that door which opens on the kitchen premises. Go first, Sartines, and order all the servants to remain away from the yard where you will have a carriage brought. Then you can remove him to La Bastille. Monsieur de Rochefort, kindly help in the business—and Monsieur de Rochefort, all is cleared between us. Go in peace and avoid politics. Now do as I direct. No scandal, no noise—not a word about all this business which is deeply discreditable to our order. We poison in secret, it seems; well, in secret we shall punish."

"Monsieur," said Sartines, delighted that the Rochefort business was over and done with, "I shall do exactly as you direct. It is best. Lavenne, open that door and give me your assistance with this."

Lavenne opened the door and they carried Camus out. Not one word had he spoken from first to last. Rochefort followed. When he reached the door, he turned and bowed to Choiseul, Choiseul returned the bow. Rochefort went out and shut the door behind him and the incident was closed.

Then Choiseul, taking the letter from his pocket re-read it, lit a taper and burned it in the grate. He stamped on the ashes and, leaving the room, returned to the *salon* on which the passage opened.

Some of the guests were taking their departure, amongst them the Dubarry party.

"We were looking for Monsieur Camus," said Jean Dubarry, "but he seems to have vanished."

"Ah, Comte Camus," replied Choiseul, "I saw him early this evening, but I have not seen him since."

"Sartines came and fetched him off," said Jean.

"Then perhaps he has gone off with Sartines," said Choiseul, "and now you are carrying off Mademoiselle Fontrailles so early in the evening. Ah, Mademoiselle Fontrailles, you are carrying away with you all the charm you have brought to my poor *salons*, and leaving behind you the envy of all the roses of Paris who have been eclipsed by the Flower of Martinique."

He bowed profoundly to the laughing girl and to Chon Dubarry.

Then he went to the card-room.

CHAPTER XII

ENVOI

A FEW days later the Comte de Rochefort was breakfasting with his friend, de Chartres, when, the conversation taking a turn, Rochefort, in reply to some remark of his companion, laughed.

"That reminds me," said he, "I am going to leave Paris."

"You are going to leave Paris? And for how long?"

"Oh, an indefinite time."

"And who gave you that bright idea?"

"M. de Duras."

"M. de Duras advised you to leave Paris?"

"Oh, no, he only gave me the idea that it would be a good thing not to become like M. de Duras. I saw myself in a flash as I would be twenty years hence, old M. de Rochefort with a painted face, living socially on the tolerance of his friends and mentally on the latest rumour and the cast-off wit of others. Besides, I was always fond of a country life; besides—I have had my fling in Paris, I have spent I don't know how many thousand francs in four years, and if I go on I will be impoverished, and I can stand many things, Chartres, but I could never stand being your poor man.

"I do not mind living on a crust of bread in the least, but I object very strongly to living with the knowledge that I cannot have venison if I want it. I have come from a queer stock, we have always gone the pace, but we have all of us had a grain of commonsense somewhere in our natures to check us in time.

"People say I am mad simply because they only see me spending my money in Paris; they do not know in the least that I have a reputation for commonsense on my estates as solid as an oak-tree. My people in the country know me and they respect me, because I know them and will not let myself be cheated. People say I am mad—silly fools—have they never considered the fact that I have always steered clear of politics?"

"Oh, oh!" said Chartres; "good heavens, what are you saying?"

"That was an accident, an uncharted rock that I struck. I have always steered clear of politics, otherwise I might be like Camus, of whose fate I have just told you—and mind, never, never breathe a word of that even to your pillow—or poor Camille Fontrailles. Well, to return to our subject. I am leaving Paris for another reason, which I will tell to you who are my best friend. I am in love, and the girl whom I am going to make my wife could not live in Paris."

"And why not?"

"Because she is a girl of the people; because she has a heart of gold and a soul as pure as the soul of a child, and a power of love simple and indestructible as the love of a dog; because she is a woman who can be faithful in friendliness as a man, because she is a child who will be a child till she dies. All that would be extremely absurd in Paris. But down there in the country, Madame la Comtesse de Rochefort will grow and live in the clear air that nourishes the flowers; she will be respected by people who know the value of worth, and when Monsieur de Rochefort is an old man, he will perhaps see in his grandchildren the strength of a new race and not the vices of our rotten aristocracy."

"Rochefort," said Chartres, "I do not know whether this is madness or commonsense, I only know that you are talking in a way that surprises me as much as though I were to hear my poodle Pistache talking philosophy."

"Precisely, yet Pistache has more philosophy in his composition than half the philosophers. You despise him because he is a poodle and plays antics, just as you despise me because I am a man who has played the fool. Yet Madame de Chartres does not look on Pistache as a bag of tricks covered with fur, for she believes—so she told me—that Pistache has a soul, and the woman whom I am going to marry does not look on me as a fool, simply because she loves me.

"Believe me, Chartres, the only people who really understand dogs and men—are women."

Footnote:

A Hairdressers alone amongst tradesmen were permitted to wear swords.

THE END.

Milton Keynes UK
Ingram Content Group UK Ltd.
UKHW050036220624
444555UK00004B/410

9 789362 098016